Silverm...

HAVE A COLLECTION OF 46 GREAT NOVELS

OF

EROTIC DOMINATION

If you like one you will like the rest

A NEW TITLE EVERY MONTH
NOW INCLUDING EXTRA BONUS PAGES

Silver Moon Books of Leeds and New York are in no way connected with Silver Moon Books of London

If you like one of our books you will probably like them all !

For free 20 page booklet of extracts from previous books (and, if you wish to be on our confidential mailing list, from forthcoming monthly titles as they are publshed) please write to:-

**Silver Moon Readers Services
PO Box CR 25 LEEDS LS7 3TN
or**
PO Box 1614 NEW YORK NY 10156

CONTENTS

Your usual full length novel:-

DOMINATING OBSESSION
Terry Smith

BONUS PAGES

Pages 213 - 236

Rewritten and expanded
the ever popular but currently
out of print

ERICA: PROPERTY OF REX
so as to be enjoyed even by those who have read
it before -

Part five on pages 213 - 236

Parts 1 - 4 are to be found in Plantation Punishment,
Naked Plunder, Selling Stephanie & SM Double value

This is fiction - in real life, practice safe sex

What is got over the devils back is spent under his belly.

An old English proverb.

For my best friend.

Les Atkins
Who has always been able to make things happen.

DOMINATING OBSESSION

BY
TERRY SMITH

SILVER MOON BOOKS LTD
PO Box CR25 Leeds LS7 3TN

SILVER MOON BOOKS INCORPORATED
PO Box 1614 New York NY 10156

New authors welcome

Printed and bound in Great Britian

Dominating Obsession first published 1997
Copyright Terry Smith
The right of Terry Smith to be identified as author of this book has been asserted in accordance with section 77 and 78 of the copyrights and Patents Act 1988

DOMINATING OBSESSION

DOMINATING OBSESSION by Terry Smith

1

Jade entered the dark room and stood by the door listening.

Was the strap there? She could not see it, but she felt that it was. It would be waiting for her in the darkness, waiting its moment, the heavy leather of it oiled in anticipation of - her buttocks trembled at the thought.

The sound of steady breathing told her that the old man was sleeping peacefully.

She walked over, careful in the darkness, found the far wall, found the straight chair, stood on its seat to adjust the curtains. The drawstring had broken and not been replaced and the curtains were so tall and heavy that they became snagged unless they were pulled at the top. Jade pulled them apart and let a two foot wide strip of brilliant silver moonlight into the room.

Outside the full moon lit up the garden and surrounding farmland as bright as day. She took a moment to look at it, listening to the sounds from the bed. The steady breathing had stopped and Jade knew that Rooter was staring at her bare bottom beneath the navy blue gymslip. She gave a last pull at the curtains and then dismounted from the chair.

"Schoolgirl tonight, eh!" Rooter's voice strained at his illness.

"I am a schoolgirl for another few weeks!" she told her Grandfather. Well, actually, of course, he was the father of her step-father, not her real Grandfather, but that was how she liked to think of him.

There was a slight tremble in her voice as she walked to the head of the bed and stood with her legs together, very prim and proper, a seventeen-year-old schoolgirl in correct school uniform of dark blue skirt, white blouse, and black

DOMINATING OBSESSION

stockings. But Jade's interpretation of the rules wouldn't have accorded with those of her headmistress. The fourteen inch skirt was far too short, so were the sheer nylon hold-ups, and the black patent leather stilettoes were a bit of poetic licence on Jade's part, as was her complete lack of underwear.

Rooter patted the bed and nodded for her to sit down. Then he placed his hand on her knee and nodded. Actually his nod was more of a thing he did with his eyes than with his head, which he could hardly move from the pillow any more.

Jade began to unbutton her blouse. Rooter couldn't manage buttons very well now, although he still occasionally liked to try. She pulled back her blouse and presented her naked bosom to him. Her breasts were large but firm, the same as her mother's, but with smaller nipples and larger areolae - shell pink, whereas her mother's were brown.

After a slight hesitation she leant forward to allow him to fondle them. At his first touch the familiar shudder ran through her body.

"I think your mother is the most beautiful woman on earth," he said, "but you are fast catching her up, and I think it will only be a matter of weeks before you overtake her... Come here!"

Jade did as instructed and in a moment his lips were on her breasts and she began to wiggle her bottom, screwing it down into the bed.

"Oh, God, no, no!"

The pain was terrible - it was beautiful. She had to keep talking to keep her mind off it, and sometimes when he nipped her, or bit too long and hard, she screamed and tried to push him away. But he was bringing her on, then holding her steady, and she knew she would go insane if the torturing bastard didn't give her release soon. She felt his hand on her inner thigh above her stocking and had to remove her left hand from her tits to stop him.

And then she began to come, feeling the ache deep in-

DOMINATING OBSESSION

side dribbling away as she rocked forward and moaned into the pillow, only marginally concerned that she might be suffocating the last shreds of life from the old man.

"I'm dying, Jade," he gasped.

"I know you're dying, Rooter, but what a way to go, eh, you dirty old bugger? Keeping mother satisfied every day and having me at your mercy."

Rooter laughed, flattered by her words, as she had intended him to be.

"On or off?" she asked, standing up.

"Off."

Jade unbuttoned the skirt, stepped out of it, and tossed it aside onto the end of the bed. "Voila," she declared.

"Voila, indeed," Rooter agreed, his greedy eyes trying to drink in the whole of her naked body at once.

Starting with her breasts Jade began caressing her body, rubbing her hands over the large twin melons and looking down to watch the way the bright red nipples immediately jumped erect again the moment they could squeeze themselves free from the steamroller's passing.

Then her hands slid down to enjoy the firm feel of her perfectly flat stomach and the gentle roundness of her young belly, before moving on to the silky soft touch of her thighs, and eventually up again to test the springy black bush of her pubes.

She moved her right palm over it, enjoying the tickling sensation. Then she buried her fingers in it. She had painted the nails green tonight. Rooter liked them green, he said that the pink of her fingers, the green of her nails, the black of her pubes, and the deeper pink of her labia as they slowly unfurled was now his favourite colour combination.

Jade continued caressing her mound while mentally willing her labia to open. 'You must think of a rose bud unfurling', Rooter had told her, 'like in those speeded up time-lapse nature films.' So that was what she had done for weeks now, practising in front of her mirror, and it worked.

DOMINATING OBSESSION

"Good girl," he murmured, and she knew it was time to bend forward and look for herself.

"Not bad!" It was bloody good, the best she had ever done. It was always better when the old man made her do it. She needed an audience, the more depraved and lecherous the better.

She placed her hands on her half open outer lips and pulled them wide so that Rooter could see the inner lips beyond and the gaping throat of her vagina gulping at him like a hungry chick begging to be fed.

Rooter nodded when he had seen enough and Jade turned round and bent right over, opening her legs wide and peering through them with her bobbed hair hanging down. And she stayed like that, caressing the cheeks of her bottom and judging his reaction, while she awaited his decision.

"Well?" she asked.

"Definitely your arse. It's all lovely, and it's not fair to make an old man choose, but that arse is out of this world."

"Is it better than mother's?"

"Better than anyone's. Now stop trawling for compliments and bring it here."

"Don't do anything rude with my bottom - please?" She was genuinely frightened at that moment, as she moved back until her soft flesh was almost in his face. Then, with her long legs open wide, she took a firm grip of her ankles. She jumped when she felt his hand on her thigh and continued to shake as he caressed both thighs and down to the crease of both knees and back before returning to examine her wide open crack. He concentrated on her clit until she was screaming for release. A sweet release that she knew he wouldn't give her for many minutes yet.

First he had to spread her juices all round, over the cheeks of her bottom and into its cleft with many teasing little jabs at her anal ring, before he was ready to make her come. Then he milked her slowly and deliberately with his index finger on her clit and his cupped palm beneath her fanny to

DOMINATING OBSESSION

catch her seeping liquid, so that they could both see how juicy she was.

It was wonderful to be milked like that. It would have been even better if she could have had her wrists tied to her ankles so that she was completely defenceless. For, when he wound her as tight as an elastic band, she felt that she must snap inside and it took every ounce of her willpower not to jump up and away from those wonderfully torturous fingers.

Rooter wiped her collected juice up the crack of her bum. She knew what he intended, but she hesitated anyway, and the next moment his index finger was entering her bum like a dart of white hot fire and she jumped away.

"Come here."

"No."

"Come here, Jade."

She came to him.

"Wrist."

"No!" But she held out her wrist.

He took it in both hands and viciously twisted his hands in opposite directions. Jade screamed and fell to the floor sobbing.

"Get up."

Jade rose and slowly turned and bent, presenting her bottom to him as she had before.

"I will need the chair," she said.

"Fetch it."

She did as she was told and pushed the low backed arm chair into place. It was little more than a child's chair, and when he forced her to bend over it her bottom would be high in the air and her head bent sideways on the seat.

Next she fetched the strap and the two curled-leather dog collars and brought them slowly to him.

"Move the curtain," he commanded.

Jade looked and saw what he meant; the moonlight was no longer quite reaching the place where she would receive

her punishment.

Jade stood on the chair and adjusted the curtain. Even in her 5" ankle strap stilettoes she had to stretch to reach the top rail, and she took her time, knowing that her position would make her body look very desirable. Then she turned and carefully climbed down so that he could see her beautifully rounded bottom in the silver moonlight and appreciate how soft and unblemished was the skin to which he intended to apply his belt.

Jade returned to him on shaking legs, and at his nod bent and fastened her left ankle to the caster of the chair with one of the dog collars. Then she spread her legs wide and fastened her right ankle to the other caster in a similar manner. The preliminaries finished, she twisted at the waist and looked over her shoulder at him, waiting for his permission to continue.

Again the curt nod. Jade bent over the back of the chair, took her breasts in her hands, pushed both straining nipples into her own open mouth, and waited.

He was stronger tonight, much stronger, and soon the nipples were having to come out of her mouth with every stroke of the strap so that she could scream. It didn't take long for him to make her come. She had hated the strap the first few times he had used it. If her need for him hadn't been so strong she wouldn't have continued to go to him night after night. But she did, and slowly she had come to need it. And now she depended on it. How else could she continue to act so depravedly and to think such dreadful thoughts if Rooter wasn't there to punish her and purify her sins?

Now she did everything possible to ensure that she received his beating at least once a week. That wasn't always possible. They had to be alone in the house before he could risk using the strap on her. And those weeks when that didn't happen were murder. That was when she got like this with the unquenchable fire in her, and so much in need of a good

session that she couldn't eat, think, or sleep.

But she would sleep well tonight. Rooter knew exactly how to deal with her, and he left her alone to jerk and shudder to her climax without interference, knowing that any extra stimulus at that moment would be too much. So she twisted and turned, grinding her clitoris against the coarse material of the chair, and groaned and moaned and gently bit her own nipples when she needed the extra pain to help her concentrate her mind away from the unbearable ecstasy. And slowly she finished and was still, with only the jelly in her legs and the burning fire on her bum to remind her of what he had done to her.

Rooter had collected her juices once more and now he wiped them on her anal cleft, and this time she made no protest as his finger entered her back passage. She still pretended to him that she didn't like this, but that was a lie, and her protestations were only a useful excuse to give him a reason to punish her. It was true that she didn't like it all. She didn't like the pain and she didn't like the problems she sometimes experienced with running to the lavatory with very little warning. But those were only minor considerations, because she now loved coming in her bottom almost more than anywhere else.

Having his three fingers inside her, like now, made her feel so weak and helpless, like a little baby. She couldn't move, she wanted only to cry, and if it hadn't been for the pain she would have had to admit that being anally stimulated was perfection. If it wasn't for the pain it would have had everything. It took so long for a start, and for all that time she was floating on a weeping orgasm, and then when the climax eventually came it was so gentle and predictable that she was always almost asleep by then, and her coming hardly woke her.

When they had finished she lay on top of the bed and Rooter cuddled her. It had been a marvellous night. Her bottom was stinging and her anus was sore, but she loved Rooter

DOMINATING OBSESSION

- she loved everyone. And she realised now that she had been worrying unduly. She was good at English, she would easily get an 'A' and if she didn't it wasn't the end of the world. There were other universities.

Jade felt Rooter shaking her and opened her eyes.

"Time for a special," he said, proudly.

"Oh, Rooter, you've not?" she exclaimed, happy for him. And when she pulled the covers aside he had the finest erection she had ever seen him have.

"My God, Rooter, you must be feeling better than ever!" she exclaimed.

"Well don't lets waste it."

Jade needed no further bidding and she scrambled round and on to her knees and took his stalk in her mouth. Rooter placed his cheek against her bottom and his arm between her legs and fondled her dangling breasts while gently kissing her bottom. Jade adjusted her position so that his arm would rub against her open labia. Then she concentrated once more on caressing his balls and nursing his erection.

For several minutes they were lost in a mutual heaven, and then Jade felt his sap begin to rise and with a few more sucks his body went rigid, and a moment later his sperm was gushing in to her mouth, thick, glutinous, and salty. She came herself again then, just a very gentle little pop in sympathy and elation and she held his sperm safely in her mouth until she had covered him up and lay down beside him again. Then she swallowed it so that he could see her throat move and beam his approval.

It was over an hour later that Rooter suddenly jerked up in bed, tumbling her to the floor. Shocked awake, Jade was in time to see him lift his arms aloft and stare into the beam of moonlight as if seeing something far beyond. For an instant she believed she must be witnessing a miracle; Rooter didn't even have the strength to lift his head from the pillow, let alone support himself with his arms outstretched like that.

DOMINATING OBSESSION

Then he cried out and she knew that it was no miracle.

"Take them. Take them all, every last one of them. Curse them down to hell where they all belong!" With that he slumped back on the bed and was dead before his head hit the pillow.

Jade stared up at the bed with white ashen face and bulging green eyes, and listened to the last chime of midnight fade away from the grandfather clock on the landing. She shuddered as someone walked over her grave. Suddenly she was cold, naked and kneeling on the draughty floor of a room that was always kept suffocatingly warm for a dying man.

2

To Miles Good the cocktail lounge of the Old Cabalanians' Club felt strangely cool and deserted now that almost everyone else had taken to the dance floor for the traditional smoochy Saturday night close.

Only he remained at the mahogany topped bar, his tall muscular frame balanced uncomfortably on the very edge of the last seat in the long row of plush red leather bar stools.

He was completely still, a half raised glass of whisky totally forgotten while every nerve end and every sense concentrated on the images his staring eyes were bringing him.

On the dance floor his wife, Robyn, was dancing with the young blond adonis who had played so devastatingly at prop forward in today's charity shield. She was dressed in the long shot silk evening dress they had chosen together for tonight's special Rugby Club dance. The silk of the dress contained all the colours in the world including some that hadn't existed before. It shimmered on Robyn's slowly gyrating body like oil on water, and fitted just as tightly, so that in the dim midnight blue light of the dance floor it was difficult to tell where the dress ended and the voluptuous

DOMINATING OBSESSION

body began.

There was no such difficulty in telling where the blond adonis's hands were though, as they lovingly caressed Robyn's near naked body, passing everywhere as unchallenged as the pale circles of coloured lights that meandered in lazy random patterns over the tightly packed dancers.

At the rear, to the point where her back swept out to become her beautifully rounded bottom, Robyn's dress was non-existent. At the front it was cut low and stretched tightly over generous breasts with prominently thrusting nipples. On her left side it lay open to reveal a tantalising glimpse of naked leg that rose in perfect curves from finely turned ankle to creamy white thigh. There was no suggestion of underwear; the thin silk mimicked the contours of Robyn's body so closely that there could be no doubt that every beautiful rise and indentation was her very own.

Robyn's head was back and her eyes were closed. Miles knew that look, and he knew how warm and generous her gently swaying body would feel as it moulded itself tightly to the hard unyielding frame of the young rugby player.

The boy's hands stopped, one in the small of her back, the other on the cheeks of her bottom, and he pulled Robyn to him as he thrust and gyrated with his massive thighs. Robyn's body quivered, then began to shake. Sensing a victory, the boy held her close, finding her lips with his and placing his hand through the split in her skirt and onto her naked bottom as he continued to dry fuck her on the dance floor.

For several moments Robyn tried to pull away, but then she was lost. For several more seconds the three of them were locked together as Miles and the boy shared in the glory of Robyn's orgasm. When it was over they were all breathless and elated. Robyn hung from the boy's arms, exhausted and subdued. The boy buried his head in her neck and continued to enjoy the soft splendours of her bottom.

Then, suddenly, she drew away and slapped his face.

DOMINATING OBSESSION

"Bloody hell!" Miles whispered, and tossed his whisky back in one gulp. He looked around furtively. No one had seen. Robyn and the boy were at the very edge of the dance floor under the open archway that divided the two rooms, and the few drinkers left in the bar were all unsighted. There was only John the bar steward. He had witnessed it too, but Miles was chairman of the club, and John, an ex-squaddie, knew when he had a cushy billet.

What Miles felt was indescribable. It had so nearly happened, after twelve years of marriage and ten years of nagging, Robyn had almost seen the light. Miles had felt the power and pride growing inside. His cock had been enormous for those few minutes. It had pulsed against his inner thigh. He had felt like ramming it through the solid mahogany bar front. He had felt so invincible.

And then she had drawn back, let him down at the last moment.

This wasn't just a fantasy with him. It might have started off that way, but now it was an obsession; an illness even. He needed total domination over Robyn. He needed to posses her completely, and the only way to do that was to force her to have sex with any man he nominated. For ten years she had refused and their relationship had suffered. Tonight had come so close.

So close...

He almost felt sorry for her. He remembered all her tearful arguments and all her protestations of love. She would never understand his motives; he hardly understood them himself. But they both understood what it would mean. They might not admit it even to themselves, choosing to hide the full truth away in the dark recesses of their minds where the evil part of everyone's soul reigns over a depraved hell of primal excess. It was that part of the mind that had to be released in a soldier to make him into a killing machine. It was that part that could make a boxer beat an opponent to pulp, and it was that part that could make a man like himself

DOMINATING OBSESSION

drive his beautiful loving wife to greater and greater depths of lustful depravity.

Miles' fist was so tight around the whisky tumbler that only the quality of the crystal prevented it from being crushed into a thousand shards. He shook his head as it filled with images; images of Robyn being shagged by street vagrants, gang-banged by misshapen dwarfs, and ... and worse, much worse. Too awful to contemplate even. He mustn't let it happen. But how could he stop it? He would sell his very soul for it. It was what he wanted most in all the world.

Except that it wasn't!

It hadn't even happened yet and already his devious black heart was leaping ahead. If he could force Robyn to obey his every command, why couldn't he have Paige also? He would be invincible, unstoppable, so why not that? Miles opened his eyes and searched out his sister-in-law's wild mop of red hair.

There she was, dancing with the other prop forward. Trust Paige to choose the one who was even bigger and built even more like a brick shit house. She looked like a beautifully painted doll in his arms. Paige was smaller than Robyn, but the light of life shone from her eyes and her mischievous giggle could turn any man's vitals to jelly. But that wasn't why Miles lusted after her. She was the most promiscuous little madam alive. It was reliably rumoured that she had been through every male member of this worthy club, from sixteen to seventy - except one: himself. She knew he lusted after her and that was the reason she denied him, and teased him unmercifully.

He had often seen her naked, walking unselfconsciously from bathroom to bedroom. She had often flounced down on the settee or crossed her legs to show him that she was wearing no knickers. She had often allowed him to hold her a fraction too long when kissing her hello or goodbye. But she wouldn't let him have her. The cow. How he longed to posses Paige and to watch some stud like this huge prop

DOMINATING OBSESSION

forward screwing the tiny little arse off her!

He would give anything to own her. His very soul even.

Suddenly Miles had a dreadful feeling that he wasn't alone. He turned slowly, his spine tingling. He felt the little hairs on his neck standing up.

A large dark stranger was watching him. Staring at him, like a cat stalking a mouse.

Now the stranger was approaching. Now he gave a stiff little bow.

"My name is deVille!" he said. "Nicholas deVille."

3

"I'm sorry, old man, no offence. You looked so - lost."

deVille laughed as Miles' obvious confusion. Then he remembered his manners, but his eyes were still laughing. "Please - let me get you a drink," he was saying now. "To apologise for my rudeness." He was already gesturing to John, the steward, who was watching the pair with a faint expression of distaste.

Miles looked at his watch. Four minutes past twelve, they were just in time, the band would be finishing soon and John would be rushed off his feet.

"That young woman is certainly something special, isn't she?" said deVille.

He meant Robyn.

Miles grinned and nodded his agreement as he turned to watch John do his best to hurry towards them with three stiff legs. Miles smiled again as he felt his own cock give another twitch. So he definitely wasn't the only one affected by tonight's happenings on the dance floor.

"What will you have?" deVille was asking, and from the look on his face and the tone of his voice it obviously wasn't for the first time.

DOMINATING OBSESSION

"Oh, sorry. another measure of the club malt, please." Miles addressed the end of his remark to the hovering barman.

"Same for me, John, two large ones."

Miles extended his hand over the corner of the bar. "James Good, but everyone calls me Miles."

"Fine - everyone calls me deVille."

Miles looked at deVille, trying to decide what Robyn would think of him. He was very smooth and impeccably dressed, suntanned, with flashing white teeth, jet black hair greying at the temples, and a ready smile. He was probably as tall as Miles, but heavier, and he looked fit. He had a slightly crooked nose and a gap in his left eyebrow where a head butt had left a permanent scar.

This was no callow youth like the blond adonis. deVille seemed harmless enough at the moment, but there was something about the set of his jaw and the flint in his eyes that told Miles that he would have little difficulty in getting his way with most people. Undoubtedly a good all rounder; good on the rugby field, in the boardroom, in the pub, and in the bedroom.

Miles felt a stab of excitement in his groin. This man had that commanding air of mystery and danger that women find difficult to resist.

"Thanks." deVille waved away the change. "Well, cheers."

The men dipped their glasses to each other and sipped their whisky. Miles' thought grew on him as if it had a life of its own.

"What?" deVille queried.

"Well, actually, I was just wondering - you were quite taken with the lady then?" Without turning Miles waved his glass in the general direction of the dance floor.

"Almost as much as you," deVille laughed. "What man could resist her? Pure animal. Raw sex. Built for it. Let any man that doesn't believe in God look at that and tell me that a perfectly formed sex machine like that came about by pure

accident. Evolution, my balls. God must be the dirtiest old man imaginable. I tell you, a man could die of lust just looking at that and go happily to his grave singing of sex." deVille laughed with enjoyment for the glory that was Robyn's body.

Miles felt exceedingly proud, but he wanted more and elected to play devil's advocate. "You make her sound like a whore."

"No way!" deVille was shocked. "I didn't mean that at all. Our little girl there takes such things very seriously I'd say. She's basically a one man woman, and that one man she would love very much and would be willing to do anything for, even act the whore if he wanted her to. She would have no qualms about being dirty with the right man. You remember those old Woody Allen lines: 'Does sex have to be dirty? It does if you're doing it right.' Well you can bet your last shag that that little vixen would be doing it right."

Miles laughed. "I think you've fallen for her."

"Yes indeed." deVille looked pensively towards the dance floor for a moment. "I could definitely do that young woman a lot of damage if she was interested."

"You reckon? She looks a lot of woman to me."

"Don't you worry - I've got a lot of pent up lust. No seriously, women are just like any other animal - a complete waste of space unless they're trained."

"Discipline, you mean?" The word was stirring something in Miles' mind.

"Certainly. They all love it. They're the better for it and they know it. Just look at that cheeky little arse. It would be a criminal shame if her present lord and master doesn't give that a regular tanning."

Miles felt the excitement stretching his cock again. "You think she would stand for it?"

deVille laughed. "I take it you don't go in for such things?"

"No." Miles felt almost guilty, as if forced to confess a serious neglect of duty.

"Well you should. I take it you've got a woman?"

Miles nodded.

"Well everything in nature has its natural pecking order, and every animal feels more content for knowing its place. You do no one and no thing any favours by letting it sort around trying to find its own reason for being. Everyone and everything likes to feel useful and appreciated, and you do that by training."

"But no one likes pain."

"Women are complicated. They might not like it at first, but no woman ever stopped loving a man because he tanned her arse. You can't neglect a woman. They have to be trained and they have to have pain. How else can they know you love them? They may think they hate you for a lot of the things you do to them. But women need that as well. They need someone to hate, someone to blame. They like to feel like a victim, and to enjoy shedding a few tears and being miserable occasionally, and it helps them if one man can supply them with the lot. One-stop shopping, so to speak. Women aren't like men. They don't need a variety of lovers, just one real swine who can make them feel like a princess one moment and as wretched as a dog the next. They can forgive a man any hurt, but they can't forgive a man that can't hurt them. They expect it. They demand it. And it's only fair for us to have the courage to give it to them in aces... well, if you ever need any help getting started with your own woman I'm only too happy to oblige."

"What!" Miles threw his drink back in surprise. "Is that a joke?"

deVille smiled, and Miles knew that it was not.

Actually," he managed to get out, "actually, I could use some help!"

deVille laughed again, but this time it was more restrained. Somehow he was not at all surprised. He reached into his inside pocket and produced a gold cigarette case which he opened and offered to Miles. Miles waved it away,

DOMINATING OBSESSION

preferring one of his own thin cigars instead.

"Well, what help do you need?" deVille blew grey smoke towards the optics behind the bar.

"She's totally untrained, so what do you suggest?" Miles countered.

"It's really up to you. Whatever you feel easiest with. If you've never gone in for discipline you'd be learning as well."

"Oh, I couldn't do it myself, not at first anyway."

deVille laughed. "So what are we suggesting here, getting the servants to see to her?"

"No - I was rather hoping - you -"

Now deVille was really enjoying himself. "Me? I hope she's good looking."

"You need have no worries there. I know you'd fancy her."

"And what would you be doing while this was going on?"

"Watching and learning."

"Would you, by God! I bet you would. She wouldn't take to it easy you know. There would be a lot of wailing and tears. Women like to make a major performance over every little freedom they have to give up. They are all prima donnas at heart, just waiting for their fifteen minutes at centre stage."

Miles nodded and grinned.

"You like that, eh? But it's not just the spanking, you know. They expect a good seeing to as well."

"I know."

deVille stopped and looked at him then.

Miles looked steadily back.

"I see - you want a threesome?"

"Not necessarily. I'll join in if you want, but mainly I want to see you give my wife a damn good screwing."

"And how about the discipline?"

"I rather think that that may be necessary to convince her to co-operate."

"How about the kisses and cuddles?" deVille paused while they both inhaled. "Women tend to find those rather crucial

DOMINATING OBSESSION

too."

"I do love her you know. I think she's the most beautiful person alive, in every way. It's just - I don't know, I've got to have this domination over her."

"And you think I'd like her?"

"I know you would, and I think she'd like you too."

"That's irrelevant," deVille commented dismissively. "Well, why not?" he agreed after a moment's thought. "It would certainly be interesting. But no chickening out when the going gets tough."

"No way."

"I shall make demands on you too!"

"Sounds fair." He held out is hand and deVille shook it firmly.

"It's a bargain," deVille said.

"A bargain," Miles agreed. "This calls for a celebration. He looked round for John. He didn't have to look far. "Same again, John," he said without having to raise his voice.

"And what do we think your wife might say when she's told she's going to shag a complete stranger in front of her husband?" deVille asked with his innocent smile.

Miles shrugged again. "Well, that's when she might need her first bit of persuasion."

"No problem!" said deVille.

4

"This is my wife - Robyn."

deVille showed no signs of surprise.

Robyn looked from one to the other. It was obvious that the two men shared some secret from which she was excluded. She looked with apprehension at the big dark haired man who stood from his bar stool to greet her.

deVille towered over her and she looked up into his eyes.

23

DOMINATING OBSESSION

Without being fully sure if she had offered it, she felt her hand clasped in a firm cool grip, and it seemed as if the rest of her was held just as firmly. Her world shrank to the size of a pair of piercing brown eyes as she became the single focus of deVille's attention, and he swallowed her up and greeted her with a gaze that radiated from his whole body.

Now there was just the two of them in an area that seemed suffocatingly small. She felt herself lifted and held off the ground by an invisible force that left her suspended and floating. She didn't know this man, and she didn't want to know him. Every fibre of her body screamed danger! She could hardly think for the red lights flashing their warning. She must hold him at a distance.

She must make him respect her. She wasn't a sex object. She wasn't his inferior.

But her body had instantly gone safety critical and now achieved the big bang with every override switch resolutely expanding away from her centre of control. She could feel her tight dress getting tighter and her taut nipples getting tauter. She could feel the pleasant dampness between her thighs growing hotter. And her legs, which she commanded to be still, were like two disobedient urchins splashing in a muddy pool. They wanted only to be left to continue dancing on marshmallow mud.

It wasn't entirely unknown for her body to react this way. It had had one or two little preliminary practices before, with other men of a certain type. deVille's type; large, distinguished, charming, confident men, who thought they ran the world and that all women were little girls who needed looking after. It was a simple matter of programming. Nature had programmed her to react to a particular type of male animal, and nature didn't give a toss that this happened to be the worst possible type for her. All women speak of the main bastard in their lives; the one mistake they will never make again - until the next time.

This man was Robyn's mistake in the making. In trumps.

DOMINATING OBSESSION

But he wasn't going to happen. She wouldn't let him happen. She wouldn't let him steamroller her. But her emotions were already off on a white-knuckle ride to destruction and she could see herself sitting helplessly in a roller-coaster screaming 'No!' while everything around her was screaming 'Yes!'

She didn't care how unfairly the deck was stacked against her - she would stop him. But there are conventions to these things - a certain social etiquette, so she wouldn't snatch her hand away and give offence, she would simply indicate that he had borrowed it for long enough.

But deVille wasn't ready to give it back. He held on gently but firmly, his pressure exactly matching her's. More sure of her now, he reversed his grip and held her hand with his fingers in her palm and his thumb on the back.

Then he pulled it towards his crotch!

Robyn watched, paralysed with horror, as her own familiar well brought up fingers approached that large bulge in his trousers and then gently bumped against it like a small boat docking against a far larger vessel.

She looked up at him again, not believing what he was doing, and his eyes were laughing at her. The bastard! He was teasing her and she had let him. Then she heard his fly unzip and felt his naked knob in her hand, and suddenly all the world was shaking. It was a terrible earthquake that had came up from nowhere and was tearing the breath from her body and rattling the brain in her head. She couldn't think. The floor was rolling and everything was crashing down around her! They would all be killed! Everyone must run for cover!

Then the chaos disappeared in exchange for white cold terror. It was too late to run - far too late. They were standing at the corner of the bar of their club, in the centre of all their friends and acquaintances, and she was holding a stranger's cock in her hand. The room was full of noise and people, but they were alone; she and the two men looking

down at her hand which was shielded from outside observation by their three encircling bodies.

Robyn looked at what she was doing. She was rubbing a man's cock. Robyn had only ever known three cocks before. Those of Ray, her former husband, and of Miles, her present mate, and of Rooter, his father. And now she knew this one, this big handsome stranger, who belonged to - who?

With no power to stop him she watched as he lifted her fingers free. But he couldn't lift her eyes and they continued to look at what her fingers had known so recently, and now had lost. It was then that the full realisation of her action rose up from somewhere deep below and emerged through the floor and whooshed up her body to leave her swooning hot and bright lobster pink.

She found her fingers again then - they were an inch from his lips. If she had retained any automotive power it would have been ridiculously easy to stop him. He was moving in slow motion, lost in a fog, carefully bending them over so that her knuckles showed white against her new shocking-pink flesh.

Then his heels were together and his back ramrod straight as his handsome head bowed to display a thick crop of very strokeable black hair. And it was the gentlest, driest little kiss you could ever imagine. Just a pair of soft dry lips that nuzzled her fingers. A bolt of electricity shot along her arm, down through her stomach, and out through her toes, locking every muscle as it passed. The shock was total, and all over in a split second. Robyn's quiet little island was wrecked; left in tatters by the passing hurricane.

Robyn knew she was shaking. And she knew that deVille knew it too; he could feel it through their fingers. It made her want to run away in shame, but she couldn't do that. She couldn't even close her eyes as the nightmare continued, and deVille confidently lifted a champagne flute from the bar. She could see the golden bubbles emerging and rising steadily upwards to explode themselves on the surface. None of them

wavered - none of them held back. Some clung to the side of the glass for a while, whilst others were more eager, but all were happy to die to fulfil their single purpose in being, that of bringing a little sparkle into someone else's life.

Robyn swam in the audacious stare of the stranger. Why had her husband allowed him to do such a thing to her? Why had she allowed it? What was being celebrated with the champagne?

Robyn knew everything now. She knew what deVille was going to do next. The champagne foamed angrily as her fingers were plunged into the elegant flute. For a moment they remained trapped there like three large pink fish in an undersized tank. Then they were gone again, leaving the half empty glass looking ill used and forsaken while they went off, sticky and chilled, to go slipping and sliding all over deVille's hot throbbing prick.

She knew how to wank him - of course she did. What she didn't know was what made her do it. But it had to be done, there was no question of that. It was something that was urgent, and which couldn't be stopped or slowed even when she felt him coming to climax. Then with a startled cry she had brought him too far and his seed snaked towards her, only to be expertly caught in his hanky.

He wiped her wrist where some of the glutinous liquid had escaped the hastily spread barrier of shining white silk. Then he cleaned the tips of her fingers and the tip of his knob, and bunching up his improvised net, returned it to his top pocket.

Robyn gazed down, and hated the disappointment she felt at seeing deVille's fly now firmly locked up and closed for business, and all there was to show for their excess was an empty glass and a small foaming puddle sinking into the thick pile carpet.

And that was it.

Robyn's knees gave way, and as her bottom dipped towards the floor deVille caught her up and swung her effort-

DOMINATING OBSESSION

lessly onto his empty bar stool.

As the two men turned their attention to the waiting champagne, Robyn tried to collect her spinning thoughts. Her display on the dance floor had been a signal to her husband that she had decided not to acquiesce to his voyeuristic fantasies. With that decision had surged a wonderful cocktail of trepidation and excitement; trepidation for obvious reasons, excitement at having suddenly stolen the initiative from him and not knowing how he would respond.

And now - THIS!

She watched the two men laughing and drinking, and shivered.

This man must not come home with them...

5

Robyn sat uncomfortably between Miles and deVille on the back seat of the minicab. Not only had Miles ensured that she was seated between them, he had also contrived to spread his legs and take up half the available space, leaving Robyn pressed against the warm firmness of deVille's right thigh. Robyn's head was swimming again, this time with the heat and lack of air. How could the others bear it? The night was still warm, even balmy, yet they didn't have a single window open. She would be ill if she had to stay like this all the way home.

Then she felt deVille's hand beneath her dress on her naked thigh.

The now familiar shock was there and she was instantly wet and shaking, but she pushed the hand away with a confidence she didn't feel.

She closed her eyes and struggled for breath. She was trapped for at least another twenty minutes until they reached home. As trapped as the air - and just as hot, limp, and damp.

DOMINATING OBSESSION

She felt the stinging lash of embarrassment at how cool and dry deVille's touch had felt against her own clammy flesh.

She opened her eyes. deVille was staring at her heaving breasts. So was the driver; the reflection of his ogling eyes huge enough to fill the rear-view mirror.

There was no stopping it now - Robyn knew that, deep down. It was going to happen. The men were beyond reason. Robyn closed her eyes tight again. She had no wish to look at her tormenters. The air was full of male testosterone. They were drunk on it. They wanted a victim.

Robyn clenched her left hand as tight as she could, and much tighter than was strictly necessary to hold the split in her skirt firmly closed. Her body was stiff and straight as she continued to stare straight ahead through tightly closed eyes, pretending to herself that it wouldn't happen, just as long as she continued to ignore it, just as long as she continued to pretend to be a statue.

Christ, what a fool - and what a statue! She could feel her breasts heaving and rolling within the confines of a dress that now felt at least two sizes too small. They were burning hot - as hot as the inside of her brain. And all the while she could feel the flames from the three pairs of hungry male eyes licking and flickering all over her like blow torches.

Then Miles' arm curled round her shoulder and in an instant her burning flesh was wrapped within its cool protective cloak and shaded from the searing heat of their lust. Robyn had always loved this man, but never as much as in that moment. Her heart went out to him. All at once she was safe. He had seen sense at last, thank God!

Her transformation was so sudden that she felt herself shudder as the heat left her body and brain, leaving her cool enough to think again. She relaxed against the man she loved, letting her body sink into his; grateful for his strength, grateful for his presence, overjoyed at this confirmation of his love for her in her moment of greatest need. He wasn't overly demonstrative, poor lamb, and this public show of affection

DOMINATING OBSESSION

was against his natural instincts, which made her all the more grateful.

She snuggled against him. He would feel her trembling, but that didn't matter, this was Miles and she wanted him to know how frightened she had been and how safe she felt now.

It was such a relief now to allow herself the luxury of relaxing. She suddenly felt brave enough to stare at deVille. It was important he understood that he had lost, but the bastard just returned her stare, supremely confident, entirely unconvinced by her silent assertions.

Miles pressed her cheek to his shoulder and stroked her arm. deVille didn't matter. She was in Miles' arms and that felt so very good. Her fingers found his thigh and stroked it affectionately. As she began to doze, Miles caught her fingers in the darkness and lifted them to his lap. Oh yes. That was what she wanted. Her little soldier wasn't so little tonight. He was big and firm, just the way she liked him. He suddenly jerked inside Miles' trousers and Robyn felt the warmth in her belly and almost mewed with pleasure.

Miles squeezed her shoulder. That silent communication between them was better than any words. They were like two halves of the same person, with the same thoughts and feelings - and the same desires. She loved the strength of him; the solid dependable reliability. She melted into him and now they were one. A perfect fit.

Miles' palm began caressing gently up and down her bare arm. The tips of Robyn's fingers found his helmet and began circling round and round on it, marvelling at how lovely and smooth it felt, even through the wool of his trousers.

Miles' hand descended to her elbow. Robyn was embarrassed to realise her muscles were still knotted and her fist still firmly clamped to the two edges of the split in her skirt. That was silly; there was no need to guard herself from deVille any longer. Even he wouldn't be arrogant enough not to realise that the rules of the game had changed.

Gentle fingers began soothing the tension from her locked arm muscles. It did no harm for Miles to realise how determined she'd been to protect herself from deVille. But he could do that for her now. No need for her to worry. deVille would be lucky if Miles let him stay for more than a single nightcap before sending him off in the same cab. She relaxed completely, feeling the last residues of tension leaving her listless body.

Then, with a sudden jerk, Miles twisted her arm up behind her back. At the same moment the fingers of his free hand closed on hers, squeezing them so tight it felt like he was actually bruising her bones.

For an instant all was still, neither of them moved, neither of them breathed. It took that long for Robyn to understand the extent of his betrayal. She was his prisoner - her skirt was wide open and her naked thigh was once more vulnerable to deVille's attack. It took only a fraction longer to blame herself for it. She hadn't made Miles love her enough. She could never have done such a thing to him. But he was like a drug addict looking to connect. This obsession of his would destroy them both.

Robyn began to struggle then, with all the rage and uncomprehending anger of a woman spurned. Her mind swirled with a red mist that lapped over everything like a thick wave of blood. She heard someone sobbing and choking with frustration - and knew it was herself. The world isn't just. Robyn couldn't possibly live with such betrayal, but the unjust world decreed that she must, and gave the power and the strength to her adversaries.

Miles held her so tight that however much she struggled she could hardly move her body let alone her arms, and between them he and deVille managed to fend off her wild kicks and use their own feet to dislodge her shoes, so that she was left without any of her weapons; a pathetic, struggling, bare foot victim.

She sobbed with frustration at her own impotence. Her

ignominy was utter and complete. She was a victim. She had nothing. They had left her with nothing.

deVille's hand took possession of her bare thigh again. Slowly it prowled up and down, looking for a way under her tight dress like a powerful feline predator hunting for a way to breach the barbed defences of a thick hedge to get to a nest of fledglings within. Then it was in, and making its way arrogantly towards her unprotected vagina. It was strange to feel this new hand on her body, moving to where so few had been before.

When it finally arrived, after an agonisingly slow approach, her body gave a great involuntary shudder as a massive tidal wave hit her peaceful island again, and she came at once.

deVille's hand didn't move - it didn't have to. It had only to remain there, cupping the fluttering little bird inside. Everything came pouring out for him. Robyn wondered how he stood the heat - his palm must be sizzling like a steak on a grill. But he didn't remove it. He left it there, as though to prove a point, like a man holding his hand in a flame.

Robyn knew what he was doing. His hand was so still while her body was twitching and weeping for him. He had done this to her without even trying, without even breaking sweat, and he could do it again any time he liked. That was what his inaction was intended to convey to her.

She didn't want to give herself to him; not any part, however small. But she could feel the power seeping from her and into him. She felt like a battery losing its charge. He was draining something from her. What it was she wasn't exactly sure. She only knew that it was necessary to retain it for herself if she wanted to remain as her own woman.

But it was too late. deVille had it now. He had too much of it. She couldn't pull it back, she couldn't reverse the flow. So she sat there, coming for him, with his hand on her vulva and her juices seeping between his fingers as the silent car sped on through the dark night towards their equally dark

DOMINATING OBSESSION

future.

Robyn became vaguely aware that Miles was shaking, and realised that her climax was carrying him with it. His palms were swimming with sweat. She could now prise herself free from his grip if she wanted to. But she didn't; something prevented her. It didn't seem to matter any more. It was too late - far too late. Miles snatched his thigh away from hers as if the heat of her body was scorching him. It probably was; she was on fire.

How many times had Miles told her how he felt? How many times had he tried to describe it to her as he pleaded with her to submit to a stranger like this? She hadn't realised. His eloquent arguments had been merely words. Poor pathetic words. Just Miles wittering on again about something she knew she could never bring herself to do. But this wasn't words any more; this was very, very, real.

deVille's fingers entered her waiting slit and reality became a dream. Not a nightmare as she had warned herself it would be, but a beautiful dream. She had willed his fingers to enter her; almost forced them with mental telepathy. And she hadn't been wrong to do so. His fingers were strangers to her. Foreign. Their touch impersonal. Disembodied. She had no power over them. She couldn't stop them doing anything they liked to her.

If they had been her own fingers, or even Miles', she could have controlled them, stopped them, directed them. But these fingers were beyond her control. They could do anything - anything. And she was helpless to resist. Not because her husband held her arms imprisoned. Not because he wanted to see and feel her submit to another man's caresses. But because she wanted this. She wanted this so much. Much more than she could ever have dreamed possible. Why? Why was it so exciting to have a virtual stranger do this to her in public? Robyn didn't know - and at that moment - she didn't really care.

Robyn moved her legs and deVille understood at once,

DOMINATING OBSESSION

and as she rose from the seat for a second he pulled her skirt back to expose her steaming cunt. Robyn had never felt this excited before. She could feel the electricity in Miles' body. She had never known him like this before. She had never known herself like this before. She was going to explode and she was helpless to stop it; didn't want to stop it.

She wanted those masterful fingers deep inside where the greatest pain was; where the greatest pleasure was. Each expert touch made her grind her bottom and thrust her thighs, screaming at his fingers to touch her harder; screaming at them to penetrate her further; screaming at them to take total possession of her.

It was unbearable. His fingers were more knowledgeable than her own. It mustn't happen. She couldn't let it. She mustn't abandon herself to him. But she wanted to - wanted to so much! Just this once. Just once. She would resist him next time. She would make herself resist him - next time. It would only be this once. After that she would be a good girl. Please let him take her higher and higher, with those clever fingers that knew so much more than her own had ever done.

Suddenly she was thrusting up. Oh yes, yes! Up and up until she thought her head must emerge through the top of the cab. That's it. Please, please. That's it! Out into the cool fresh air where every breath she took didn't scorch her lungs.

Then it hit her, and went on hitting her again and again. Oh, my God. Oh, my God! This was like nothing she had ever experienced before. She was trapped between them - deVille and Miles. They were feeding off her. They were devouring her like starving hyenas. They were starving and she was their feast. She could feel their heat and their hunger. She bucked and twisted between them. Her head thrashed from side to side. She would die...

... And then it was finished, and she wanted to be free. She couldn't bare their touch any longer. She couldn't take any more.

She slumped, exhausted, into the seat, throwing her head

back and crying for them to stop. They had to stop; had to leave her in peace. She could take no more. But even as she heard her words from a distance like the voice of a familiar stranger, she knew they were unnecessary. She knew the only reason she was now able to articulate her need was because the crisis was past, and it was a need no longer.

She began to shake and quietly whimper; it helped to whimper. She was amazingly wet. She could feel the perspiration cooling on her skin. That was quite nice really. But she didn't want the other wetness to cool - not yet. She hugged it to her, drawing up her knees and closing her thighs on its warm stickiness. That was a comforting wetness which she wanted to hold on to a little longer, while she had a little doze.

6

This was turning out to be the best night of Miles' life!

He had anticipated this moment a thousand times, often with the inevitably sticky consequences, but even his vivid lust induced imagination had never devised anything as wildly erotic as this. Miles couldn't have asked for anything better. deVille was a master - a real bastard.

Miles looked at the back of deVille's head, now driving. He had only given him brief directions, but deVille seemed to be experiencing no difficulty in navigating his way through the unfamiliar Cambridgeshire lanes. In fact, driving seemed to barely tax his attention at all, leaving him free to stare at Robyn as the driver had done before they changed places - through the rear view mirror.

Miles wondered at the calmness of the man. His body was perfectly relaxed, almost motionless, and his expression was blank and inscrutable.

In contrast, Robyn was full of movement and tension,

DOMINATING OBSESSION

thrashing about on the back seat as volatile as a pulsating cylinder full of trapped steam.

Miles had his left hand behind Robyn's back pinioning both her wrists together. His other arm was under her chin with his hand flat against her cheek, pressing her head firmly into his shoulder. His own cheek was on top of her head, and he was kissing her damp hair and whispering constantly to calm her while his own excitement crept towards crisis point as he stared down at the cab driver's head in her lap.

The interior light was on. deVille had seen to that so that Miles could witness every last detail of his own wife's violation. And that was exactly what Miles was doing - enduring every last agonizingly erotic detail of it with bulging eyes, wide open ears, and the biggest erection he had ever experienced.

The unkempt mass of black greasy hair continued to twist and turn between Robyn's creamy white thighs as the cab driver fought to keep his mouth tightly clamped to her vagina, and she fought just as desperately to be free. The noises made Miles shudder with disgust. The man was insane with lust, grunting over Robyn like a wild bore over his kill; snorting and slobbering, gurgling and swallowing, and all the time calling her 'whore' and 'bitch' and telling her how many depraved ways he was going to fuck her. The man was a monster, and Miles knew that he himself was no better - worse in fact, because watching another man licking and eating his wife was bringing him close to a wonderful ejaculation.

He was breathless at the prospect of this animal actually screwing her. It was almost too much for his spinning mind to comprehend. It wasn't just a dream any more, it wasn't just a fantasy - it could actually happen - probably would. He and deVille could invite this perverted beast into the house with them and actually watch and assist as he did the awful things he'd vowed to do to Robyn.

Suddenly Robyn stopped bucking and bobbing and sat

bolt upright. Her tormented moans stopped and left behind a moment of intense silence so sharp that it seemed to penetrate and freeze Miles' thoughts. The hairs on the back of his neck stood up, and he waited in irrational shock to know if she was still alive.

She was. Robyn's pinioned hands snatched at his shirt, twisting and trapping the flesh at his waist in a grip that made him exhale in noisy agony. Then, like a vampire, she bit deeply into the heel of his hand and clamped him in an agony that drove every thought from his head and every other sensation from his body.

The driver grunted in satisfaction and raised his head for a moment. His swarthy unshaven chops were smeared with Robyn's juices. His sunken eyes were black and dull like those of an addict deep into a wondrous trip, but his leer was triumphant, and Miles could see why. The man had his thumb in Robyn's vagina, and at least two of his nicotine stained fingers in her anus. He closed his grip and jerked his hand and Robyn screamed again. So did Miles - as long fingers once more twisted his flesh and chisel like teeth clamped down afresh on his already numb hand.

The cabby used the thumb and index finger of his other hand to carefully reveal Robyn's clitoris. It was as though Miles was seeing it for the first time. It looked so big and so vulnerable, sitting there like a fat pearl winking from the centre of a freshly opened oyster.

The cabby smiled maliciously and clicked his incisors together dramatically. He sneered as Robyn twisted and squirmed in panic of what was to come next.

Miles carefully detached her fingers from his waist and pulled her chin up, forcing her head back so that her teeth could do him no further harm. He caught deVille's calm eyes through the rear view mirror, and then followed their reflected gaze down to the grubby face which was slowly sinking between his wife's widespread thighs.

Robyn's breasts thrust forward, as round and firm as

DOMINATING OBSESSION

melons, with light brown areolae the size of gold crowns, pierced by hugely erect nipples. She looked magnificent with those Amazon breasts displayed proudly - as defiant as the figurehead on the prow of an ancient sailing ship gallantly cutting through wind-tossed waves.

Robyn shrieked. She began to jerk and thrash about, and then to shake like the ground in the path of an approaching earthquake. At first it was all too much; too violent, too awkward, too disjointed. But then the cabby found her natural rhythm and took control, twisting his fingers and thumb inside her and alternating his teeth and tongue on her clitoris until he could make her rise and subside at will.

Miles had no need to keep her head imprisoned now. He let his arm drop to her breasts and flicked his fingers back and forth over those hard, firm nipples.

Robyn was mewing and rocking her head gently from side to side in an attempt to cope with the ecstasy. Suddenly her eyes opened, glistening with moisture. She blinked a few times in the gloomy yellow light, found what she was looking for, and then concentrated on them as she continued to tremble and shudder.

deVille stared back at her through the mirror, his eyes totally cold. They both knew what this was about; she suddenly wanted him to see her submission. She was his now, to do with as he liked. He had ordered the cabby to change places. He had ordered Miles to hold her while they did so. And he had ordered Robyn to stay where she was and not to resist. They had all done as they were told, and they were all continuing to do so - dancing to his tune.

The eyes in the mirror dilated, and Robyn came. Her mouth opened, her eyes closed, her body shuddered, and then she slumped back into the seat. Miles released her wrists.

The cabby rose and gazed triumphantly upon the scene of his victory like an army general surveying the field in the aftermath of battle.

Robyn looked strangely serene, totally still, and totally

at peace. The cabby gripped her hair and twisted her to face him. He wanted her to look at him - he wanted to gloat.

But Robyn didn't open her eyes.

The cabby spitefully brushed Miles' hand from her breasts and drank upon their beauty, before pouncing on them with mouth, and fingers, and thumbs.

This was too much. Surely deVille must stop him? Surely the man must show some mercy? But deVille was different - a true bastard without conscience or compassion.

Miles watched his wife's poor exhausted body begin to spasm and twist again as she tried in vain to wrench the cabby's face from her bosom. What hope was there for her, locked in a moving car with an animal and two bastards for company? But Miles didn't have long to wait for an answer as Robyn's hands stopped wrenching at the cabby's greasy hair, and amazingly opened and clasped his head to her breasts. She was gasping and panting to a steady rhythm.

Miles' gaze lowered further. Robyn's dress was rucked tightly around her hips which were raised and thrusting. Her legs were wide open, and her damp bush of chestnut curls was dissected by a hairy wrist which ploughed in and out of her with the steady piston strokes of a steam hammer as the cabby fist-fucked her into final submission. In his free fist, the cabby was urgently pumping his fat stumpy cock. His face was twisted absurdly with intense concentration.

It was all over very quickly. Robyn cried out, her poor features racked with pain and ecstasy. As the cabby's cock spat thickly onto her bare stomach she slumped back against Miles and lay still, the only indication of life remaining was the slow swell and fall of her mauled breasts.

The cabby sat up and re-buckled his trousers. He grinned broadly and turned from one man to the other, anxious for their applause, as he wiped his fingers on a three hundred pound strip of crumpled silk.

Miles looked at deVille in the mirror as the car slowed and then stopped. The cabby and deVille changed places

DOMINATING OBSESSION

again. It was all over. Miles wouldn't have believed it possible that Robyn would let the cabby take deVille's place - but she had. deVille had brought her to the edge of orgasm before ordering the switch, and true, Robyn had resisted at first. But the cabby had been as equally determined as she, and her defiance had only lasted a minute or two against his brutish insistence. Now the cabby was back in his accustomed seat, and Miles could hardly believe it had happened.

"Drive on," deVille commanded.

The cabby switched off the interior light and took a few moments to try to ascertain where they were. deVille smiled at Miles, silently admitting that he had got them lost, just driving without having a clue where he was going. The driver wasn't bothered, it was all on the clock and the next signpost would reveal all. He shrugged his shoulders and the car started slowly away again, carrying three very happy men ... and a tormented, sleeping woman.

Miles and Robyn had travelled a lifetime in a single cab journey. They had changed completely - irreversibly. But Miles knew there was more to come - much more. He shuddered with fear, knowing they had hardly started to plumb the dark depths of his terrifying depravity.

Evil is a drug, which once savoured, is hard to resist.

7

As the front window lowered and Miles stooped to pay the cabby he almost gagged from the stench of bodily odour. He hadn't really paid that much attention to the man before; not surprisingly he had been focusing on his own gorgeous wife. The cabby had been nothing more than a convenient tool. True, he was quite repugnant, and that had certainly appealed to Mile's depravity; the beauty and the beast.

Miles added generously to the charge on the meter, and

DOMINATING OBSESSION

the driver had the grace to grin sheepishly as if acknowledging that it should be he paying Miles.

"Have you a card?" He winked. "We might need you again."

"Sure thing." The cabby scrabbled around in the glove compartment and emerged with a scrap of printed pasteboard. "How about now, boss? It would be cheaper, no return trip."

"Not now, I'll phone." As the taxi crunched away down the drive, Miles looked over at deVille and Robyn.

They were standing together in a strange way, as if something secret had just passed between them. They were only three or four yards away, but Robyn seemed very remote. deVille was standing behind her and holding her arms behind her back. She looked like a prisoner under arrest.

That was the first time that Miles felt the loss. He loved Robyn, and perhaps she had always been right when she had insisted that this way would lead to her losing him. But it had never occurred to him that it could also lead to him losing her, and just how very much that would hurt.

At that moment Miles heard the heavy front door thrown back on its hinges, and the three of them were suddenly bathed in sparkling white light from the huge crystal chandelier in the hall. He swung round and saw Jade as he had never seen her before. Perhaps it was because he was still incredibly aroused.

His slightly ungainly teenage step-daughter had blossomed into a breathtakingly gorgeous young lady. She was wearing a silk dressing-gown which clung to every beautiful curve of her young body, and the light from the hall made it virtually transparent. Miles' gaze was drawn, as though by a magnet, from the promisingly generous contours of her breasts to her long and shapely legs, which were teasingly visible through the shadowy silk.

"Rooter's dead!"

With mouth gaping - but not from the news of the demise of his father - Miles turned to look at Robyn, but as he

DOMINATING OBSESSION

did so she came rushing past him holding the hem of her dress high to enable those beautifully long legs to fly up the short flight of granite steps that led to the front door.

Miles followed into the house and stood watching as mother and daughter raced up the curved marble staircase in their panic not to keep a dead man waiting.

"Trouble?" deVille's gently cultured voice made Miles jump, more in guilt than in surprise at the other man's silent approach.

"My father," Miles explained.

"Oh, I am sorry."

"I'm not."

"Well, nevertheless - in the circumstances -"

"What?"

"The cab has only just gone. If we phoned quickly, it would only take -"

"No, no need for you to go." Miles turned. "Besides, I could do with the company."

"I really think I should go. Can you remember the name of the firm?"

"No." Miles slipped the cabby's card into his jacket pocket. "Look, I mean it. I don't want to be alone at the moment."

"I understand, but won't you want to go up and pay your last respects, and all that?"

"No. I hated him, and I have no intention of playing the hypocrite. But I've no qualms about toasting his demise with some of his best whisky."

Miles started across the capacious hall, leaving deVille to close the front door. It was large and heavy and formed from studded oak planks with a central window made from dark bottle glass bullseyes covered with a black wrought iron grill.

"Bolt it," Miles said over his shoulder, and he heard deVille sliding the two four foot long cast iron bolts home as he opened the door to his study.

DOMINATING OBSESSION

So his father was dead at last. Well, he was glad to hear that. But as usual the old bastard's timing had been impeccable. The events of this night had signalled the start of the rest of Miles' life. Even more so now the old sod was out of the way. But he had already done his best to ruin it. There was every chance that Robyn would make this an excuse not to come down again and the moment would be lost. He had to find some way of keeping deVille here and retaining his interest.

Miles stopped halfway to the drinks table and smiled broadly to himself. He had the perfect answer. deVille was in for a treat.

8

Sir Rupert Good was dead.

All men are bastards. At least, Robyn had never met one who wasn't. But as bastards go, Rupert was capable of leaving the rest of them standing, even to the very end. And yet, seeing him lying there, cold and white, and as brittle as a shrivelled leaf, she still felt a sense of loss. Was it for him, or for a life which used to be and would be no more?

Robyn had brought Jade to live in this house when Jade was just five and the little girl's emerging vocabulary had been unable to cope with the complexities of pronouncing his Christian name, so to her Miles' father had always been known as Rooter. And the name had stuck, and become universally accepted. Especially by Rupert. He had liked it. It was affectionate, having a nickname which had been bestowed upon him by an angelic little girl. It appeared to imbue him with all those human and humane qualities which he had never been known to possess.

Rupert had known what everyone was thinking; that Rutter would have been more appropriate than Rooter, but it

DOMINATING OBSESSION

was close enough, and that had amused him. Rupert had always been a dirty old man who liked nothing better than rutting, preferably with the very young and defenceless.

Robyn looked at Jade standing on the other side of the king-sized bed. "Do your gown up properly," she said, "you're gaping."

"Sorry. Who's that man?"

"He's nobody, he'll be leaving soon. But we've still got your father to consider. You're too old to be running around half naked."

Jade nodded her acceptance of the reprimand, but didn't look particularly chastened by it. Now wasn't the time to argue, however, and Robyn looked down at the old man again. Even now she still couldn't look at him without experiencing familiar twinges of shame; shame for all the cover-ups concerning parlour maids and nannies she had been forced to conspire in. The young innocent faces of the girls involved still haunted her sleep at night. But that wasn't the worst of it. The real shame was that she had had to conspire in the cover-ups, because she had allowed the grizzled old bastard to be intimate with her as well, and he'd threatened to tell Miles if she didn't co-operate.

All men are bastards. They all have that little devil burning away in them, even when they're sure in their own minds that they are thinking of something entirely innocent. The difference with Rooter was that he felt no need to try to control the little devil, so its appetite grew and became more cruel, and he used it to prove his power over people. This evil old man had driven his wife to an early grave, and then set about ruining her two fine sons. He had done a good job of it, too. He had sapped their confidence and convinced them both that they were totally dependent upon him. He had given them just enough to make their lives tolerable, but in return they were forced to acknowledge his supremacy over them.

Robyn knew she ought to hate this old man who had ru-

ined Miles' life. Robyn didn't particularly care for - or about - Elliot, Miles' elder brother, but she could see that Rupert had ruined his life as well; driving him into the arms of that promiscuous money grabbing little bitch, Paige. But she didn't hate him. She felt the tears grow heavy enough to break away from her lashes and begin their meandering journey down her cheeks to her quivering chin.

Jade came round the bed to give her a comforting hug. That made the tears worse and Robyn tugged a tissue from a box beside the bed. They clung together, and Robyn looked at her beautiful daughter. Jade's face was puffy and her eyes were also rimmed with pink. At least the old bastard had two women to shed a tear over him.

When the two had calmed a little, Jade moved back to the other side of the bed. They each held one of Rooter's stone cold hands. None of Rooter's evil seemed to matter any more. He had needed them, and they had loved him in the only way possible - on his terms. It was a love that only makes sense to women, but they knew now that they had done the right thing.

"Were you there, when he ...?" Robyn looked into her daughter's eyes.

Jade nodded. "It was frightening. I think I'd almost dozed off, because I suddenly looked up and there he was, sitting bolt upright and looking up at the ceiling. And he shouted -"

"What?"

"It was horrible."

"What was it - what did he shout?"

"He shouted, 'Curse them all down to hell!'"

Robyn paused for a moment. "You're kidding?"

Jade shook her head. "No, that was it, and then he flopped back on the bed and was gone."

The two of them froze and looked at each other for some moments.

"What do you think he meant?" Robyn eventually broke

the unsettling silence.

"I think he meant it. I really think he meant to curse us all down to hell." Jade shivered. "I don't mind telling you, Mum, it scared me half to death. It sounds silly now, but it seemed very real at the time, all alone in this big house with a dead man's curse ringing in my ears."

Robyn moved to Jade and hugged her reassuringly. "Don't worry - everything's going to be OK now. But why didn't you call us? You knew where we were."

"There was no need really. There was nothing you could do, and I felt better downstairs locked in the kitchen. I switched all the lights on and didn't come back up here until the doctor arrived. You've only just missed him."

"What did he say?"

"He said it was his heart. We knew it would be."

"Yes." Robyn dabbed her eyes again and tried to cheer herself with a little smile. "So - what time did Rooter - what time was it?"

"That was another funny thing - exactly on the last stroke of midnight."

"Oh!" Robyn hugged herself. "Very eerie."

"Very. But guess what else was strange?"

"What?"

"Did he ever tell you to look under his pillow when he died?"

"Yes!" Robyn nodded vigorously.

"And did you ever look when he was asleep?"

"Yes!" Robyn continued nodding.

"There was never anything -" They stopped. They were both talking at once and saying the same thing.

"Well," said Jade mysteriously, "look now!"

Robyn questioned her silently, and Jade nodded for her to do it.

Robyn gingerly lifted the pillow so as not to disturb the dead man too much, and slid a long buff envelope from its hiding place.

"How is it possible?"

"He must have known," Jade said with another shiver.

"But even so, he couldn't walk. Did you help him?"

"No, it came as a complete surprise to me too... look at page two."

Robyn did so. "Good God!" she squealed. "I don't believe it! He's left the lot to Miles, to us! Practically everything!"

9

Robyn kissed the tip of a finger and placed it on Rooter's cold lips. "Thank you, Rooter," she whispered, "you old bastard."

She switched off the table lamp and stood in the dark staring down at the lifeless shape on the white pillow. She was very unsure about what to do next. Jade had been packed off to bed. It was her 'A' level English exam tomorrow. Robyn looked at her watch - today, in eight hours time, she mentally corrected herself. Jade wasn't bothered any longer, but as Robyn had cautioned her, even rich young heiresses can benefit from a university education.

It seemed incredible. From the age of five Robyn had been a latch-key kid being brought up by a single parent in the back streets of Birmingham without any money and no education to speak of. And now, here was her daughter a millionairess before her eighteenth birthday, and with very good prospects of being accepted into Cambridge.

Robyn wanted to dance a jig. She desperately wanted to tell someone. She wanted to tell Miles; to see the expression on his face when she told him what had happened. But he was downstairs in his study getting drunk and believing that he and his family would shortly be out on the streets without an allowance unless Elliot did the decent thing, when in-

stead, it was the other way round. It was Elliot and Paige who had got practically nothing, and Miles who would be dishing out the hand-outs.

Was that awful man still with him? Robyn shuddered. It had suddenly become cold. She smelt herself, screwing up her nose in disgust. She smelt sour. She smelt used. She shuddered again and shook her head in denial as the memories of the taxi cab came flooding back. How could she? How could she? Say it wasn't true. Oh, to be able to go back, to just a few hours ago when she was happy and free, dancing with hardly a care in the world. Before she had met that awful, that, that irresistible man.

She ran from the dark towards their lighted bedroom at the end of the landing, hoping that Miles would be there waiting for her, so that she could tell him the news and they could make love until it was time to get Jade up for school.

But Miles wasn't there. The evidence that he had been there was all around her on the floor, but he had already showered, changed and gone back downstairs.

Robyn slipped her dress off, screwed it into a ball, and threw it across the room to join the other mess. She walked over to the full length mirror and surveyed herself. her body showed the marks of her tussle with the cab driver. There were love bites on her breasts and thighs, and the usual burst of bright chestnut between her thighs was matted and dull. She patted the curls and her fingers came away sticky with secretion.

How could she?

She fairly ran to the shower cubicle, kicking her shoes off on the way. She scrubbed herself rigorously with a flannel, and didn't stop until her hair was shampooed and every inch of her body had been washed a dozen times.

When satisfied, she stood again before the mirror and towelled herself down. Now her flesh was pink and clean. The area between her legs was like a sunburst of autumn colour again, and very soon, when she had finished spraying

DOMINATING OBSESSION

herself with scent, she would smell like a young man's idea of heaven once more.

Robyn sat at her dressing-table and brushed her hair until it shone, letting it fall into its natural heavy curls. She watched how her breasts swayed enticingly with every movement she made. Unable to resist the wicked temptation, she threw the brush down and placed her hands on her breasts, pushing them down and letting them spring back again. They were as over-sprung as a Cadillac. She giggled at her own thought, and tried to cover the nipples with her index fingers. It was an hopeless task. The large nipples twisted away and flicked upright again, anxious to be proudly surveying the ceiling once more.

She ran her fingers over her flat stomach, letting the nails leave a thin curving white line across the pink flesh and showing her progress to her pubis. She parted the chestnut curls and outer labia. It was no good - the thoughts were there again. The man was still inside her brain. She closed her eyes and let her mind drift back...

deVille had slid her from the back seat of the cab and supported her while she found her feet. For some bizarre reason she had wanted him then as she had never wanted any man before. How it had happened she didn't quite know, but she remembered being suddenly on her knees in front of him with the sharp gravel of the drive cutting into her knees. Her hunger was dreadful and she could already taste his cock in her mouth as her trembling fingers reached out to undo the magic zip.

Then he had hit her hard - once on either cheek. She hadn't understood what had happened, but the next moment she was on her feet with her back to him, with the shock of his slaps still ringing in her ears and making it difficult for her to hear him whisper venomously: "Behave yourself! Wait for permission!"

He had laughed then, not nastily, but not genuinely enough

DOMINATING OBSESSION

to take the sting from his words.

But she couldn't wait. He knew that. All she could think about was the weapon in his trousers pressing against her bottom - and soon her bottom was stroking up and down its length. It was a monster, she was sure of that. She still hadn't seen it fully, and using the deep valley between her buttocks might not be the most accurate way of measuring the size, but she was still in no doubt. She shuddered at the memory of holding it, hot and purring in her hands...

Yes, he had got to her all right. But she would banish him now. Her fingers were flying over her clitoris and she could feel her juices coating her thighs. The ache was deep inside. She needed to be penetrated. She reached for the brush and pushed the handle home, feeling the sharp nylon bristles tease her. Almost there - only a few seconds more. Oh, Yes! Oh, yes! He was with her now, but in a moment he would be gone - exorcised once and for all, and she and Miles would be safe!

The hand caught Robyn's flying wrist and swung her round and to her feet. Her heart was in her throat, and her eyes stared at the black hearted bastard. The shock couldn't have been any worse had it been the arisen Rooter standing there. The pending orgasm was snatched from her. She felt the brush slip from her and heard it thud quietly on the carpet.

"Come on, no need for you to be doing that." deVille jerked her past him and propelled her towards the door. "You've been keeping us waiting."

Miles was leaning against the doorjamb, smiling at her. He had changed into a casual shirt and slacks. He looked very calm and cool, and hardly drunk at all. The sight of him brought Robyn up short.

deVille took her wrist again and pulled her arm up behind her back. He slipped his free hand between her legs from behind, and caressed her where the brush had been only

a few moments before. No one said anything. Robyn and Miles simply stared silently at each other while the stranger groped her freely.

"Now, we don't want any noise while we go downstairs," deVille said confidently. "We wouldn't want to wake your lovely daughter, now would we?"

10

Robyn stood naked and to attention in the centre of the kitchen.

This was her favourite room in the whole house. It was where Miles had first brought her and little Jade. She was to be cook and housekeeper for his aging father. Her bedroom had been off the pantry then, in what had originally been the butler's quarters in the days when the house had many live-in servants. But those days were long past and most of the rooms were closed up with dust sheets over the furniture, and this room, her domain, had quickly become the centre of the house.

The old man had already been semi-invalid and he never came here, and Miles had given her free reign to furnish it as she wanted. So she had pushed the large pine refectory table to the end nearest the cooker and sink to make a kitchen-dining area, and the other end of the thirty foot room had then become her very own country cottage parlour. It was all very cosy, very chintzy, and cluttered with a medley of mismatched easy-chairs and sofas, and boasting a large open inglenook fireplace that had a roaring log fire every winter.

Now Robyn was standing with her back to the refectory table as ordered, staring straight ahead over deVille's head. deVille had turned her favourite easy chair around, and she didn't actually have to see him clearly to know that he was still surveying her with an easy and relaxed manner. He sat

DOMINATING OBSESSION

with his legs crossed, and lying across his lap was a short thin gardening cane that had presumably come from the conservatory. There could only be one possible reason for a man like deVille to be holding a cane, and the realization of that made Robyn's body hum with a strange excitement.

"Miles showed me your video," deVille said in his easy conversational way.

Robyn stiffened even more, if that was possible, and her eyes instinctively flitted back, even though she knew it was impossible for her to see Miles and give him an accusing glance. She heard a movement from behind to her right and knew that Miles was still leaning against the wall and sipping his latest drink.

"You do like to be inventive, don't you?" deVille said.

Robyn blushed at the thought of this awful man seeing the private video Miles had made of them together. She said nothing.

"You certainly do like it dirty," deVille goaded. "Many people would find that sort of behaviour disgusting."

Robyn still said nothing.

"You may answer," he prompted.

"I have nothing to say."

"You're embarrassed."

"Not of what we did. It was private."

"'Was' being the operative word," deVille said. "Nothing you think or do is going to be private from me in future, is it?"

"Isn't it?"

"No," deVille smiled arrogantly. "Those days are over for you. You know why, don't you?"

Robyn shook her head - genuinely puzzled.

"Because before tonight is over you will belong to me - completely."

"You're mad," Robyn said, without conviction.

"You're mad, Master," he corrected her. "You will call me Master from now. We may as well start as we mean to go

on."

His tone was so easy. It was almost possible to believe that there was no harm in the man. And the things he offered her with this easy style - they made her head ring with confusion. Would she like to call him Master? Wouldn't it be so easy and pleasant to surrender to him? No! No! No! She was being crazy! He was her enemy. She hated him. She detested him. She couldn't bare the thought of him touching her.

"Never!" she said, with more passion than she had intended to betray.

"All right. No matter. You will eventually. When you come to think of me that way - as your master."

He paused, but Robyn said nothing. Her body was red hot again. She was so hot she could hardly breath and it was all she could do to stop from shaking. Did the bastard know what he was doing to her? She closed her eyes in shame. He knew all right. But he was wrong if he thought that meant he must win. His words were only going to make her more determined. But she wouldn't tell him so. It was enough for her to know - she would never let him win. She would rather die first.

"What were you thinking about when you were masturbating?"

Robyn blushed furiously again. The bastard. Why, oh, why, had she let him catch her like that? Why hadn't she taken the simple precaution of locking the door?

deVille lifted the cane up and flicked its tip down hard against the heel of his right shoe, making Robyn flinch at the dull crack of bamboo on leather.

"I'm waiting."

"Nothing." It was a stupid thing to say.

deVille stood up slowly. Now she could see his eyes. She almost panicked then, with every instinct in her body stumbling over each other in their unseemly haste to rectify her mistake. But she said nothing, and she wasn't sure whether that was due to bravery, or because she was petrified.

DOMINATING OBSESSION

deVille walked slowly past her. She listened to every casual stroke of the cane against his leg. Then it stopped, and she knew that he had turned.

The blow when it came was almost a relief. She heard it whistle through the air, and the crack of it exploding against her taut skin echoed around the walls of the kitchen. Robyn cried out and stumbled forward - and then she turned on him with fury flashing in her eyes.

deVille raised the cane and pointed it at her chest. It was only an inch from her breast bone in the deep cleft of her heaving bosom.

"Stand to attention!"

Robyn glared at him defiantly. He meant it, the bastard. This man had no qualms about hitting a woman. They had only just met and he had adequately proved that already, and that single stroke with the cane had been far harder than anything Rooter had ever administered with his strap.

deVille was now looking at her sex-lips. She knew why. Beneath her rage churned immense arousal - and she knew it was apparent to the two men. She took a quick glance at Miles. Poor man, he had no idea that his depraved father had trained her to be sexually aroused, and even satisfied, by a well administered beating. He was looking at her in amazement - as if she was someone he didn't recognise.

Robyn turned without a word of complaint and assumed her previous position, staring at the chimney breast at the far end of the kitchen, and wondering which smarted the worst - her bottom or her wounded pride.

deVille walked round to stand in front of her.

Robyn lowered her eyes.

deVille took her chin and squeezed until she looked at him. Then he smiled at her. "I like administering discipline to beautiful young women, and I'm very good at it. I don't mind if they show spirit. I'm what they call a sadist." He articulated carefully as if explaining something to an idiot. "That means I get a sexual thrill from hurting people. So

DOMINATING OBSESSION

you see, the more you defy me, the more it gives me the opportunity to enjoy myself." He paused, and gave her chin one last cruel squeeze, and let go. "But then, you knew that already, didn't you? After all, you're a masochist, aren't you?"

Was she? Was that why she was so attracted to bastards like him?

"What were you thinking about when you were masturbating?"

"You."

"Me?"

Robyn looked down again, and eventually whispered quietly so that the two men had to strain to hear, "Your cock."

deVille probably nodded his understanding, but Robyn couldn't see. She wasn't sure any more which she found the most exciting, their talk, or his silences, which seemed to go on for ever and give her plenty of time to think about how she must look standing there naked for him to examine at his ease.

"Well, we interrupted you before you were finished. Please resume."

What should she do? She suddenly knew that it was the thing she wanted to do most in all the world. To masturbate for him while thinking of his giant cock. Her hands moved from her sides, but she couldn't do it.

"Start with you breasts," he offered, as though jogging her memory. Or was it to prove to her that they had watched her entire performance in the bedroom?

She nervously placed her hands on her breasts and ran her palms around them.

"Can I look at you?" she asked timidly.

"Master," he prompted.

But she wasn't ready yet. She would manage without looking at him if the bastard wanted to be awkward. She twisted her nipples between fingers and thumbs, then ran her hands down over her taut stomach to her waiting vagina.

deVille rose and walked behind her again. The cane wasn't

long in coming. This time it was an encouraging stroke, not a punishing blow. And it worked. Her body jerked, her back arched, her hips thrust forward, and her fingers became the greatest lover she had ever known.

He moved away, but she heard him return within a moment to stand behind her again. Then he passed something to her. Robyn nearly died! It was a cucumber! Not a smooth-skinned greenhouse variety, but one of their own from the kitchen garden. It was shorter - no more than a foot long - but far thicker, and nobbled all over as if plagued with boils. He must have sent Miles to fetch it after watching their homemade video.

Robyn obeyed his silent instruction and rubbed its tip up and down the lips of her vagina until she knew she was ready to receive it. She pressed it inside. She felt deVille's hot breath on her shoulder and the top of her breasts as he leant over to watch. Instinctively she thrust her hips forward so that he would see. The vegetable slid smoothly in for three-quarters of its length, and then stopped. deVille bent his arm around her, and placing his fingers on hers, pushed until it was all the way home. He rested his fingers there, silently instructing her not to relax the pressure. Robyn swooned. Her insides were full, her clitoris was singing, deVille's breath was hot on her body, and the overwhelming aroma of his perfume was clouding her brain.

He moved back and delivered four more strokes with great deliberation. Her shaking legs could hold her no longer. She spiralled to the floor, urgently pumping the vegetable and grinding her nipples into submission. It was now that she needed the pain. Now that she needed the punishment. She was a filthy animal that needed to be whipped mercilessly. And deVille knew that. He understood her need. It complemented his own exactly, and for what seemed like several minutes the cane became the key as they locked together in a brutal act of sexual excess.

At last Robyn could no longer scream or jump to his

stinging blows.

She heard him move away and slump back into the chair. He was breathing hard, but whether from physical exertion or sexual arousal she wasn't sure.

She relaxed her muscles and eased the cucumber from her vagina, and then twisted round and opened her eyes. deVille was staring back at her with a look of satisfaction. He was so lovely - so desirable. She hurt all over. It was difficult to tell which had done the most damage - her own wicked fingers or his wicked cane. But it had been worth it. She had never come like that before. She had been disgusting, disgraceful, and he had punished her for it. And now she felt wonderful.

She had a new Master - a wonderfully cruel and merciless Master. She wouldn't call him that yet, but she knew it was true.

11

"Get to your knees."

deVille was too close, and all Robyn could see were his shoes and the bottom few inches of his trousers. She wasn't sure that she could move without assistance, but he was waiting, so she had to try.

Unsteadily she forced herself up. The floor was stone flagged and she was lying in the narrow gap between the two large oriental mats. The stone was hard on her knees, but comfortingly cool against her breasts and sore nipples. She remained crouched for several seconds, gaining strength, before raising herself fully on her knees and placing her arms behind her back. Then she raised her head and looked deVille in the eyes.

deVille smiled down at her. "Very good," he said.

Robyn felt her breasts swell with pride. She tried to deny

DOMINATING OBSESSION

it, but it was no use - she could feel the warm trickle of juice deep within her vagina, and the ache in her anus, and she knew that she was born to please this man. However much she fought it, however much she denied it, that was nature's truth.

deVille lifted one of her best doilies from the chair, and took a silver penknife from his pocket. He made a short cut and tore the cloth in half. Robyn tried to stifle her horror at such wilful vandalism as he moved behind her and used one of the strips to tie her wrists together. It was strange. Here he was tying her wrists and making her his prisoner, and yet the act seemed so intimate.

"Now, kiss my feet."

Robyn felt the colour drain from her face as wild reality came crashing in. She felt her body shrink inwards away from danger. Her back arched even further, lifting her swollen breasts towards him like a peace offering. The hairs rose on every part of her body and she suddenly felt cold from her breasts to her buttocks. She was covered with goose bumps. It was all coming true; the fantasies that had thrilled her dreams since she was a little child!

"Left shoe first."

This was unbelievable! Robyn felt the tightness in her chest and her head began to spin again. She linked the fingers of both hands together and shuffled forward on her knees, and then she carefully bent forward over his left foot. As her lips touched the shiny leather her body rocked with a tremendous shudder. At first she tried to convince herself that it was simply the sensation of her nipples touching the cold stone floor again. But it wasn't. This was it! This was the real thing!

As she shuffled to kiss his other foot the strange fever raged deep inside her. Her lips were bone dry, and she licked them futilely with her parched tongue. She was so hot and dry she could have been in the depth's of Hell itself.

She had to stop this. She had to deny him. But could she

deny herself? She choked back a sob. Oh, God, help me! she prayed, I want this, oh so much!

But it was as though God wasn't listening. Her body continued to tremble with an excitement it had never felt before, and she realised she was more sexually aroused than she had ever been in her life.

"Now, you kiss each hand," deVille reached his left hand forward with its back towards her.

Robyn remembered how he had kissed the back of her hand when they had first met. It seemed a lifetime ago now, yet it still made her tremble inside to think of it.

His hand was large with long artistic fingers and beautifully manicured nails. The skin was smooth and lightly tanned with prominent cord like veins and a coating of short black hairs of uniform length. An inch of brilliant white shirt cuff divided the soft olive skin from the dark black of his jacket sleeve. The cuff sparkled with gold, and a quick look confirmed that the sculptured jet motif on the gold cufflinks exactly matched that on the ring he wore on his little finger; a beautifully crafted scorpion in the shape of a six.

His hand was perfect. Robyn couldn't have made it any more perfect if she had designed it herself. She knelt forward and kissed it. That was perfect too. It made her stomach go all squelchy and she knew that she wanted to cry.

deVille removed his left hand and presented his right, and when she had kissed that too she rocked back onto her haunches, and that part of the simple ceremony was over. But this time when she raised her head and looked up at him there was a lump in her throat, and his smiling face was surrounded by a halo of golden light which fragmented into a dozen jagged shards by the teardrops in her eyes.

"Now you press your cheeks to my crotch, one at a time, and then you give me a single kiss - here," he touched his fingers elegantly to the tip of the bulge in his trousers. Robyn looked up at him in awe, but he was looking away, presumably at Miles, as if totally oblivious to her presence at his

DOMINATING OBSESSION

feet.

No! No! Her brain screamed. You mustn't! You mustn't! But it was too late. Nothing in the world could deny her this. Her smooth left cheek came to rest against the rough cloth on his thigh, and her face pressed into the throbbing monster that lurked beneath.

The monster immediately rounded on her and jerked forward. Robyn closed her eyes and nibbled her lower lip. All she had to do was plant a little peck on the tip of his erection and her ordeal would be over. This man filled her with terror; she could feel it now like a pain in her chest. But deep down she also knew she wanted him - desperately!

deVille coughed, and Robyn accepted that his patience was exhausted. She rocked back and looked up at him sheepishly.

His look was stern and cold. "I think you could do with a little practice. However, there will be plenty of time for that."

Robyn's heart leapt at the statement. Did he intend staying with them then? Or visiting them regularly for more evenings like this? And how did she feel about that?

deVille's voice cut into her thoughts. "Now, you will call me Master and beg permission to rise."

The room closed in until there was only a narrow tunnel between herself and those dark brown eyes. Robyn's brain started to spin again, and deVille's eyes continued to darken until they were as sharp and black as the sparkling chips of jet in his jewellery.

He was waiting for her reaction. Miles was waiting for her reaction. She was waiting for her reaction.

This was the most important decision she would ever have to make.

12

"No."

The single word hung in the air while the room sucked in its breath and waited for deVille's reaction.

"I beg your pardon?"

"I won't call you Master." Robyn's voice quivered with fear, but now the decision was made the rest was easier.

"You're very brave."

Robyn didn't feel very brave. She felt like running to a safe little corner and hiding herself away.

"But very foolish also. I really can't allow you to defy me any longer. Miles, come and make yourself useful. But first you'd better get undressed."

As Miles obeyed without question, deVille disappeared past her and went to the sink.

Robyn bowed her head and the sound of her husband hastily disrobing filled her ears.

"Good," deVille was speaking confidently again, "now help her up."

Miles, totally naked, came and helped Robyn to her feet.

deVille was busy ripping a tea towel in half. She would be lucky to have any linen left if he did stay for long. He started quickly towards them. "That's it, take her to that side of the table," he instructed Miles. "Then tie her ankles to the bottom rail with these." He was opposite them now and tossed the strips of torn towel onto the refectory table in front of Miles. "Make sure her legs are as far apart as possible."

Miles did as he was told. His hands were hot and shaking, and he took the opportunity to surreptitious rub them up the insides of her thighs and kiss the left cheek of her bottom as he stood up.

"Now untie her wrists and come round here."

As soon as Miles had obeyed deVille spoke to him again. "Hold out your wrists."

"Me?" Miles queried, incredulously.

DOMINATING OBSESSION

"You," deVille confirmed.

Hesitantly Miles complied and deVille tied a strip of towel to each of his wrists.

"Now cross your arms and lean over the table."

Again Miles complied, albeit with some degree of uncertainty.

"Robyn - cross your arms in the same manner."

Robyn did so and deVille tied their right wrists together and then their left ones, so that a divorce was out of the question for either of them; at least until the ceremony deVille had in mind was all over.

"Excellent," deVille said, as he walked to the armchair and picked up the cane. "We are almost ready to start." He walked to the head of the table, waited some moments like a headmaster waiting for their attention, and then suddenly brought the cane swishing down to land with a resounding crack on the pine boards. Both Robyn and Miles jumped and cowered, displaying their collective trepidation.

deVille gave the cane several more vicious experimental swipes, then walked determinedly towards Miles. Robyn saw the colour drain from her husband's face. He crouched, trapped like a cornered animal as deVille, apparently oblivious to the consternation he had aroused in his new friend, walked past him and on to the food preparation area.

Selecting a large kitchen knife from a rack on the wall, he placed it on its back on a chopping board and carefully positioned the tip of the cane on its sharp blade. Then he pushed down on the cane and split it in two as far as the first growth node.

"You wouldn't believe how tricky this is," he confided, as if it was something they were waiting to learn. "It's very easy to split it unevenly, and then the thing's a total write-off."

It took him some time to split the cane into four strips right down to the lowest node. This now gave him a cane with a two foot split shaft and a six inch handle.

This time when deVille brought his new improved weapon whizzing down to smack on the table top he seemed far happier with the sound it made. He grunted contentedly.

Miles groaned.

Robyn watched her husband. He looked in pain - poor love. She wriggled in her bonds until she could place both her hands round his arms and gave him a reassuring squeeze. Miles looked at her and tried to smile, and then returned her conspiratorial signal.

deVille was on the move again, but this time he walked down Robyn's side of the table. He stopped behind her and she shuddered as he laid the cane against the soft ripeness of her bottom. Robyn held her breath as he lifted it away in an arc and executed a number of slow-motion strokes, whilst cocking and un-cocking his wrists until he was perfectly happy with distance and technique.

Robyn couldn't help groaning - from fear or excitement even she couldn't be sure - but Miles took it for the former and squeezed her arms again.

"That is undoubtedly the most delectable bottom I have ever had the pleasure of laying my eyes on," deVille said, with all the authority of a connoisseur. "Can you stop it from trembling?"

The bastard. Robyn knew that she couldn't. She heard the condescending laughter in his voice and closed her eyes in shame as she tried her best to do as he asked. But the bastard knew what he was doing. She had never been more excited, and thinking about her predicament only made her tremble all the more.

"Never mind." deVille tapped his cane on her bottom like a conductor bringing a vast orchestra to order. "Now, I want you to understand that this is for your own good, my dear. An untrained woman is an unhappy wretch," he announced pompously. "Sam Johnson I believe - or perhaps I just made it up."

"You bastard, deVille," Robyn managed.

DOMINATING OBSESSION

"Yes," he agreed, "make the most of it now. Get it all out of your system while you have the opportunity. You've got the right idea; this will be almost like a religious experience for you. A total conversion that will ensure that you never think these misguided thoughts again."

"You pig!"

"Come, come. Be reasonable. I defy any real man to stand where I am now and not give that darling little bottom at least one lash."

Robyn said nothing. His words had the ring of truth about them. Besides, deep-down she could equally well say that she defied any woman to be lying trussed and naked as she was now, and not to have her bum screaming out to experience the cut of at least that one lash.

"You must recognise that I'm not your enemy Robyn - I'm your friend. A very good friend that only want's to see you happy. I want you to have a joyous and fulfilled life. I want you to experience many things and enjoy wonderful erotic sensations that are denied most people due to their own inhibitions."

"You want to beat me for your own gratification, you mean." Robyn summarised it for him.

"Yes, there is an element of that, I cannot deny. But it's clear to me that you still don't understand your own true desires. Just as I desire very much to beat you, you desire very much to be beaten. However, you will only recognise this truth once you learn to conquer your deep-rooted guilt."

"Guilt?!"

"Yes - " deVille said with absolute confidence, "guilt," and he pressed the flat of his cane against her bottom to emphasize his meaning; Robyn was still shaking with excitement. She closed her eyes against the shame of knowing that her tormentor spoke the truth.

"To my mind there are three legitimate reasons for a man to beat a woman. The first is to train her to the whip, of course - and that is no matter to be taken lightly. Once started

DOMINATING OBSESSION

it must be carried out religiously, on a daily basis, and there are days when a man is just not in the mood, or doesn't have the time. Luckily, in your case you have a loving husband who can carry out this task, leaving me free to enjoy the second and third reasons.

"The second reason is for mutual enjoyment before and during love making. And the third? The third is perhaps my favourite of all. That is for reasons of punishment when the little lady's done wrong."

deVille savoured these last words and let the thought hang in the air for them all to consider. Then he continued: "Of course there are those women who take to it readily and don't need much training before they acquire a taste for it. And there are those unfortunate, spirited, stubborn few, who have to receive a great deal of punishment right from the start." He allowed a moment more for his ominous words to sink in. "But let us bear this in mind ... I have no wish to thrash a woman beyond the point where she truly ceases to find it enjoyable or necessary."

He laid the cane on the table, and the sudden touch of his hands against her poor shaking bottom was so gentle and unexpected it almost made her come.

"Shush, shush," he intoned. "Calm yourself, little one."

As his hands caressed round and round her cheeks and up and down her shuddering thighs she eventually stopped shaking and achieved some semblance of calm. When she was still he laid his strong body over hers as though he wished to protect her from a cruel world. His hands ran up her back, making her spine arch. He massaged the tension from her shoulders before placing a gentle kiss in the small of her back, and then he moved away again, taking much of her new found warmth with him.

He now paced back and forth, and Robyn could only see him from the very corner of her peripheral vision each time he reached either extreme of his chosen course.

"Now listen. When you know that you've been punished

enough, you will call me Master, and I will stop. It's as simple as that." He turned and paced again before continuing. "But you must mean it. Don't be tempted to lie, because I will know, and that will make me very angry. If that happens I will punish you further for your wrong doing." He turned, and Robyn could feel his stare slicing cruelly into her very soul. "I will not tolerate lies!"

His words were shocking. She had no doubt that he was speaking the truth, and it was a terrible blow, for she had been intending to lie as soon as she safely could. She felt she could never honestly call him Master, and now her only hope of avoiding unspeakable pain had been removed.

"Don't worry that you won't know the correct moment to stop me. The first time that you think of me as your master, rather than deVille, is the precise moment of your conversion."

The lecture and the preliminaries were over. deVille picked up the cane again, and it was in that moment, as the full meaning of everything he had said sank in, that Robyn knew for certain that Miles had delivered them both into the hands of a madman. The man was a megalomaniac. Jade would wake up in the morning to find her mother and stepfather naked and butchered.

13

Robyn took one last look at Miles before closing her eyes. It wasn't really his fault. He had been obsessed. If only she had seen that earlier and agreed to sleep with one of the rugby team while he watched. Miles did his best to look reassuringly at her, but he was obviously even more certain of impending doom than she was - if that was possible.

deVille laid on then.

Robyn screamed - she could do little else. She writhed

and thrashed and begged him to stop - but she would have killed him if he had done so. It was wonderful. It was unbelievable - and it was getting better and better!

The glow spread from her bottom and moved into every inch of her body. She knew she would regret it in the morning when her clitoris was too sore for her to move, but it felt so good rubbing hard against the edge of the table, and the pain and the ecstasy were a perfect combination.

And then she was coming and deVille was bringing her on. There was no thought or knowledge; only the light and the movement as she twisted her head and body from side to side, trying to screw herself down away from the flame of the pain which kept lapping her body with its urgent command. She was moving and screaming, but she couldn't break free. There was nowhere to go - except to give in. So she stretched one last time as high as she could, and then let everything cave in as she started to weep. Her tears filled her world and lasted for ever. Then everything was rushing and in a moment she was a person again, crying on a hard table top.

And then she was Robyn, and deVille had stopped beating her.

The table was now cold and inhospitable, almost as cold and inhospitable as her new found knowledge. It was wonderful. deVille was wonderful. There had never been anything like that before. Would there be more? She was sure there would. Her clitoris was on fire, and so was her bottom. Her breasts were two soft cushions lying in a puddle of perspiration. She closed her mouth and moved her head. Oh, Christ! The pain in her clitoris shot into her anus and then up to her brain. It was excruciatingly unbearable. She tried to bite the table, and not being able to do so she beat her forehead against it instead. The unbearable moment passed and she tried to concentrate on the glow in her bottom instead.

She sensed Miles was looking at her, but she didn't want to see him. Not now. Not yet. Miles belonged to a different

DOMINATING OBSESSION

part of her life.

She wanted deVille! She wanted him inside her where her empty vagina was screaming to be filled. She had to have him! She couldn't wait a second longer!

"Please... please..." Where was the bastard? Where was deVille?

The bastard was behind her. She shuddered at the touch of his hands on her waist. Then his helmet touched her anus and she tensed. He leant towards her, pulling her hips back. He was naked, and that was bliss. She lifted her head. His cock was between her legs and his pubic hair was tickling her sore bottom. Then his belly was against her and his heavy balls were slapping against her upper thighs. Eagerly she wriggled herself down onto the length of his rod, trapping it between her legs and squeezing it hard.

It wanted to move. She didn't want to release it, but she wanted it to move too. It slid back and forth against her pouting lips, taking on a thick coating of her juice. Then it touched her clitoris and she cried out and thrust her bottom back at him.

"Please, please, please, you torturing bastard! Put it in! Ram it in me! Fill me! Fuck me! Help me!!!"

Robyn couldn't think - she couldn't move. She was helpless. He must help her! He must give her this! In a second she knew her agony and waiting were over, and a new agony was about to begin. His body dipped, and the next instant the demanding monster was at the entrance to her vagina. There was no need for delay, his credentials were fully in order. She opened the mouth of her vagina and thrust back, taking him inside at the first attempt. "Ohh...!!" She had never been so stretched - no one ever had. There was no stopping it now. He was inside and travelling upwards. This foreign thing was moving and stretching her insides almost beyond her limits of endurance.

"No! No! You can't...!"

Sweat trickled down her spine and into the deep valley

between her buttocks. More dripped from the tip of her nose. She had never been so hot - her blood was boiling. She could taste salt on her lips and in her parched mouth. She couldn't have been more thirsty if she had been in Hell itself. Her vagina was still struggling to admit the monster, and deVille's hands squeezed her shoulders in readiness to pull her back further as he thrust even deeper.

It took him only moments to bring Robyn to her first, screaming climax - and then she came again and again until she thought she must die. She pleaded with him to cease, but she knew he wouldn't.

Eventually, as Robyn drifted into satiated semi-consciousness, deVille's movements slowed and stopped. As the monster left her she smiled contentedly, sighed and relaxed. Now that he had tasted her delights she had him - deVille now belonged to her.

"No, no, no!" The tight entrance of her anus was already stretched when Robyn reared up in horror. There was a moment of searing white heat, and then her beleaguered bottom reluctantly accepted the intrusion and closed tightly around the collar of his huge helmet. He must be insane! He must know he would tear her in two; rip the thin membrane and rupture her anus. But she was too staggered to react. Her body was paralysed and so was her brain, but it retained a dull ache in which lived the knowledge of what he intended to do, and the terrible realization that she had no way of stopping him.

His ring tapped and scraped on the table-top as he cupped her perspiring breasts. It was strange that with everything that was happening, Robyn noticed such an insignificant detail. He kissed between her shoulder-blades and licked her backbone lightly. Her eyes were wide and wild. They wouldn't focus properly but she could vaguely see Miles' face and knew that he was devouring every last detail of his own wife's vile violation. The hands on her breasts were a gentle comfort, as were the cheek on her back and the soft gentle kisses,

but her anus was full of a huge, hungry, uncaring, arrogant monster that was paralysing her spine.

"Please, please, no -"

deVille began to move a fraction and Robyn felt she would die. She began to hum through her nose as the scream left her toes and rose up her legs. She rolled her forehead on the table in tormented unison with his moving inside her. Backwards and forwards he moved, a little deeper each time, so that the paralysis going down met with the scream coming up. Then his cock became more vibrant and his movement more urgent and the scream reached her throat and exploded from her mouth at the second she fainted.

When she came to she was still impaled upon his demanding cock, but they were moving together again now and it was wonderful to be back in tandem with the one she loved. The pain was still there, but that didn't matter any more. She knew he loved her and wanted to fill her with his seed, and she wanted that too - more than anything on earth.

When they erupted together Robyn felt more complete than ever before. She was without any thought, but her body felt it. This was true marriage. This was two people becoming as close as two separate entities can be. They clung together in paralysed stillness while love took part of one and hid it away in the other, so that neither would be only their self ever again.

Eventually - a long time later - she remembered Miles and looked up. She lifted her weary head and looked at him properly. He appeared to be absolutely dumbstruck, and had she the energy she would have laughed at his gawping expression.

"Are you all right?" he asked with genuine concern.

Was she all right? She thought she was all right. There was just one thing; one thing to worry her and mar her total contentment. There was something she had sensed while deVille's monster was ravaging her bottom. Something supremely important that she couldn't remember now, some-

thing dark and sinister. She thought very, very, hard, but no, it wouldn't come. Miles was waiting anxiously for her answer.

"Me?" she said. "I feel wonderful!"

Unseen by Miles, the corners of her smile trembled uncertainly.

14

Robyn woke with the dawn.

A scurry of starlings was already arguing bad naturedly in the sunlight on the balcony outside the french windows. Her body was glowing with warmth and contentment, but she knew there was something wrong.

She mentally searched for what it was. Rooter was dead, she suddenly remembered. And relaxed. That was all right then. Then she suddenly remembered the real reason for her concern. The Master! The Master had arrived last night, but had he gone again while she was sleeping? She jerked her head from the pillow ready to wake Miles to ask him.

Then she sank back down at rest. It was The Master's slumbering body next to her.

How did she feel? It was incredible. She slowly shuffled her way across the bed until her whole body was only a fraction from his. She didn't dare touch him. But if he moved in his sleep he would brush against her.

Robyn remained looking at his back for some minutes. Her mind was empty. He was too close for her to think. It was enough for now to know that he was still here in her bed. Slowly she peeled the duvet away from his body. It was like drawing a sheet from a magnificent work of art for the first time and knowing that it was all hers. That seemed inconceivable. Why would he want her?

DOMINATING OBSESSION

Robyn placed her hand on her bottom and fingered the cane marks. Then she touched the ring of her anus. He had wanted her last night all right. And he was lying in her bed. He must want her. She let that thought sink in for a few moments before going any further. Was it permissible to touch him while he was asleep? She leant forward and lightly kissed his spine. He didn't wake, he didn't move. Emboldened she kissed down and over his shoulder blade, Then she let her nipples lightly brush his back.

Once started it was impossible to stop and soon the whole of the front of her body was pressed against the back of his. He was so firm and solid. Mens' bodies were so incredible, not at all like her own. They were soft and smooth on the surface, but so hard inside. Robyn ran her hand over deVille's bottom, then over her own, and marvelled at the difference. How could men like women's bottoms? Her own felt soft and squishy, whereas deVille's was tight and firm. It was lovely. She ran her hand on to his thigh feeling the muscles just below the surface. Every part of him was lovely.

Robyn looked at deVille's hand on the pillow. It was olive brown against the brilliant white Egyptian cotton. She reached over his recumbent body and placed her own hand on top of his. It was tiny and white by comparison. That reminded her of something and she removed her own hand and looked at his once more. She had still not had a good look at deVille's cock, but she knew that it was just like his hand: long, wide, dark, and beautifully marked with just the right amount of prominent veins.

Her hand went off to search for it, and found it with a shock that set her heart pounding. deVille might not be awake, but his cock was. She held it in her fingers marvelling at the feel of it. She tucked herself more firmly into his bottom and tried to imagine how wonderful it must feel to own such a thing. No wonder deVille was so dominant. Who wouldn't be with a thing like this hanging between their legs all day long? Just touching it like this made her feel so powerful.

And bad. It was like fingering Dillinger's gun while he slept. Just think of all the women it had subdued. And everyone of them glad to lie down before it and offer it homage.

Robyn knew what she wanted to do, but the thought terrified her and she remained where she was for several minutes hoping that deVille would wake up before she had time to put her crazy plan into action. But he didn't, so she relinquished his wonderful cock for a moment and stole round the bed to kneel on the floor on the other side where she could look at it.

It was beautiful. The most beautiful object in the world. She looked at deVille's sleeping face. God, he was beautiful too, too beautiful for words. Robyn slipped under the duvet and made her way back up the bed until her head was level with his cock. Then she reached forward and kissed its knob. Slowly, gently, she fondled it with her tongue. Then she took it inside. She knew that deVille must eventually wake up and find her lying there sucking his cock, but she couldn't help herself. If she was doing wrong, and needed his permission before doing this, then she would gladly take any punishment he wanted to give.

Slowly she felt deVille's excitement growing. Her own was growing too. Her left hand was on deVille's balls to support them and gently caress them, but her right hand was inside her vagina stirring up the abundant juices she found

Robyn felt deVille stir. His hips urged forward a fraction, and Robyn leant closer and swallowed more of him into the warm depths of her willing mouth. She felt so naughty as her forehead docked gently with his hip, and his thighs edged up to cradle her glowing cheek. Her face was firmly embedded in his groin. In the darkness she used her tongue to skilfully massage round and round his smooth helmet.

This was wicked! Should she really be using her mouth to milk the poor man, without his consent - and while he slept?! She remembered being the little girl who crept into the larder to help herself to her favourite sweets which were

always kept in the tin on the top shelf. A spark of trepidation and beautiful excitement swept through her - as it always had in those far off, halcyon days.

deVille moaned quietly from beyond the heat of the thick duvet. Robyn rubbed herself urgently - and whimpered quietly. deVille rolled over in his sleep pinning her head to the soft mattress with his groin. She could not move as he pumped into her, filling her mouth with his sperm. She drank from him as she too climaxed. She fed from him. She swallowed again and again. He was filling her with his seed - and his strength...

deVille rolled away and snored very quietly; he even did that with class!

Robyn backed out from under the duvet and remained kneeling on the floor looking at him. She had taken his seed. The warmth of it was in her stomach, the taste of it was in her mouth, and the knowledge of it was in her heart. A woman can never truly be possessed by a man until she has drunk of his seed, and only then if she has drunk willingly. Her heart knew that, and felt it again now.

She had drunk willingly. Never had any woman drunk more willingly. The room was not cold, yet Robyn felt herself trembling. This large frightening man possessed her now. He had not even woken; barely stirred even; but it was true, nevertheless. Her future now lay with The Master.

The thought terrified her, but it also filled her with wicked excitement.

15

Two days later, just after 9 o'clock when she had seen the last of the daily cleaning staff out, Robyn went to join Miles in the study as he'd asked.

As she opened the door she heard deVille's deep choco-

late brown voice. Robyn felt her heart jolt to a stop, then begin surging ahead, racing at double time. The two men were standing looking into the stationery cupboard which had both doors gaping wide.

"Ah! there you are, Robyn," Miles said.

Robyn closed the door. Both men had turned to greet her and both were smiling at her warmly, yet she felt strangely frightened and shy in deVille's unexpected presence and it was a strain to force herself to walk over to them.

"You're back," she said, stupidly.

"Yes, I said I would be," deVille reminded her, as if he was surprised that she had been in any doubt. "There were just a couple of things I had to do. I'm completely free now."

"deVille's agreed to remain with us until your training's completed, Robyn," Miles explained.

"I will be your master, but Miles will conduct a large portion of your training while I supervise and act as advisor," deVille added.

Robyn's whole body was humming now. They really meant to continue with this insanity. They really intended to turn her into an obedient little sex slave for anyone to enjoy. Anyone they decided to give her to for an hour, or a day, or for as long as that person wanted her.

Robyn's head began to spin and she watched her own breasts begin dramatically rising and falling as she struggled for breath.

Totally oblivious to her emotional state, Miles continued to reveal more of their arrangements. "deVille will use the blue guest room for now. But he's ordered a new four poster bed." Miles smiled indulgently at deVille who smiled happily back. "And when that arrives he will be moving into my father's old rooms."

They were going too fast. It was all signed, sealed, and agreed. She was just a pawn in all this. She had already become just a slave, an object with no feelings and no say in her own future.

DOMINATING OBSESSION

Unable to take it all in Robyn turned away and looked at the open cupboard to see what they had been doing. Immediately, she wished that she hadn't. Where once there had been nothing more exotic than paper, pens, and printer ribbons, there now hung a fine and fascinating array of whips, straps, and canes. The sight of them and the knowledge that the sole reason for their introduction into the house was so that they could be used to beat and torture her own naked body was terrifying, but not as terrifying as the sight of the other item that shared the cupboard with them.

Standing propped upright on one of the lower shelves was a large oval salver and engraved on its sparkling silver surface was the most terrifyingly erotic scene Robyn had ever seen.

The central engraving was of a young woman beset by horned devils. Each of the devils had a man's head and upper body, but below the waist they were cloven hoofed bulls with long tails, and rampant penises. They were of varying sizes. Those that held the girl's ankles wide apart were full grown males, whereas the two that held ropes tied to her wrists were of the size of young children. They were pulling her arms apart and towards the ground so that although her legs were straight her body was bent at a right angle. The devil that whipped her poor exposed bottom was a giant with huge bulging muscles, as was the one which had its monstrous cock stuffed in her mouth and was grinning with menacing glee at his wicked violation of her.

Robyn felt the cold hand of death on her heart and she knew that even if she never ever again had to stare at the look of hopeless terror on that young woman's face, it was already too late. Robyn needed no artists caption to tell her what the picture represented. That was a poor naked and defenceless lost soul in torment being dragged down to hell to spend the rest of eternity suffering unspeakable acts of brutal violation and torture.

"I see you're admiring our whip cupboard." deVille's voice

came drifting into her awareness as if carried on a breeze from another world.

Robyn looked at him. He was smiling at her - except that he wasn't. He was laughing at her. He knew what she had seen and he knew why it terrified her so much.

"Let me explain your routine." deVille suddenly sounded all businesslike now that he considered the preliminaries to be safely out of the way. "At the time appointed for you to receive your daily instruction, you will come to this whip rack and take down a selection of three whips. You will place them on the silver tray, and you will then offer them to your pupil master who will choose the whip he wishes to use first on that particular day to carry out your instruction. Do you understand?"

deVille and Miles were both looking at her expectantly. "Oh, I - I'm sorry. What did you say, please?"

Fury flashed in deVille's eyes for a split second, but he paused, calmly repeated the instruction word for word, and waited again for her to confirm her understanding.

"I, um -" Robyn tried to repel the response she knew was inevitable. "Yes, Master."

"As you see," deVille continued, "Miles has fixed the mirror tiles inside the cupboard so that you can watch yourself take down the day's whips. It is important for you to witness your own actions at all times, and for you to appreciate that you are carrying out your duties willingly."

Robyn was confused. She was hearing deVille through a cloud of cotton-wool.

"Whoever is acting as your pupil master will be addressed by you as Master or as Mistress - depending on their gender. You will adhere to this for the full period of the instruction. Do you understand?"

Robyn's poor head was spinning. She couldn't take her eyes from the awesome images on the tray. "Yes, Master."

"I hope you do, Robyn. Have you been obeying the previous instructions I gave you?" deVille said, ominously.

DOMINATING OBSESSION

When Robyn's brain caught up with his words she nodded dumbly, unable to speak.

"Show me."

The blouse she had chosen to wear that morning was almost transparent, so she was wearing a bodice under it. She pulled them both from the waistband of her skirt then lifted them so that both men could check, that as deVille had instructed, she was wearing no bra.

"Good, and the other?"

Robyn released her blouse and slip and slowly lifted the hem of her short skirt. Under it she was wearing bronze suspender belt and stockings, and nothing else.

"That's very good, Robyn," deVille told her.

He sounded as if she should be proud that he was pleased with her. Robyn felt as if her whole body was shaking, including her brain, but strangely, the fact that he was pleased with her made her feel calmer.

"How do you feel?" deVille asked.

Robyn started to shake again. How did she feel? - she felt ill. But she knew that deVille wasn't asking after her health. She also felt like a tart, but she knew that he wouldn't want to hear that, either. "Available, Master," she replied, hollowly, after several seconds.

"Yes," he confirmed with a nod. "That is how you look."

Robyn blushed. She knew that her labia were stretched wide and must be glistening with her secreted juices.

"Did you have your enema?"

Robyn nodded.

"And you've obviously taken great care with your makeup and presentation. I'm pleased. You obviously did listen to my instructions after all. Now you understand, don't you? You are now as a woman should always be - not only available, but also very desirable." He smiled like a tutor with a favourite pupil. "You may drop your skirt. You've done very well." He turned to Miles. "Your lovely wife is going to be a credit to us both, Miles," he said, and Miles smiled with

pleasure and nodded his agreement.

"Now, each of these instruments has its own name," deVille said, returning to his former subject as Robyn struggled to adjust her dress and send her racing mind to catch up with him. "When I have time I will write their names on little cards which Miles can pin up next to them. But in the meantime, let me show you which three you are to take down for today." deVille moved closer to the cupboard and Robyn followed him as though he was magnetic.

One by one he pointed to a paddle, a strap, and a multi-tailed whip made of knotted silk and leather strands.

deVille looked at his watch. "What time do you make it, Miles?" he asked.

"Ten past nine."

"Excellent - so do I. Would you leave us for five minutes, Miles, but remain in the hall? Return at exactly nine fifteen."

"Of course." Miles looked curious, but said nothing. He turned to leave.

"Close both doors behind you please," deVille called after him.

The study had an inner and an outer door with a six inch gap between. The outer door was like all the other doors that led off the hall; wider and taller than a conventional door and made of heavy carved oak panels. However the inner door, although of the same height and width, was very different. Other than a six inch border of oak all round, it was covered in padded wine-red leather on both sides. The leather was fixed to the door by brass bun-headed parliament pins that formed it into diamond shapes that were a perfect match for all the leather furniture in the room. In all the years that Robyn had lived in the house this inner door had always remained open, and she watched now with a curious feeling of changing times as the brass door-knob twisted back into place to secure the door with a strange finality.

"Let me look at you," deVille directed.

DOMINATING OBSESSION

Robyn turned to him feeling the heat rise.

"Those really are magnificent breasts, Robyn," he said.

Robyn looked at him in surprised confusion.

deVille nodded, silently instructing her to turn towards the mirrors in the back of the open cupboard.

Robyn turned and looked. Her aroused state had ensured that her blouse and bodice were drawn tight around her breasts. At the centre of each was an enigmatic hint of blood engorged nipple. Robyn looked at deVille's eyes in the mirror and for the first time she saw her breasts as he was seeing them and realised just why countless men found it impossible to disguise their desire to worship their seductive beauty.

deVille moved close behind her, reached round, and gently lifted and caressed them. Robyn felt her breasts swell and rise proudly for his inspection. She dreamily laid her head back against his shoulder and watched through lowered lashes as his powerful hands moulded and squeezed. deVille kissed her neck without taking his penetrating eyes from hers in the reflection. With slow deliberate movements he pushed her blouse and bodice up until Robyn's breasts were free for them both to admire. deVille cupped them again and squeezed, as though testing the ripeness of fruit at the market. He flicked Robyn's erect nipples with his thumbs, and she groaned into his neck.

She could feel the heat of his huge erection against her bottom. deVille pulled both garments off over her head and watched her magnificent breasts pounding against each other as she encourage her heavy chestnut curls back into place. When she was ready, and her eyes were back on his again, he released her skirt and let his eyes drink in the wonder of the rest of her body as it slid down her smooth nylon clad legs. Robyn turned to him eager to clasp him round the neck for a kiss.

deVille stooped and kissed each raised nipple. "Go and fetch the cane," he ordered.

"Master?"

"Do it!"

Robyn turned back to the cupboard, and taking down the cane, handed it to him with bowed head. "Why -" she felt less comfortable with his title now that it was morning - a little ridiculous, "why, Master, have I done something wrong?"

"Be quiet, Robyn. I expect unquestioning obedience."

Robyn looked at her feet like a chastened child.

"Go to the desk and bend over."

The room contained two desks. The one in the large bay-window overlooked the walled garden. This was by far the grandest and had always been known as the 'master desk' - even before the family had acquired a true master to use it. The other was at the opposite end of the room, in line with the door, and directly facing the master desk. This desk was known as the 'lady desk' and was far shorter and narrower than its companion. Both were made from oak and finished in the same red leather as that on the inner door. Both had captain's chairs, also made of oak and red leather that matched the chesterfield settee and club chairs and wing chairs that were the other main furniture in the room.

It was the lady desk that deVille was pointing at, and Robyn nervously made her way to it and stretched herself across its centre. It was so narrow that although her breasts were squashed against its leather top, her head was free to hang over the edge so that her eyes had an unhindered view of the intricately patterned Persian carpet beneath.

Robyn gripped the edge of the desk firmly and waited.

deVille took several practice swipes that made the air whistle and kiss her exposed bottom. Then he laid on with a stroke that exploded on to both cheeks of her bottom with a blistering white hot flash of pain and heat.

Robyn screamed. She jumped up and turned on him angrily, while frantically trying to rub the acute pain from her assaulted buttocks. deVille grabbed her and slung her across the room. She tumbled on the carpet and thumped against

DOMINATING OBSESSION

the chesterfield settee.

deVille was angry - very angry. It wasn't nice to see, and Robyn wondered what had possessed him. She rubbed her bruised shoulder.

"Come here!"

Robyn couldn't move. His mood swing was so sudden. He looked insane.

"I won't tell you again!" he pointed to the vacated desk. "I will brook no defiance. Not now. Not ever!"

Robyn wanted to call out to Miles; to anyone. She was terrified of what this maniac was going to do to her next. In this mood he could do anything. But Miles was no help, not any more. He was completely under deVille's spell. He would stand back and do nothing.

Feeling dreadfully alone she scrambled to her feet, and without looking at him, gingerly draped herself back over the desk. She sobbed quietly. Her punishment was going to be terrible, and there was no way to stop it. It had been only a minor act of defiance, and she now knew that she would never do such a thing again, but there was no way to show him that or to let him see how sorry she was.

The vicious stroke came and she screamed and jerked. But this time, she didn't jump up or release her desperate grip on the desk. When her scream had faded and her senses returned, she waited fearfully for the next hiss of the cane and the wicked lick of pain that would accompany it.

... And she waited. And then she realised that deVille was no longer behind her, and she listened to his movements over at the whip cupboard. She held her breath as she listened to his footsteps approaching again. What had he fetched? What instrument of torture was he going to use on her now?

deVille pulled her upright, and as she swung round in his arms, he hugged her tight.

Robyn cried. She cried more than she had ever cried before. She cried from sheer and immense relief, and for grati-

tude to her master for being the loveliest, gentlest, most merciful master any slave could wish to have. She was crying so much she barely heard the knock on the door.

"Come in," deVille called evenly.

The second knock was louder, as was deVille's command to enter.

The door eventually opened and Miles popped his head round. "Is it all right to come in," he enquired.

Robyn began to laugh through her tears, and deVille joined her.

Miles took that as an affirmative and joined them, eyeing Robyn's condition with a little curiosity.

"Did you stay in the hall, as I instructed?" deVille asked.

"Sure did, right outside the door," confirmed Miles, eager to please. "Just as you told me to."

"Good. And what did you hear?"

"Hear? Not a thing."

"Excellent." deVille was obviously pleased. He picked Robyn up and sat her on the desk. She winced uncomfortably at the soreness in her bottom.

"I'll have this study as my own. It will be out of bounds to everyone else unless I send for them. However, as you, Miles, will be in charge of Robyn's discipline, until we've fixed up a proper punishment room you will use this room each morning at ten o'clock. You Robyn, will arrive here at nine-fifty-five precisely, take down the whips, and present them to Miles on the silver tray. I will remain here at first to supervise." deVille looked at them both to confirm that no last remnants of resistance remained to be dealt with. They both nodded their understanding and compliance.

"Now, haven't I seen another room with doors like these? Isn't it the music room?"

"Yes - well not quite," Miles began and then corrected himself. "It's the piano room. A sort of smaller practice room off the music room," he explained.

"I remember," deVille said thoughtfully. "Yes, I think

DOMINATING OBSESSION

that'll do very well for the official punishment room. Lets go and have a look."

Robyn stooped to pick up her discarded clothes, but before reaching the door deVille turned and spoke to her. "While we're away you can take the books down and dust them off. Wear that." He pointed to a green butler's apron with a yellow duster protruding from its pocket. "And only that."

16

Robyn stood looking at the closed door for a moment before going to fetch the ladder from its narrow purpose built cupboard at the far end of the line of shelves.

"Dust the books. Who does he think he is?" she asked the empty room. The room made no reply, but they both knew the answer. He thought he was her master with an absolute right to command her to do anything he wanted. And he was right, Robyn thought, as she wondered about his final instruction.

Deciding that it was best to err on the side of prudence she lifted her left leg and propping her foot against the angled ladder she wound down her stocking. When she was completely naked she slipped the apron over her head and tied the laces behind her back.

She looked at her slippers. It would be painful to be bare footed on the steps - but not as painful as having her bum thrashed again. She tidied them away with the rest of her clothes.

The study had far fewer books than the library, thank goodness, but there were more than enough for anyone who had to dust them regularly. A lot of them were reference books, but most of them were Rooter's personal choice. Robyn mounted the steps.

Up here the books were mainly Rooter's collection of

DOMINATING OBSESSION

pornography. Robyn removed them from the shelves a handful at a time and placed them on the shelf below while she dusted first the bare shelf and then the spine and top of each book as she replaced them.

She had dusted them several times in the past while Rooter worked at his desk and watched her and she had no inclination to open any of them any more. Except one, which she flicked through until she found the page she vaguely remembered.

The left page showed a black and white line drawing of a maid standing on library steps similar to the ones she was using. The maid was dressed in the Victorian style in a black and white maid's outfit with a little white lace cap, but the skirt was very short and raised at the back to show her pert little naked bottom. This too looked as Robyn's own must look, with the stripes of the cane across its cheeky little twin moons. Robyn studied it for a few moments and then put it away. Times might change but men didn't, she concluded, and continued with her work.

After only a few minutes the two men re-entered the room. Robyn looked over her shoulder at them. They were both looking up at her, obviously pleased with what they saw.

"Set the chessboard up, please Miles," deVille said. "We'll have a game in a moment. Robyn, come here, I've got a surprise for you."

Robyn descended the steps obediently and went over to the master desk.

"Take the apron off," deVille instructed.

Robyn obeyed without a murmur and once more stood deliciously naked before her master.

"Do you like jewellery?" deVille asked.

"Yes, Master." She was anxious to see what he had for her.

First he used a plastic template to confirm the correct ring sizes for both her little fingers. Then he produced a small velvet box which contained two matching gold rings.

DOMINATING OBSESSION

Robyn lifted one out of the proffered box and lifted it up to examine it in the morning sunlight streaming through the bay-windows. It was beautiful, like an engagement ring with a jet scorpion on it holding a very short thin chain on the end of which there was another much smaller ring.

deVille looked over his shoulder, and seeing that Miles had finished setting out the chess pieces, called him over to participate in their fun.

Both finger rings were identical in design, and deVille showed them that the two tiny rings on the end of the chains both had a spring loaded hinged section. He used one tiny ring to press this section down on the other. Once the first ring had passed through the gap in the other the hinged parts sprang back and the two were linked together.

deVille held one of the finger rings up. Its twin was now attached to it by three-quarters of an inch of thin gold chain joined in the middle by the two tiny interlocking rings.

"They're beautiful," whispered Robyn.

"Do you know what they're for?" deVille asked.

Both Robyn and Miles shook their heads.

"They're for naughty little girls who masturbate."

"Oh!" cried Robyn.

"What do you think, Miles?"

"I think you came along just in time, deVille." Miles said. "I can see that dear Robyn is almost totally out of hand."

"I agree. Turn round, Robyn," deVille commanded.

Robyn did so and he crossed her wrists and used her new rings to link her little fingers together.

"How does that feel?" he asked.

Robyn turned back to face him. "Very strange," she said uncertainly. "There's virtually nothing there, and yet I can't use my hands at all."

"They aren't that efficient," deVille informed Miles. "A clever girl can undo them or pull one ring off her finger, but it does seem to give some of them a strange feeling to be imprisoned by such light bonds."

Miles nodded.

"What you must remember is that they are to stop masturbation only. Don't use only these if the girl is being whipped or having sex. If she was to become over excited it would be very easy for her to dislocate a finger."

Miles nodded his understanding again.

"See if you can undo them," deVille suggested, and Miles did so without any problem.

"Good. Now look at these."

deVille pushed two small velvet bags along the desk and left Robyn to remove the contents from the first one. It was a simple gold bangle, but it was exquisite. On the outside it had a bigger more substantial version of the little chain and small hinged ring arrangement that her finger rings had. The outer rim was also ornately chased with her name, six scorpions, and the words: 'The Master' and 'six'. Inside it was engraved with the date for the previous Sunday; the day that Rooter had died and Robyn had become deVille's slave.

The second velvet bag contained a matching bangle, and by narrowing her hands Robyn slipped one onto each wrist. deVille adjusted them by squeezing them one click at a time until their diameters were too small for Robyn to be able to pull them back off over her hands again. Robyn examined the left bangle closely. As it had tightened one end had slipped inside the other, but the bangle was so well made that it was almost impossible to see where it had entered without looking very carefully.

"How do I take them off, Master?"

deVille shook his head. "You don't."

deVille allowed Miles the honour of pulling Robyn's arms behind her back and locking her wrists together.

"You'll probably find these and a pair of ankle restraints all you need for when you're carrying out her daily instruction," he told Miles. "But I have a full set of straps and ankle bracelets here for you should you choose."

Robyn was anxious to see, but with her arms locked be-

hind her back she was helpless as he put everything else into a large jewellery box, closed the lid and slid the box to Miles.

"Now," he clapped his hands and the mood changed instantly, "if you would like to release Robyn, Miles, she can resume her cleaning whilst we enjoy a challenging game of chess... and don't forget, young lady," he smacked her naked bottom, "be ready for your instruction at ten o'clock sharp. That should give me plenty of time to achieve check-mate," he added with absolute confidence.

At three minutes to ten Robyn descended the steps and put them away. She went to the bizarre cupboard, took down the paddle, strap and whip deVille had earlier indicated and placed them on the silver tray. Carefully she closed the cupboard, checked the old clock on the panelled wall, and approached the chess players.

For almost a minute she stood in tense silence. Nobody moved, so she had no idea who's turn it was and her mind was far too excited to be able to take in the disposition of the pieces. At the last stroke of ten from the clock, deVille raised a finger and Miles looked up and paid attention to her and the contents of the tray. After only a moment's hesitation he selected the paddle.

Robyn placed the tray on a side table and went to stand in front of the lady desk. The two men followed her over.

"Bend over the desk," deVille ordered.

Robyn did as she was told, stretched her arms across its width and gripped the opposite edge. She shuddered at the touch of the cold leather and wood against her warm breasts and stomach.

"Come round here," deVille directed Miles.

Robyn saw both sets of legs appear, but she didn't look up.

deVille took her right wrist and un-clipped the little hinged ring from her bangle to let the thin chain hang free. This he threaded through the brass drawer handle before clip-

DOMINATING OBSESSION

ping the ring back to the bangle. Robyn tried jerking the chain, but whatever it was made of was much stronger than she. Miles attached her left wrist in a similar manner and now she was spread on top of the desk.

"We'll need your jewellery case," deVille told Miles.

When Miles returned with it they used straps to attach Robyn's ankles to the legs of the desk.

"Right, I think you're ready to begin," deVille announced.

Miles' first strokes with the paddle were hesitant, but soon he was laying on with considerable and painful force. From the corner of her eye she saw deVille undressing; laying his clothes neatly on the captain's chair as he did so. His precision seemed alien to the moment. Once he was fully undressed he took over from Miles to allow his pupil to do the same.

After a couple of strokes on Robyn's exposed bottom, deVille stood aside and Miles selected the strap. Robyn twisted on the desk, and she knew she wouldn't be able to stand too much of this.

deVille knew too, and as her excitement rose he placed himself in front of her. He gripped her hair and lifted her head. His eyes bored deep into hers; deep into her soul. He urged his hips forward, and slowly stuffed his bobbing cock into her wet mouth. Robyn groaned around its powerful girth and heard Miles drop the strap on the floor behind her bent and bound form. A moment later she groaned again as Miles' insistent cock penetrated her vagina fully with one urgent thrust.

Robyn's brain began to spin. She had never experienced anything like this before. The sensation was incredible. She knew she couldn't last long. Miles grunted over her shoulder and came first, and almost instantly deVille filled her mouth. As she felt the hot sperm jerking into her at both ends of her body she whimpered and shuddered helplessly on the desk. She suddenly felt totally fulfilled. Having two men grunting over her like this made her feel like a beauti-

DOMINATING OBSESSION

ful and powerful goddess.

The two men changed places, and while Robyn struggled with her mouth to stop Miles' cock from deflating, deVille used Miles' sperm to lubricate his entrance into her vulnerable anus. Robyn groaned loudly as he inched into her. She couldn't deny him his pleasure, and as he grew inside her the pain and the discomfort were gradually swamped by sheer pleasure.

deVille skilfully brought himself and Robyn to another climax together, and then, still with his cock fully implanted in her bottom, he instructed Miles to release her.

deVille easily lifted and turned her limp body, and with Miles helping to support her with his hands beneath her armpits, lowered her carefully onto Miles' rejuvenated cock. Robyn's head flopped back onto deVille's shoulder as Miles' cock forced its way into her vagina which was stretched by the presence of the huge lodger in the passage next door. But the men didn't stop - she didn't want them to stop.

At last Miles was fully embedded. Robyn whimpered and found herself suspended on two huge cocks, and bathed in sweat between their hot bodies. Then deVille bent his knees and let her slowly down until her toes touched the carpet.

Slowly at first, but then gaining momentum, they all began moving together. Robyn rubbed her breasts against Miles' chest. Miles' contorted face was a picture of ecstasy.

"Come, Robyn," deVille whispered, his voice remarkable calm.

"Yes, yes pleeease!" Robyn ground herself desperately against the two men, and then shuddered uncontrollably as she felt Miles fill her cunt with his seed.

As the two panted and wilted deVille rose to his full height, almost jerking her free from Miles. With an alarming roar he exploded into her battered bottom, and the exhausted and entangled threesome became a heap on the floor.

17

Jade awoke early. It was well over a week since Rooter had died and three days since the funeral. She had hardly been to college since, and seldom been up before noon either.

Jade wasn't surprised that she always awoke thinking of Rooter. It wasn't due to sentiment or love. It was purely a physical thing. Rooter had had his uses and now that he was gone she couldn't remember when she had last felt so frustrated.

Jade was a virgin. Could you believe it? Almost eighteen and still a virgin. None of her friends were. Well, that might not be entirely true, she told everyone that she wasn't, so there might be one or two of them that were doing the same.

It wasn't any moral reason that kept her chaste, it was just circumstance - she hadn't met the right boy at the right time. Then she had decided to save herself for Miles. It sounded crazy. All little girls fall in love with their father. It's natural. They all grow out of it. Except Miles wasn't her real father - and she had no intention of growing out of it.

The closest she had come to losing her virginity was when she was fourteen. She had been best friends with the Mortiboys twins. They were very beautiful, very sophisticated, and very bad. Being friends with the Mortiboys twins made you a somebody. She hid a secret cache of adult clothes round at their place. She used to tell her mother that she was staying over, then they would get dolled up to the nines, put on lots of make-up, and go to the clubs and pubs. One night she ended up in a car with three really old men, they must have been in their thirties surely, and she got pushed into the back and nearly raped, and that had really scared her. Shortly afterwards the twins got into drugs and dropped her because she wasn't adventurous enough for them any more.

So, her time for experimenting with boys passed while she hadn't any friends, and by the time her new friends came along she was too much in love with her Dad. That was what

DOMINATING OBSESSION

she still called him. She would like to call him Miles, but she couldn't. He would think she didn't love him any more, because he wasn't her real father, and she couldn't find the courage yet to tell him that she loved him too much - in the wrong way.

That was why she was missing Rooter so much. Jade threw back the duvet and sat up crossed legged looking at herself in the mirrored doors of the wardrobe. She had jet black hair cut in a bob, beautiful tits and tremendously long shapely legs. She was wearing a man's shirt. It was one of Miles' favourites. Jade had heard him giving her mother hell for misplacing it. He had worn it so much that it was frayed on the collar where his hair had rubbed against it. She always slept in one of his shirts and nothing else. She had lots of his things that he didn't know he'd lost.

Jade unbuttoned the shirt and looked at her breasts. They might not ever get bigger now that Rooter had gone. She began to rub them, looking at her reflection in the mirror and feeling sorry for herself. She was a normal healthy girl - perhaps a little over-sexed, but being in love with Miles and not having a boyfriend had meant that she only had masturbation to fall back on - until she had discovered that Rooter regularly masturbated her mother... she rubbed her hand over her pubic mound a few times and then parted her labia and dipped her index finger into her wet quim.

At first the discovery about Rooter and her mother had upset her and she'd wanted to tell Miles. But then she knew that Miles hated his father so much that she would never have the courage to tell him what Rooter was doing to Robyn. Watching them together in those early days had dismayed her. The thought of Rooter's grizzled old hands touching her mother's firm young flesh had made Jade shudder. And the first time she had watched him make her mother suck his wizened old prick Jade had almost been sick. Yet she couldn't stay away, and eventually she knew that she wanted to substitute herself for her mother - just to see what it was like.

DOMINATING OBSESSION

That first time, Rooter had seemed to know why she had come from the moment she entered his room. She waited until she was sure that Miles and her mother weren't going to return for something they had forgotten, and then she changed into a short stretch skirt and tight fitting white blouse. With her black stockings and suspenders and a pair of her mother's ridiculously tartish high heeled shoes, it perhaps wasn't surprising that Rooter knew - he was infirm, but he wasn't blind. Jade remembered his lecherous smile as he had knowingly patted the bed.

Having the old man masturbate her had been fantastic. She knew it was wrong, she knew they might get caught - but that made it all the more exciting.

Her thoughts of Rooter had brought her to the edge, and it was time to finish herself off. She removed her rotating finger from her clitoris, and began to strum her nails across her labia like a heavy metal fanatic finishing the final few bars of a rock anthem. She began to come, and she threw herself back on the pillows and lifted her hips high into the air, grinding them from side to side as she urgently rubbed her clitoris once more. At last she could stand no contact at all and she rested her hands on her flat tummy while she gently rocked to fulfilment. She allowed her body to slowly sink back down onto her crossed ankles, and with a final squeeze of her nipples it was done for another day - or perhaps only until this evening, when she was bound to feel frustrated again.

It really was a pig being young and sexy. Fuck Rooter. Fuck the old sod for dying.

Jade decided she couldn't be bothered to bathe or dress. Now that this morning's important business was out of the way, and she could think straight again, she remembered why she had set the alarm - she had something to do. There was something very strange going on in the house since that deVille person had invited himself to stay.

She rose, and without bothering to rebutton her shirt or

to pull on a dressing gown, she made for the bathroom. As she came out of the bathroom she saw her mother descending the stairs. That was another thing. Since deVille had come Robyn had taken to wearing very short skirts and tight tops with no bra. Jade gave her mother a moment to reach the hall and then started down after her. She crept up to the kitchen and peeped in, but there was nothing to see - just her mother preparing the breakfast.

If she had taken the trouble to dress properly she could have gone in and eaten. She pulled at the open shirt. It was no good, there was no way she could get away with this, she would have to go back upstairs first. As she approached the foot of the stairs she heard someone coming down, so she quickly ducked out of sight in the servants' corridor.

The corridor gave access to most of the downstairs rooms, plus two flights of back stairs, the cellar, and the unused butler's pantry. It also led into the kitchen. That door had a central wooden panel and two matching side panels of frosted glass. Set into the wooden centre panel, about three-quarters of the way up, there was a small circular window of coloured glass. Purely ornamental of course, but at sometime, someone - probably a suspicious butler - had arranged for the centre of the leaded circle to be replaced with a teardrop of clear glass. By stooping slightly, and putting her eye to this, Jade was able to see into the kitchen without being observed.

The teardrop gave a much enlarged picture of the centre of the room, and a slightly curved and distorted picture at its edges. Consequently, when deVille entered the kitchen, his figure grew long and thin, and then shrank almost to nothing before suddenly leaping into the area at the centre of the room.

Her mother looked round, put down the pan she was holding, and fairly ran over to fall to her knees at his feet. Jade suppressed a gasp as her mother bent and kissed deVille's feet - actually kissed his feet! Next she kissed both his hands, pressed her face to his crotch, and finally kissed him where

Jade presumed his penis to be.

The young girl couldn't believe it. Without thinking she slipped her hands under her shirt and agitatedly massaged her breasts. She couldn't resist the bizarre tableau as her mother rose to her feet, turned her back to deVille, bent at the waist. That flicked her skirt up. Jade was treated to a magnified view of her mother's bottom, and her heart missed a beat as she saw it was criss-crossed with angry dark stripes. Her mother had been whipped, or caned!

deVille ran a hand lovingly over the stripes and then down between her mother's legs, where it remained for some time. Jade watched her mother's bottom twitching, and moaned quietly with fascinated longing, before moving her hand down to massage her own clitoris. God that woman! She had everything! She had Miles, and yet she insisted on prostituting herself with everything in trousers. Wasn't whoring with Miles' own father disgraceful enough, without bringing another man into the house before Rooter was hardly cold in his bed?

To Jade's surprise - and disappointment - the two suddenly parted and tried to regain a degree of normality. deVille took a seat at the table whilst her mother returned to preparing the breakfast.

The watching girl's heart leapt as she saw a way to finally get the happiness she longed for. Telling Miles about Robyn and his father might have been impossible, but this wasn't!

The thought was hardly in her head before Miles entered the kitchen. He had only just missed discovering them himself, but Jade was glad he had. She wanted to be the one to tell him the bad news.

Miles sorted a newspaper from the recently delivered pile by deVille and went to sit on the opposite side of the table.

Then it happened. deVille called to Robyn, and without question she left the cooking and displayed her bottom to Miles in the same way that she had for deVille. This time

DOMINATING OBSESSION

she faced Jade. Miles seemed pleased with her bottom and Robyn seemed pleased at what he was saying about it.

Jade didn't understand. How was it possible for Miles to let her behave like that, flouncing about without any underwear and exhibiting her bare bottom to the house guest?

The knowledge that there was something between these three that she didn't understand kept Jade patiently glued to her spyhole while the two men ate their breakfast - and her diligence eventually paid off.

As soon as deVille had finished eating he stretched back with a cigarette. Her mother looked round and left her work unfinished. She stood before him asking something, but deVille shook his head and pointed back at the unwashed dishes. Her mother turned dejectedly and began retracing her steps, but deVille called her back. Once more she stood before him while he spoke to her, and in a moment she had pulled off her top and was proudly displaying her naked breasts for him. At his bidding she leant forward and allowed him to fondle and kiss each of them in turn. Then he spoke again and she stood upright, and undoing the zip at the side of her skirt, let it drop to the floor. Stepping free of the untidy bundle she turned and flounced back to the sink.

As soon as her back was turned, Jade saw Miles lower his paper and deVille return his wink and grin. Robyn stayed at the sink cleaning the dishes in only her high heels, suspender belt and black stockings. The two men observed her putting-away, which seemed to involve a lot of stretching and bending, and Jade realised that her mother was revelling in the attention - and she envied her beyond endurance.

Jade's fingers were firmly embedded in her wet vagina and her legs were weakening by the time her mother had finished her chores and returned to deVille's side.

deVille looked up from his paper, took a moment to check that her work was truly done - as if he hadn't surreptitiously watched every second of it - and then gave a curt nod of consent.

Jade watched her mother slip elegantly under the table, open his flies, and hungrily feed his semi-erect penis into her mouth. She laid her face on his thigh and her cheek hollowed as she slowly sucked him deeper.

It was all too much for poor Jade. Her legs buckled and she sank silently to the floor of the chilly, dank corridor. With her back against the kitchen door, she stuffed one hand into her mouth, and used the other to give herself a shattering, silent orgasm.

18

Robyn didn't want Jade to be at the reading of Rooter's will.

The funeral had been bad enough, but she was sure that Paige was saving her real onslaught for a showdown in front of the staid frail old Mr Hanbury, senior partner of Dewberry, Rowbottom and Pride who's normal genteel demeanour and ancient mode of attire combined perfectly with the faded Victorian splendour of his large oak veneered office.

Mr Hanbury might have the look of one who has seen it all before, but Robyn secretly suspected that nothing in his past life had quite prepared him for this particularly virulent form of ginger hell cat. Ever since deVille's arrival, Robyn had been trying to persuade Jade to go to spend the summer with a school friend in Norfolk, but Jade had stubbornly refused to commit herself. Robyn expected to encounter similar resistance from her daughter concerning the reading of the will, and was pleasantly surprised and grateful when Jade not only agreed to stay away, but also agreed to cook deVille's breakfast for him.

In normal circumstances Robyn might have been more suspicious of her daughter's easy compliance, especial as Jade had suddenly and unaccountably begun referring to deVille as Uncle Nick, but these were frantic times for Robyn

DOMINATING OBSESSION

and she was simply grateful to have two items slot into place so neatly.

So with trepidation in her heart for the coming ordeal, but serenity in her mind at leaving deVille in capable hands, Robyn sailed forth into the car and waved back to her daughter who stood on the steps happily waving goodbye until they were completely out of sight.

19

The moment her parents' car rounded the bend in the drive Jade stepped back inside the house, slammed the large oak door, and slid both bolts across with a flourish of finality.

She took a moment to look up towards the bedrooms, listening and thinking, and then she raced quickly upstairs to change.

This was it! The butterflies had started. She pulled off her normal day clothes, threw them into the corner, and replaced them with a black suspender belt, black stockings and a little tartan flare skirt.

Then she went to the wardrobe and took out the shoes she kept hidden under some old school jumpers right at the back. They were a pair of her mother's in black with ankle straps and incredibly high stiletto heels. Tart's shoes, Jade thought to herself. The sort of shoes she had told herself she would never ever wear in public however desperate she got to get a man. But already she could feel it, and when she stood up after putting them on, there was no denying the excitement in her body.

She looked at her legs in the mirror, starting at her feet and travelling slowly up an incredibly long expanse of black nylon that was almost as shiny as the patent leather of the shoes. When she reached the hem of her skirt she lifted it just ahead of her eyes like a great artist unveiling a master-

DOMINATING OBSESSION

piece for the world's critics to marvel at for the first time.

Even she had to admit that the high heels made her legs look fantastic. They now had a perfect shape and seemed to go on for ever; way past the lace patterned stocking tops and right on past the jet black 'V' of her pubes until they eventually stopped at the waist band of her skirt.

Jade turned so that she could look at her bottom. Even that had a totally different shape. It was now a much more pronounced and pert little thing. Next her eager gaze followed the back of her legs and traced down again, slowly dropping the hem of her skirt back in place as her eyes passed by, until finally she arrived back at the web of criss-crossed straps that held her slender ankles caged.

No man could possibly mistake the clear message these shoes were sending and no woman could possibly stand tall in them without feeling incredibly sexy and powerful with her motives and desires on full display.

It had seemed so perfect when she had planned it. It had seemed so straight forward when she had practice it. But now that the time had come to carry it out, she faltered, as even her massive self confidence deserted her for a moment.

What if he laughed at her? What if he told her to go back up stairs, wash the paint off her face, and get back into her school clothes?

That reminded her. She opened the top right hand drawer of the dressing table and lovingly unwrapped her new angora crop top from its neatly folded covering of crisp tissue paper. Then she pulled it on over her head and moulded it to her naked breasts. When she had finished her tits looked even better than when they were naked. Their outline and her raised nipples were clearly visible through the thin canary yellow wool above six inches of bare midriff and navel, but now the beautifully rounded orbs looked so soft, warm, and cuddly that even her own palms itched to fondle them. Expensive, but worth every penny, she decided at last. Our Mr deVille would very much appreciate those and he would

DOMINATING OBSESSION

be in no doubt that there was nothing between the thin well stretched angora and her own firm pliant flesh.

But would he get to see that flesh? Jade lifted the tiny skirt again. And would he get to see this downy little mouse's nest? Or would he stop her long before that? How old was he, anyway? Forty? Fifty? Much older than Miles. Much older than Robyn, even. And she herself was not even eighteen yet.

Jade walked up and down the room a few times, thinking about him. He was a lot to take on. She barely knew him, and he didn't look like the type of man to trifle with. She was going to try to seduce a man that was more than twice her age and who she hardly knew. And why? Because some female intuition told her that he was the answer to all her prayers. Some instinct told her that by using deVille she could get the one thing in life that meant anything to her. The one thing she had to have at all costs.

But turning him on was one thing: holding him at bay afterwards was another. Jade stopped in front of the mirror and raised her skirt again. If she went to him like this, with no knickers, that was an invitation that couldn't be ignored, surely? The bush that covered her pubis was jet black and as thick and soft as a mink pelt. She ran her fingers lightly over it watching the hairs bend down before them then jump smartly back to attention after their passing like rows of well drilled guardsmen.

She was still a virgin. Rooter had insisted on that. When the time came it would be more prized than the most generous dowry, he had told her. Whether he was right or wrong she didn't know. Men set more store by such things, she knew that. But if she had to give it up in order to hook deVille would she be willing to go through with it?

Jade took another quick look at her wristwatch. It was now or never. Well, she was a young woman hungry for her life to start; and there was no other way!

deVille would go for her, she was sure of that. But what

would happen when Miles found out that his trusted friend had waited until they had left him alone with her in the house and then taken advantage of such a sweet innocent little child? And he would find out, she would make damn sure of that. Jade smiled maliciously at her co-conspirator, her own reflection. He would go insane. deVille would get kicked out immediately, and with any luck he would take Robyn with him.

Jade smiled again at the prospect. That would open Miles' eyes for him. That would make him look at her the way deVille was going to look at her soon. That was all she asked. She just wanted to see him look at her that way; as a man looks at a woman rather than as a father looks at his child. That was all she was asking for, a fair chance to compete with Robyn on equal terms.

Jade smiled at her reflection again, then suddenly squealed and laughed, flipping her skirt up to expose her nakedness. She was going to do it! And she was going to win! She knew she was. Some people, she thought, the Robyn's of this world, never have to bother. They have everything presented to them on a plate without even having to break sweat. But the rest of us, us mere mortals, we have to grab what we want any way we can.

Jade fairly flounced down the stairs and into the kitchen to start preparing breakfast. Now she was sure: it was right. No more wondering. No more dithering. When deVille came down she would do it. Just do it! without even thinking about it, she told herself.

She didn't have long to wait. Within ten minutes she heard deVille in the hall picking up the newspapers and slapping them together as he arranged them in the order in which he liked to read them. Always the Sun first followed by the Times. Jade shook her head and smiled wondering which he actually preferred if he was truly honest.

deVille entered the kitchen with his head still down flicking through the different headlines. Without hesitation Jade

DOMINATING OBSESSION

ran over to him and sank to her knees in front of him.

Now he looked at her. And already he was staring at her with the look she so desperately longed to see in Miles' eyes.

Jade expected him to speak or draw away, but he didn't. He simply waited. Well that was OK, she knew what to do. Since deciding on her plan she had practised it often enough in front of the mirrored wardrobe doors in her bedroom. But this was different, as often as not when she had practised it she had ended up on her back laughing. But she wasn't laughing now...

This was strange. She was paying homage to a man, treating him as if he was her lord and master. And suddenly, as she bent to kiss the toe of his left shoe, she knew that she wasn't play acting any more. This ceremonial act of submission suddenly felt shockingly real. She had never believed that any man was superior to her - except, perhaps, Miles. But as she moved her head to hover above the tip of deVille's right shoe, she knew that she might be capable of worshipping another human being.

A tremendous shudder ran through her. God all mighty, did she want to be equal, or did she want a man who could fill her with overwhelming primal feelings like these? Nothing she had ever done before had ever come close to this.

deVille threw the papers down heavily on to the end of the table and held out his left hand.

Jade looked up at him and she knew that her eyes were cloudy.

"Don't look at me - keep your head bowed," he barked, as if she should have known better.

And she should. Instinctively she placed her arms behind her back with the wrists crossed as if they were bound together, and as she leant forward to kiss the back of his hand, she knew that this was the way it should be done. As her lips touched the warm flesh she groaned inside. It was as if she had been doing this all her life.

deVille turned his hand and she kissed the centre of his

palm. Then he placed the same palm on her left cheek and gave her the gentlest little squeeze. She knew without him telling her that this wasn't part of the ceremony. She knew that this was to take the bite from his earlier harsh words of reprimand and to reward her for doing so well. Now she could hardly breath. deVille held out his right hand and somehow she found it with her lips without even opening her eyes.

Then she stopped

She knew what she was supposed to do next, but she couldn't move.

deVille placed his hand on the back of her head and guided her forward. Jade heard herself give a little involuntary cry. There was nothing non-sexual about this and nothing false or hidden about her actions. If she did this she would be admitting his superiority over her before their sexual relationship had even begun. And there was no question about her not doing it. Her body was humming with more power than it had ever known before.

Jade let her head be moved forward and when her left cheek touched deVille's thigh there was something there against the side of her nose. It wasn't erect, but a thing that large and solid didn't have to be. She could feel it pulsating, just the other side of the thin piece of worsted that separated them. It was warm and alive; and it was waiting for her.

deVille moved her cheek to his other thigh. Then he removed his guiding hand from her head.

Jade forced her eyes to open and remain open as her pouting lips started their long journey towards the solid bulge in deVille's trousers. In slow motion she watched every detail as it got closer. Then her lips touched it and she felt something snap in her womb. Whatever it was, was attached to her brain, because it twanged back with the speed of a piece of broken elastic to explode in her head so that she no longer had any idea where she was or what was happening. She might have toppled then if deVille hadn't caught her shoulders and held her upright for a moment.

DOMINATING OBSESSION

"Very good," he said.

Jade's befuddled brain noted his compliment, but she couldn't reply. She had no breath to spare for exhaling let alone speech. And now she kept her head bowed; not from respect, but for simple survival.

"But, you've forgotten one thing, haven't you?" he asked.

Jade didn't know. Had she? She didn't know what was happening, let alone what she might have forgotten."

"Where's my, 'Good-morning, Master'? or didn't Robyn tell you about that?"

"Mother didn't teach me any of it," Jade replied, addressing her words to his knees.

"Master," deVille said, incomprehensibly.

"What?" She began to look up, then remembered that she mustn't.

"You address me as Master," he explained.

"No I don't," Jade explained back and now she looked at him.

deVille lifted her to her feet. Jade couldn't stop shaking.

"So how do you know this much? - you spied on us?" deVille guessed.

"Yes. It was very informative," Jade told him.

deVille had the grace to smile. "I imagine it would be - you're what? Fifteen," he suggested.

"Eighteen!" Jade replied, angrily.

deVille nodded. "Eighteen, eh? All grown up. So you will know what happens next."

He was laughing at her, daring her to do it. And he didn't care whether she did or not. He thought she had nothing to show him, the arrogant pig. He would see!

"I hope you're dressed for the part," he said, adding to his derision.

That was enough. Jade swung round angrily, turning her back on him. Then she bent and placed her hands on her knees.

Several seconds passed in silence before Jade realised

that he wasn't going to do anything. He didn't have the guts. But he must do something! She had to have something to tell Miles. She wiggled her bottom. She had put herself into a position where that was the only thing she had left to entice him with.

"Put your hands on your ankles," his cool voice directed her.

He had stopped laughing at her. She had achieved that much. But she couldn't do what he was demanding now. Hands on knees was bad enough, but hands on ankles...

Jade felt a hollowness in her stomach and her head began to spin. Slowly, trying not to think about how exposed she would look once he lifted her skirt, Jade began sliding her hands down the smooth shiny silk of her legs until her fingers touched the tops of her ankle straps.

deVille waited again. Jade felt her body begin vibrating uncontrollably and knew what he had been waiting for. The man was a bastard - an absolute bastard she thought as she watched and felt the hem of her tiny skirt shaking like the fringe on a racing surrey.

deVille flipped her skirt back.

Now he knew that she was correctly dressed for the occasion. Jade felt herself begin to colour. And it wasn't only her facial cheeks that were blushing. She didn't have to try very hard to imagine what deVille was seeing. She had practice this part too, over and over again in the wardrobe mirrors. Now that it was actually happening she realised that she had never really believed that it would.

And then came a part that she hadn't practised.

"Beautiful. Absolutely beautiful," he said. His voice sounded distant and his words seemed to slip out unintended like those of a prospective buyer who wants to appear unimpressed, but finds it impossible not to express his desire for the article he is being offered.

"Eighteen you say?" he added, after a moment.

"Almost eighteen," Jade confirmed, her natural confi-

DOMINATING OBSESSION

dence returning with every second that passed.

"Almost, is better," deVille said in a throaty voice that made Jade's heart flutter.

Then she almost jumped out of her skin and clutched hard at her ankles to stop herself rising as his cool hands descended gently on to the hot cheeks of her bottom.

deVille's skin was amazingly soft and smooth, and his touch gentle and confident. Like a skittish thoroughbred filly, Jade instinctively knew that she was being admired and assessed by a professional and was calmed immediately.

As the unaccustomed palms began slowly circling the half moons of her bottom Jade clenched her teeth, closed her eyes, and tried to hang on, but soon she felt a familiar crisis beginning to arise in her tummy.

deVille stopped his circling and drew his fingertips lightly across her taut flesh. Jade's face began to burn again. He was tracing the fading marks of Rooter's final beating. Somewhere deep inside her loins her coming orgasm started making preparations. She felt it nagging away at her dam, opening up a little hole. It was such a tiny little hole, no bigger than the tip of a man's finger, and the fabric of her dam was wide and solid. But she knew the fissure had started.

"You know how to accept discipline then?" deVille asked.

"Yes." Jade desperately tried to make her tone as matter of fact as his.

"Who from?"

Oh, no, she couldn't tell him that!

deVille's right hand suddenly descended with a loud crack on her bottom.

Jade sprang up with a cry and turned on him.

He didn't move. He didn't spring back or attempt to protect himself and the eyes that bore into her's were totally unconcerned.

Jade dropped her own eyes, and her raised hand, and lifting her skirt she rubbed the singing skin where he had struck her.

DOMINATING OBSESSION

"That hurt!"

"I'm waiting," deVille replied, and his voice implied that he wasn't a patient man.

"Rooter," Jade said, looking up so that she would be in time to register his shock and disgust.

It didn't come. deVille's face was impassive.

"Your grandfather," he said, to show that he knew who she meant.

"No! He wasn't my grandfather. He was Miles' father. No relation of mine. Not really."

deVille nodded. "Bend over again," he ordered.

"Why?" Jade asked, quickly and defiantly.

deVille's left eyebrow moved a fraction as if it wanted to register its shock. But deVille wouldn't let it.

"You shouldn't have risen without permission. I'm going to have to discipline you for that," he explained.

They stared at each other for several long moments. The bastard! Jade wanted to flounce out of the room. Every fibre of her being, every thread of her upbringing, screamed at her to do so. But there was a stronger voice. 'Remember why you're here - remember what you're after,' it cautioned.

Jade turned quickly and resumed her former position. God, he is going to get such a beating when Miles finds out, she consoled herself. She might even join in herself if she got a chance. The thought was comforting until his hand slapped her bottom with more force than she would have dreamed possible.

He hit her three times on either cheek. She didn't cry out; she wouldn't let him have the satisfaction. But with the last one she couldn't stop a tear breaking free from her left eye and skitting down her cheek.

She sniffed.

"Get up," deVille commanded.

Jade did so and stood with her back to him, praying that he would let her go to get on with cooking his breakfast.

"Turn round."

DOMINATING OBSESSION

She couldn't, he would see her tears.

"Turn round," he commanded again.

"I can't - my nose is crying!" she wailed, and for a moment she knew that she sounded exactly like her mother.

"Do it," he said more kindly.

Jade turned and did her best to look at him defiantly with her cheeks and upper lip wet and her eyes full of the tears still to come.

deVille handed her a handkerchief.

Now she cried and wiped quickly at her face as deVille pulled her to him and held her in his arms while she wet his chest with her tears and prayed that nothing worse stained his shirt.

When she had fully recovered and blown her nose and dried her eyes she tried to hand him his handkerchief back.

"Keep it and wash it," he instructed.

Jade smiled and nodded and tried to hide the offending article behind her back.

"I think you'd better go and get my breakfast," he told her.

Jade smiled and nodded again and scampered gratefully away.

She ran and put his handkerchief in the washing machine, and washed her hands, then tried to think what she should do next. She hadn't a clue. Her bottom was throbbing and her dam was still crumbling. She picked up a frying pan and spatula that someone had left ready, but she couldn't remember what she wanted them for.

"Come here," deVille instructed.

Jade put the cooking implements down and went back to him in a dream. She couldn't think. She knew she ought too, but her brain wouldn't function.

"Sit down," he said.

Jade sat on the first chair at his end of the table. She was just in time. Her legs began shaking uncontrollably.

"Take off your top," he commanded.

DOMINATING OBSESSION

Jade looked at him, struggling to understand what he wanted. Then she pulled the tiny garment off over her head.

Her breasts were huge. She could see them jiggling in front of his eyes.

deVille was watching them too. She could see the light dancing on his pupils as they moved in rhythm with her bouncing boobs.

"Shake them again," he instructed.

Jade did so. And again, over and over, until he decided he had had enough. He liked her tits. Jade sniffed and smiled again. She was pleased he did.

"Lift your skirt."

After a moment Jade lifted the hem and raised it to her lap holding on to it for grim death with both hands in a vain attempt to control her shaking body.

deVille was looking at the top of her legs. He shook his head as if something wouldn't do.

"Take it off," he instructed.

Jade stared at him for a long time then she pulled at the button and slid down the little zip. While she still had the courage she lifted her bottom from the chair for a split second and sent the skirt skidding towards her ankles.

Her whole body was shaking. Her thighs were pressed tightly together and she could hear the continuous silky tearing sound made by the nylon of her stockings as her legs moved up and down past each other. She couldn't stop her legs rising and falling: she was a shipwrecked mariner treading water and praying for someone to rescue her.

deVille wasn't that someone. He was looking at the top of her legs: still not satisfied.

"Open them."

Jade looked at him through large frightened eyes and did nothing.

"Open your legs!"

Jade shook her head. She couldn't. They had to stay together. They were the only thing that was holding the rem-

DOMINATING OBSESSION

nants of her dam in place.

deVille leant forward and pressed her knees apart.

For the first time her vulva was fully exposed to his stare and she could feel the heat of his interest.

"Beautiful!" he said.

He raised his eyes to hers and he was smiling.

"It's an absolute little darling." His eyes returned to admire it.

He meant it. His eyes hadn't been lying. Jade felt a tremor run through her as the imprisoned waters threw themselves against her dam.

deVille's hands were still on her knees holding her legs apart. He pressed them wider. It made his face come closer to her own. His eyes were big and soft and brown.

His lips moved. "Take care of your tits," he said.

What could he mean?

Jade's hands went to her breasts and cupped them uncertainly. Then her fingers and thumbs found her nipples and closed on them. "Ahh-hhhhh!" she cried. And her eyes closed and her body made her cry into a sigh as her dam creaked and prepared to give up the unequal struggle. Sensing victory the impatient waters pushed forward and for a long moment she was drowning under their dark swirling surface. Then she was suddenly spinning back up towards daylight carried along in a wildly circling eddy.

She surfaced and deVille's large soft brown eyes were there to greet her. She squeezed her fingers and thumbs together and the pain helped her retain control of her senses, but the dam was gone and her juices were free to pore into her waiting vagina.

deVille didn't leave her. His hands remained on her knees and his eyes remained staring into hers as she let herself come.

With a final jerk it was all over. She gave one last squeeze to her nipples and signed heavily.

"Better?" deVille asked.

DOMINATING OBSESSION

Jade nodded and waited for his invite. A slight pressure on her knees was all she needed. She was in his lap in a moment with her head on his chest and her arms round his neck.

His right hand found her chin and lifted it, and in another second their mouths and tongues were attacking one another like Siamese fighting fish.

Slowly Jade swam back to reality. Everything was normal. The clock was still ticking; the sun was still streaming in through the high Georgian windows; Miles' smiling face was still beaming down at her from his photograph on the mantle; and she was still sitting naked on their house guests lap in the middle of Robyn's kitchen.

deVille's body felt firm and cuddly beneath her. She rubbed her naked breasts against his shirt. It felt strange, but very very nice to sit here little and naked on his lap while he was fully dressed. All he had done was smack her bottom and gently hold her knees apart, and she had come for him. She had read all the sex manuals so that she would be ready, but where did it say that you did what deVille had just done to make someone come?

deVille lifted her chin again.

She looked into his eyes and she knew that her own eyes must be as wide as saucers with wonder and trepidation.

"Breakfast," he reminded her.

When he smiled at her like that she knew that she would do anything for him if only she could work out what his words meant and remember what to do about them.

Slowly, very slowly, it made sense. He was hungry. He wanted his breakfast. He was waiting for her to get it for him.

"Oh!" Jade sprang up and started casting round for her clothes.

"Don't bother with those." He took them from her. "You don't need any clothes. Just make sure you're careful with the hot fat," he said.

DOMINATING OBSESSION

Dully Jade nodded. She wanted to go back and kiss his hand and sit safely on his lap. But she knew that she couldn't; there was something she had to do. She began walking towards the Aga.

She heard deVille rise and she looked back at him. He didn't see her. He was walking the other way, towards the fireplace.

Jade turned away again and continued her journey. It was hard. It was all uphill through encroaching grey mist, but she forced her feet to continue putting one in front of the other. They weren't built for walking on springy white clouds, but it didn't matter, there was no hurry, and eventually she reached her destination.

She needed to smile at deVille to show him how clever she had been.

deVille was just turning and returning a bunch of small keys to his pocket. Her clothes were no longer in sight and she realised that he must have locked them away in one of the alcove cupboards.

His action was incomprehensible, but he smiled reassuringly at her and she knew everything was as it should be.

20

Jade was preparing deVille's breakfast and she was in the nude.

It gave her an unbelievable feeling. No wonder her mother had liked it. It would be just the sort of thing for her, showing everything off. She was such a slapper, surely Miles must be able to see that?

Jade could hear the rustling as deVille turned over the pages of the newspapers, but she wasn't fooled, she knew he was watching her.

Her plan wasn't going quite as she had envisaged. But

DOMINATING OBSESSION

this was better. She had never even considered that she might like it quite so much. Or rather, that I might like deVille quite so much, she corrected herself, stealing another look. If I wasn't so much in love with Miles I might quite like being in love with you for a while, you beautiful dark handsome bastard. She stole yet another glance at him. He was so distinguished; so superior and forbidding; so wonderfully handsome and debonair. It's obvious that I need older men, she decided. Men need time to learn how to mature into real bastards.

deVille had known exactly what to do and he had gone easy on her. She had seduced him, all right, but he hadn't made it very hard. It was almost a pity that Miles would have to fight with him and throw him out. Especially when he likes me so much, Jade thought with glee, giving herself a mental hug.

Perhaps all men would be as easy? No! you mustn't think like that, she scolded herself. You love Miles. You're only doing this for him, and you're only doing as much as is absolutely necessary to get what you want.

But that didn't sound right. She had already done enough to show Miles what sort of man deVille was. She could go and lock herself in her room now and wait for Miles and Robyn to return. But that might not be for hours. If they made friends with Uncle Elliot and Aunty Paige they would go to the club to celebrate. If they didn't, they would go there to let off steam. Either way, she could be locked in her room for hours thinking of deVille and what might have been.

Jade arranged deVille's full English breakfast on a large warm plate and took it over to him.

deVille put his paper aside and cleared a space so that she could set it down. They smiled at each other.

"Sit down. I want to look at you," he ordered, and Jade's decision was made. She was going to stay and find out more about being a woman. Much more - she hoped.

Jade sat in the same chair as before and tried to teach

herself not to blush when he looked at her.

"You're very beautiful," he decided after a couple of mouthfuls of bacon and egg.

Jade beamed.

"Even more beautiful than your mother."

"Oh!" Jade's head began spinning. Was that possible?

"No one's more beautiful than Robyn," she protested.

"You are," deVille said, as if it was an undeniable matter of fact. "You're younger, you're more vibrant, you're more confident. You're all together more interesting."

"Oh. I thought you meant my looks."

"Oh, those too," deVille said, dismissively, "but you must have realised that for yourself. And the fact that you already surpass your mother in physical beauty is all the more significant for the realisation that Robyn must now be at the absolute zenith of full bloom whereas you are only just budding into blossom."

"Oh!" Was it true? Was that what Miles would see? Jade beamed again.

"Masturbate for me," deVille said, forking another mouthful of food from his plate.

"Pardon?" Jade was shocked.

"Nice and slow. I like to enjoy my first cigarette of the day after breakfast and I don't want you to finish until I've finished that."

Jade looked at him wondering what to do.

deVille turned the Times over and finished the article he had been reading.

Jade put her left hand on to her left breast and her right index finger on to her clitoris and looked at him blankly. She felt like a trainee pilot asked to take the controls for the very first time.

deVille looked at her and nodded.

Jade began.

deVille cut an inch of bacon, forked it on to a prepared square of fried slice, and conveyed them both to his mouth.

DOMINATING OBSESSION

Jade wriggled her bottom down on the cushioned seat and leant back. This was going to be a big one. She would show him what a real wank was. She opened her legs wide and used both hands to pull her labia apart.

She had his attention now. Using the thumb and fingers of her left hand to hold her sex lips wide she began to slowly masturbate herself. With each stroke she let three fingers of her right hand travel way up inside her vagina before she brought them back to delicately circle her clitoris.

deVille finished his breakfast, pushed the plate away, and lit a cigarette.

Jade was still happily engaged on the task he had set her. She was now using both hands on her clit, fanny, breasts, and nipples. Her eyes were cloudy and closed to narrow slits and her head was slowly rotating from side to side as she softly groaned her way to climax.

deVille crushed out the remains of his cigarette and blew out the last of the smoke in a long blue stream. "Very good," he said, smiling. Then he grabbed her hand and yanked her to her feet.

"Come on."

"I haven't finished," Jade cried, trying to hang back.

"Yes you have," deVille replied, with a note of finality.

Jade was livid. She pulled against him and finally jerked her hand free. She stood half bowed, with her breasts shaking and her face white with anger, gasping for breath.

deVille hit her hard across the face with no holding back. Then he slapped her again, this time with a downward stroke that forced her to her knees.

Jade's world was suddenly split wide apart. In a brilliant flash of white light she learnt in an instant of naked brutality everything she had not been taught in a short lifetime of privileged and pampered existence. No one had ever hit her like that before. No one had ever felt the need. She was an intelligent civilised human being with absolutely no defence against such unprovoked, incomprehensible, and unneces-

DOMINATING OBSESSION

sary violence.

She sat on her haunches with her arms in front of her face, waiting for his further blows to reign down on her.

They didn't come. deVille took her hand again and pulled her to her feet. Despite her ridiculously high heels he suddenly seemed very tall and solidly built. She had always thought of him as very similarly sized to Miles, but now she could see that he was taller and much more heavily built.

"Truth time, Jade. What are we doing here?"

"I - I don't understand. Why did you hit me?" Jade realised that she was very close to tears.

"That was to show you what will happen."

"When?" Jade coward back from him.

"If you don't tell me the truth - first time - every time. I don't like being jerked around. Not by a self willed, selfish, spoilt little brat - not by anyone!"

Jade nodded. She could see he didn't. She could also see that he was big enough and brutal enough to ensure that it didn't happen very often.

"Let's start again. What are we doing here, Jade?"

What could she tell him? She couldn't tell him the truth. She waited as long as she dared, which was only another two seconds. "There's something I want," she blurted out.

"What?"

"Someone."

"Who?"

She couldn't tell him that. This was all going horribly wrong.

"Who?!"

Jade jumped at the violence of the single word. She pressed her hands between her legs and twisted round, jigging up and down and looking for some sort of salvation. She wanted to plead with this dreadful maniac not to hit her again, but what good would that do? The man was a monster; a psychopathic monster.

"Miles," she wailed.

DOMINATING OBSESSION

For a moment deVille didn't understand her. He thought that her cry must be a plea for help and he looked towards the door as if he expected to see Miles there. Then his eyes filled with understanding.

With an ice cold chill Jade realised that deVille wasn't the least bit frightened of Miles. When he had thought that Miles might be about to come to her aid, he hadn't even turned a hair.

"Miles," deVille repeated.

Jade nodded. "You don't seem surprised," she said.

"Most little girls get a crush on their fathers," he said, simply.

"He's not my father! I'm not a little girl! It's not a crush!" Jade said, with pauses between each statement as she slowly worked out that every piece of his assertion had been incorrect.

"Especially a little girl like you," deVille continued as if she hadn't spoken at all.

"What do you mean, a girl like me?"

"You want Miles because he's the one man in the whole world you can't have."

"That's a lie!"

"And because he belongs to Robyn."

"I don't care about Robyn. That's got nothing to do with it."

"Yes you do. She might be the only thing you do care about. For all the wrong reasons. You've already had Miles' father - because Robyn had him first. And you've done your best to cause friction between Miles and your mother so that their marriage would fail. And now you want Miles. You're jealous of your mother. You think she's got everything. Sophistication, beauty - Miles!"

Jade wanted to throw herself on him. She wanted to punch and kick and scratch him. She wanted to hurt him as he had hurt her. But she couldn't. The man was a brute. He would throw her off and beat her into submission. She fled to one

DOMINATING OBSESSION

of the arm chairs and throwing herself on to her stomach she began to howl with frustration and pain.

"Come here, Jade."

Jade continued to cry with her shoulders and chest shaking as the terrible injustice of everything in life racked her body with dreadful sobs.

"Don't make me come and fetch you."

Jade wiped her eyes on a cushion. Then on a sudden impulse blew her nose on her mother's hand embroidered antimacassar.

Without looking at him or raising her head she walked slowly over and took up her former position in front of him.

"Miles is your father, Jade. You must know you can't have him."

"He's not. My real father left us when I was very young. He just disappeared. No one knows where he is. Miles is just Robyn's husband. He's no blood relation to me."

"That doesn't matter. He brought you up as his daughter and that means that the law says you can't have him."

"The law's wrong."

"Maybe it is. It often is. But only you and the other's concerned can decide that in this actual case. Do you really believe that it's not wrong to lust after your own father, Jade?"

"It's not like that. Well, it is, but you're just trying to make it sound worse. We're not related and I don't think of him as my father any more. I think of him as a man. The man I love."

"I'm not your judge, Jade. You don't have to lie to me. But please don't lie to yourself. You only have one true judge - yourself. What you are proposing could hurt many people; Robyn, Miles, yourself. Try to forget your natural bias. Try to judge your own petition fairly. If you don't, it will end in tears. It could end in destroying somebody; perhaps you all; especially Miles.

Jade looked at him defiantly.

"Do you believe in the Devil, Jade?" he suddenly asked

incomprehensibly.

"What!" The man is weird, Jade decided. Can't he see how important this is to me? What the hell has the Devil got to do with anything connected with real life?

"All right. Do you believe that in the end people who do wrong get punished in one way or another for what they do?"

Jade shrugged. "Perhaps - sometimes."

"And don't tell me that sometimes, when you want something very much, or you really need someone else's help, you don't say some sort of prayer to some sort of god?"

Jade shrugged again. Maybe that was true. Didn't everyone?

"You've been brought up in an Anglo Saxon country, Jade. You know that you can't expect to enjoy yourself without having to pay for it in the end. That fact, true or false, has been imbued into your very soul. So you know that if God exists, then so does his mirror image: the Devil. You can't have one without the other. You can't pray to one without making the other exist, if it's only in your soul. And if you lie to yourself your soul will know the truth."

He stopped and they stared at each other for several seconds while the clock ticked on unaware that anything life changing was happening.

"So, I will ask you again, Jade, don't you feel that it's wrong to lust after your father?"

Was it wrong? He wasn't her father. He had been her father, but he wasn't now. He was Miles. But even if it was wrong, she had no choice. She couldn't go through life, or even start it, without him. Perhaps people who had never had something they must have at all costs wouldn't understand and so would judge her harshly. But she couldn't judge herself that way. She wasn't a free agent and even if she did destroy them all and condemn them all to languish in Hell's fire for all eternity as deVille said, she didn't care. She had to have Miles.

DOMINATING OBSESSION

"It's not wrong. Anything that feels so right could never be wrong. I may be a selfish and spiteful self willed woman as you say, but I'm not a little girl. I haven't been a little girl for many years and it's not my fault if I know what I want and have the guts to go for it. And make no mistake, I will get Miles, one way or another."

"Fair enough." deVille didn't seem angry, he seemed impressed. Jade relaxed a little, certain now that he wasn't going to hit her again. Not for a while anyway.

"I don't doubt your determination any more, but you still have a major problem, you know? Miles won't want you."

"I'll make him want me."

This time it was deVille's turn to shrug. "Perhaps you will. And perhaps I put that badly. What I meant to say was, that unlike you, Miles will know that he can't have you."

The man was a nerd. Jade couldn't think why she had ever thought any differently. Did he think that she didn't know that? He was a bloody insufferable interfering knowall and she was sorry now that she had ever involved him in her business.

"A little thing like that. I'm surprised you can't tell me how to deal with it just like that," she said, sarcastically.

"Maybe I can."

"Oh, yes. I'm sure."

"All right then - I definitely can."

Could he? Jade's heart leapt at the knowledge that deVille thought there was a way round that part of her problem that had always given her the most heartache. She had always tried to convince herself that once Miles saw her as a woman he would also be able to ignore Robyn's feelings and the law of the land. But she knew really that Miles wasn't like her.

"How?" Jade asked, trying not to show her excitement.

"Hold your horses. I said I could, not that I would."

"I knew you couldn't," Jade said derisively, then regretted it when she saw deVille's eyes narrow. "I'm sorry," she said, instinctively standing up straight and coming to atten-

tion. "Won't you help me?"

"Of course I'll help you - if the price is right."

"What do you want - money?"

deVille laughed heartily. "I'm certainly richer than you with all your newly acquired millions," he informed her. "I have been rich for so long that I have lost all desire to acquire any more wealth. No, it's a very different pastime that interests me now."

"I'm a virgin," Jade said, taking an educated guess at what pastime he was referring to.

"Are you indeed? And you're doing what - offering me your cherry?"

Jade nodded.

"Don't you want to save it for Miles?"

Jade blushed and nodded again.

"Maybe you have something else?"

"What?" Jade asked, confused.

"Turn round and clutch your ankles again," deVille instructed.

Jade obeyed uncertainly.

deVille came to stand at the side of her. He placed his left hand on her neck and his right one on her bottom.

"What sort of relationships have you had with boys, young Jade?" he asked. His hand began circling on her bottom and Jade quickly remembered how close she had been to climax when he had interrupted her lovely wank.

"Not much. Only heavy petting and that."

"What does 'that' include?"

"Nothing. Just touching each other. You know."

"Like this?" deVille's right hand entered her vagina while his left began fondling her breasts.

"Yes," Jade replied with difficulty.

"Did you masturbate them?"

"Sometimes - a few."

"How many?

"One," Jade admitted, shamed that he had forced such an

DOMINATING OBSESSION

embarrassing confession from her.

"Once?" deVille guessed easily.

Jade nodded, her shame now total.

"Did you suck his cock?"

Jade was shocked. "No! I was only thirteen!" she asserted angrily.

"How about Rooter?"

Now she blushed again. "Yes. Sometimes."

"Did he do anything else?"

"You know he did - he used to beat me with a strap."

"Anything else?"

"No. I told you. I'm a virgin."

deVille placed his left hand on her neck again and his right hand came up to play with her bottom. Jade began to jump every time he touched her there.

"Did he ever touch you here?" deVille pressed her anal ring again.

"Yes."

"Did he ever put his finger inside?" deVille's finger entered her anus and Jade jumped, but deVille held her down with pressure on her neck.

"Sometimes."

deVille's finger was moving quickly up and down inside her anus. She was very hot and wet in there and she knew that he had her close to coming.

"Did he ever put his dick in here?"

"No."

"No?"

"He couldn't. We couldn't get it hard enough."

"Good."

deVille masturbated her in the bum letting her sidle to the floor as her legs gave way and then finally lie on her stomach as he finished her.

"I may be able to help you," deVille said. He was drying his hands like a doctor after an examination.

Jade tried to lift herself from the floor, but it was easier to wait until he came and took her hand and pulled her up.

"This is what I want." deVille pulled her to him and placed both hands on her bottom.

His cock was fully erect now. Jade could feel it hot and pulsating against her stomach. It felt enormous, far too big for her front passage let alone the rear.

"It wouldn't fit," she said with a tremor in her voice.

"We will make it fit. You will agree to become my slave, and once Miles has deflowered you in front I will do the same to your beautiful little rear. Agreed?"

"No! You're going too fast."

"You want Miles don't you?"

"Yes, you know I do."

"Well I can't get him for you, but I can help you to get him for yourself."

"You mean it? You really can do that?"

"Together, I'm sure that we can put Miles into a position where he is forced to choose - you, or Robyn."

Jade froze.

"What's the matter?" deVille asked. "Frightened of Robyn?"

"You're such a bastard!"

deVille laughed. "Yes, aren't I?" he agreed as if she had paid him a great compliment. "But I think that's exactly what you have need of at the moment."

"He will never choose me," Jade said, wearily. She had set out with such confidence in herself, but her performance with deVille had proved to her that she was still a child as compared to a woman like Robyn.

"Don't worry about that. I'm sure that we can even up the odds - even stack them in your favour a little. Don't for-

DOMINATING OBSESSION

get I know your mother - intimately. I know her strengths and weaknesses."

Jade's heart rose up like a phoenix.

"Ahh, I see I have your interest again."

"Please, Mr deVille, don't play with me any more. Please, tell me what to do."

"Good." He applauded her interest. "But first, the bargain. You will agree to become my slave and you will put this beautiful little orifice at my disposal immediately after your business with Miles has been completed satisfactorily. For my part I will train you to be more than a match for your mother and engineer the circumstances in which you can put that training to good use."

"But I can't become your slave, I love Miles," Jade pointed out, bitterly disappointed that his proposal was so full of holes that it had fallen at the first hurdle.

"Miles won't mind. In fact he will insist on it. Miles likes to see his women ravished by other men."

"Oh!"

Jade was totally nonplussed. But that explained everything. That explained why Robyn had been behaving that way with deVille and why Miles had let her. It also meant that she herself could have Miles to love and at the same time she could also be slave to this wonderful frightening man. She looked at deVille with new eyes then, and that huge cock that she hadn't even seen close up yet, and that she had thought she must deny herself, suddenly loomed very large in her thoughts. But then she remembered what he intended doing with it.

"He won't fit," she repeated. "We won't be able to make him."

"Don't worry," deVille said, easily guessing what she was talking about again. "Nature is a wonderful thing. It's better than any other form of magic in bringing about the seemingly impossible. You'll see, my cock and your arse will prove to be the perfect size for each other."

DOMINATING OBSESSION

Jade knew that her eyes were wide with fear and he laughed. "Yes, you've discovered my weakness. You have to have Miles. I have to have little girls' bottoms. As many as possible and the younger the better. But seventeen is my favourite age at the moment."

"And you won't do it if Miles doesn't choose me?" Jade asked, to remind him of his words.

"No. That way, when I take this lovely prize I can feel that I have truly earned it." He crushed her to him and as they kissed his right hand gently stroked her bottom with all the reverence of a life long competitor handling the champion's cup that he believed might at last be his.

"But how will we do it?" Jade asked at last when they eventually broke free.

"Ahh! You can safely leave all that to me for the moment and concentrate on thinking how nice life will be when you and Miles are lovers. Is it agreed? Is it a bargain?" deVille held out his hand.

He doesn't know how he's going to do it yet, Jade guessed, but that didn't dim her optimism much. Her feminine instinct had been right. deVille was the missing piece in her puzzle and now that she had slotted him into place she would soon have everything she had always wanted.

"Agreed," she confirmed, taking his hand. Then she giggled delightedly and threw herself into his arms for another wonderful kiss.

"Well, time to get started" deVille said as they finished their kiss. "I think we better start by introducing you to your real master."

Jade looked at him without understanding what he meant.

Ignoring the question in her eyes deVille stood up and placed her on the ground. Then he walked to the centre of the room and turned to stand with his legs slightly apart.

"Come and meet him. It's time you introduced yourself," he instructed.

She was going to meet his cock!

DOMINATING OBSESSION

She walked over to him with all the confidence she could muster, her performance marred a little by the fact that she wobbled on those high heels.

When she arrived deVille merely looked at her as if he was curious to know what she had come for. He was playing the bastard again and Jade knew then that her training had begun and that this was how it would be with Miles. deVille would provide the circumstances, but if she wanted any of the goodies that were on offer she would have to learn to take them for herself.

Well that suited her. She was seventeen. She had never opened a man's fly or handled a real man's cock, but there was no way deVille would shake her resolve. She had a lot of catching up to do. She hadn't officially left school yet, but if deVille was right, in a few days time she wouldn't be a virgin any more, she would be one man's slave and another man's mistress, and she would have two darling cocks to call her own, one for each tight little passage.

Jade sank slowly to her knees.

Calling upon her deepest reserves and with her eyes fixed firmly on the top of his fly, Jade watched her own shaking hands reaching out towards it. Her fingers were alive, there was no way they could possibly cope with this first hurdle. She clenched her fists and concentrated on slowing her breathing. When she reached forward again her fingers trembled less violently. They soon reached their destination and found that they had buttons to deal with, and not a zip as she had expected. Each button was a separate ordeal, and as each one popped free, the tension in her chest and brain rose exponentially.

Jade closed her eyes and took several large breaths. The vision inside her head was of a huge waiting serpent that could snap her wrist with one twist of its body.

Her hand disappeared to the wrist as she fumbled inside deVille's trousers. It was waiting there, out of sight in the dark. She could feel it through the material, pulsing slowly

against her timid fingers. It felt like nothing she had ever touched before. It was large, and warm, and strong.

She moved her hand a little, and suddenly her fingers slipped through the slit in deVille's underwear and she felt it for real. She squealed and withdrew. She needed a moment - just a moment. Her breasts and forehead were bathed in perspiration.

deVille remained quiet and perfectly still - enjoying her naive efforts. The bastard. The total utter black hearted bastard. One day she would get him back for this. One day she would make him beg and shake and almost faint with emotion.

Jade let the anger shake the trepidation from her body and slowly she became calm and cool again. This time. This time would be different. This time she would do it.

Jade's hand slipped into the darkness once more and curled around the waiting monster. She felt she must faint; the feel of it was unbelievable - a huge vibrant column of flesh far bigger than she had ever imagined. So big that to release it from its lair took a great deal of firm but gentle squeezing, and urging, and guiding. But at last it rose majestically before her face. She couldn't believe she was holding such a magnificent thing in her hands. It was beautiful - the most beautiful thing she had ever seen.

"Say hello to your true master."

Jade looked up at deVille.

He reached out a hand and pressed his palm against her glowing cheek. It was fatherly and comforting. She moved one hand from her precious prize for long enough to capture his hand and hold it still while she pressed her lips to the centre of his palm.

"Thank you, he's lovely," she whispered recognising the sound of awe in her own voice.

Jade turned deVille's hand and kissed the reverse. He had beautiful hands. She looked at what she held in her own other hand. He had a beautiful cock too. Seeing them to-

gether it was easy to tell they belonged to the same man. She bent his cock towards her and looked at its top side. She let his hand go and lightly traced her fingertips along the crazing of veins on the top of his cock. It twitched. It wanted her. She looked up at deVille through misty eyes. She pushed her tongue out and carefully lifted away the silver jewel that glistened from his cock's single eye. It was immediately replaced by another. Growing in confidence and still holding deVille's gaze, she licked round the curved edge of his swollen purple helmet, before stealing that jewel too.

It was time. Submissively she lowered her eyes in recognition of deVille's authority over her. Her hands trembled. She leant forward, and dipped her head in one inexperienced movement until the huge column of flesh filled her mouth completely. Oh, it was heavenly. The surge of power filled her body until she was a superwoman. She closed her eyes and rocked back and forth on her heels, swallowing hard to devour the gorgeous taste of him.

deVille touched his hand to her forehead and eased her away until his cock popped from her mouth and slapped back against his shirt. "Very good Jade, but you've still a lot to learn." He stood deliberately before her spellbound face, his cock twitching above her moist lips, and slipped out of his shoes and trousers. "Come on," he admonished, "don't just kneel there."

She rose as if in a dream and started on his shirt buttons. She eased them open and her nipples rubbed against his hairy chest whilst she studiously dealt with the cuffs. She ghosted behind him to slip his shirt off, and her small hands took the opportunity to dwell on his broad shoulders.

He had an incredible body. It was hard and sculptured. If it hadn't been for his suntanned skin she would have believed it had been chiselled from pure marble by a classical artist. She couldn't resist pressing her breasts to his back and running them down to his waist as she placed her hands inside his boxer shorts and pulled them down his legs. She

heard his cock slap against his stomach as it sprang free. She lifted each of his feet in turn to remove his pants, and then slipped his socks off whilst kissing his buttocks. He had a lovely bottom and seemed to have no objection to her forwardness.

Emboldened now, Jade gripped his buttocks and prised them apart. Her heart pounded, and she knew just what she wanted to do. She slowly ran the tip of her tongue from his waist down into the valley between his buttocks. She wrapped her arms around him and weighed his awesome balls in one palm whilst firmly stroking his pulsating shaft with the other. She heard a low groan from above. She had him now. She could feel the beat of him entering into her own body. Now it was his turn to wait and wonder.

Her tongue flicked forward and touched the tight ring of his anus. He jerked powerfully in her hand and threatened to break free - so she took a firm hold with both hands.

She licked again - and again - making each thrust stronger, until at last his entrance opened completely and welcomed her inside. She began to thrust long and deep until she felt his knees weakening and knew he could stand no more. With dextrous agility and perfect timing she slipped between his legs and milked him urgently with both hands. deVille looked up at the ceiling and roared like a man possessed as his sperm spat violently into her face.

Jade continued milking him - milking him until he was empty. His sperm lay on her face and breasts, and the final few drops dribbled onto her stomach and trickled down into her silky black muff.

When she was sure he was spent she scrambled to her knees and licked him clean. He was still erect. He should have deflated by now - Rooter would have done. But this wasn't Rooter - this was a young man, with a real cock in its prime.

She took him inside her mouth again. Although he had only just enjoyed a shattering climax, she now had the power,

DOMINATING OBSESSION

and she could make him climax again. She knew what he was thinking: there she was covered in his seed, kneeling dutifully at his feet with his cock in her mouth. He thought that he had the power - but he didn't. It was all with her now. She wasn't a child any more. She was beautiful, and invincible, and she could make any man shoot his precious load into her.

deVille held her head and thrust into her with all his mighty strength. Jade held on bravely and rode with him, sucking him into submission until he could move no more and pulled away from her grunting like a fatally wounded bull. But she wasn't going to let the bastard escape that easily. He had humiliated her, he had derided her, he had treated her like a child, he had beaten her and terrified her - and he had made a woman of her. A woman that knew no mercy.

Jade gripped his buttocks, urging him on and thrusting her mouth almost the entire length of his shaft. She felt his excitement rising again, and with each pump of his organ he groaned with undiluted pleasure as his whole body stiffened and he raised himself up onto his toes. Jade was learning. She relaxed her grip and massaged his aching balls whilst rhythmically sucking and drinking his priceless seed...

deVille gave a huge sigh and rocked back onto the balls of his feet. His hands rested limply on Jade's head while she licked him delicately back to a state of ease.

Jade was suddenly awash with euphoria. She had done it - and how she had done it! At times it had felt like someone else possessed her body - but she knew it was her. She knew she could do such things again - and more, much more.

She looked up to see deVille's smile of approval, and when he lifted her chin she held his stare and proudly allowed the last of his salty offering to glide smoothly down her throat.

22

deVille washed his cock at the sink.

Jade remained on her knees watching him and remembering what it had been like to have the full length of her tongue way up inside those massive heavy hewn buttocks.

deVille took a few careful moments to dry his tool, then he threw the soiled towel towards the laundry room and looked at her. His massive weapon was still half raised. Jade shuddered at the memory of what it had felt like to have it deep in her mouth with its knob bumping demandingly against the entrance to her throat. Then she remembered what it was like to have her mouth full of gushing sperm and to release her throat and feel its thick salty goodness sliding effortlessly down towards her stomach.

She used her index finger to scrape some of his spunk from her face and bring it in front of her eyes where she could look at it. She ran her lips and tongue along the back of her finger to capture it and transfer it to her mouth where she savoured it like a connoisseur with a fine vintage wine. Was there anything more wonderful than drinking a man's seed, unless it was to feel it squirting on to your face and tits?

She rescued some more of the precious liquid from her left breast and was about to convey it to her mouth when deVille stopped her with a command like a rifle shot.

"Stop that!"

Jade jumped and looked at him in amazement through wide round eyes.

He came to stand in front of her, taking hold of her wrist and holding it up as if examining the evidence of some heinous crime.

"Make this your last," he said, thrusting her finger at her so that she could suck it like a penny lollipop. "I want to see my spunk on your body. It's a badge of possession to show that I've marked you. While it's there it will help to remind

DOMINATING OBSESSION

you why you are naked and what your only purpose in life will be from now on." He walked several paces away before turning to stare at her intensely as he spelt out exactly what that was. "To make me and my friends very very happy at all times in any way we demand." Jade looked at him dumbly. For all his talk of slavery she hadn't understood what that meant until this moment.

She had agreed to two things. To become his slave and to allow him to ram that huge monster of his up her bum. She had always intended to find a way to renege on the second of these, but now she knew that she must renege on them both. There was no way she would become this man's slave. There was no way she would ever allow herself to become any man's slave.

Jade felt the excitement in her breast. She wouldn't give up Miles and she wouldn't submit to deVille; a man that had the physical power to make her do anything he wanted. It was going to be a hard fought battle in which deVille appeared to have all the big battalions, but he hadn't given full weight to her cunning and treachery. She would win in the end, because she had to. She couldn't live as anyone's slave.

"Now collect up my clothes and bring them here."

Obediently Jade did as she was ordered and helped him dress.

"Right. We can't be sure when your parents will return so we had better adjourn to the cellar."

"Oh no!" Jade tried to pull back. "Don't make me go down there!"

"Why ever not? What is the matter with you?"

"Because of what happened."

deVille stopped pulling her. "What happened?" he asked with interest.

Jade felt a bit silly now. "I saw a thing," she said uncertainly. A black beast as big as a man, but with wings and glowing eyes."

deVille laughed. "When did you see this?"

DOMINATING OBSESSION

"When I was ten. We were playing down there - hide and seek - and somebody put the lights out."

"And this thing jumped out on you?"

"No. It was in one of the side cellars. The daylight threw its shadow on the wall. I didn't actually see it. I only saw its shadow, but I know that it was there and that it had been watching us, waiting for one of us to go into its tunnel to hide. There are smaller cellars and tunnels that go everywhere you know right out in to the garden and even down to the road and that's a quarter of a mile away."

"I know."

"You know?"

"But I shouldn't worry about your black beast." He began dragging her towards the cellar again.

"Please. I really am scared, Uncle Nick!"

"Uncle Nick, is it?"

"I have to call you something."

"Very well... I believe you are scared, but not of that black beastie. How did you know that it had glowing eyes if it was only a shadow?"

"I don't know. Perhaps I was wrong about that - but I did see it!"

"Perhaps you did, Perhaps it was a child's premonition," deVille conceded, unconcerned for her obvious terror.

What did he mean, premonition? "Wait, wait. Please let me have some clothes if we're going down there, there's rats and all sorts of things," Jade tried stopping him again.

"I've told you, you aren't having any clothes until I've finished training you. And maybe not then, either, if you insist on annoying me any more. Now don't stop me again or you will receive your first beating up here and have to crawl down the cellar steps as best you can on your hands and knees."

It was no use. He was determined and completely heartless and already they were at the door at the far end of the kitchen, the one that lead to the servants passages, and the

DOMINATING OBSESSION

very same one that a very naive teenager had stood behind to spy upon her mother, deVille, and Miles only a very short lifetime ago.

They entered the servant's area. It wasn't as richly decorated as the rest of the house, but it was fully carpeted and centrally heated and kept scrupulously clean by the gang of cleaners that came in from the village every morning at six to clean, cook, and polish everything.

In the old days, before Rooter had decreed that he wanted no live-in servants and only wanted Robyn, Jade, and Miles to attend to his needs, this had been the heart of the house. It consisted of two long corridors in the shape of a cross. One ran sideways through the house with a spiral stair at either end. The other ran from back to front, beginning to the rear of the curved marble stair case in the hall and running all the way back to the back door. That was the one they were standing in now.

Ahead of them was the cellar door with the door to the unused butler's pantry to its right. To their left was the main part of the passage that lead to the front hall and to their right a shorter length that lead to the back door.

In the old days these passages allowed the servants to reach all parts of the house very quickly and to avoid meeting guests or members of the family in the main part of the house. And in those days it wasn't at all unusual to see servants emerging through concealed doors in the panelling to bring drinks and food and all sorts of comfort to their employers.

deVille extracted a bunch of small keys from his pocket and took a moment to select one. The cellar door was still the same one that had always been there, but now it was secured by a modern five lever deadlock. deVille unlocked the door and ushered her inside.

They were now standing in total inky blackness at the top of the cellar steps. Jade made a blind grab for deVille. He chuckled at her panic but guided her hands to his waist

DOMINATING OBSESSION

and waited while she wrapped her fingers through his belt. When she was ready he stretched out for something in the dark.

Suddenly there was the sound of hell rushing up the stairs to engulf them and down below the cellar began to glow with a flickering orange light.

"What is it?" Jade asked when she realised that they were going to live. "I thought something had exploded." She removed her hands from her ears to listen to his reply.

deVille chuckled. "Gas torches - aren't they magic?" He took her hand. "Come on, come and have a look at all the lovely things I've got for you."

Jade descended the stone steps with mounting disbelief. As she saw more and more of what the cellars had become her mouth fell open and remained that way until they reached the cellar floor. "Where did all this come from?" she finally found the courage to ask.

"You were all away at the funeral for quite some time."

"You couldn't possibly have done all this in a day!"

"I did have a lot of help," deVille admitted. "I do have a lot of friends, and, as you probably realise, once someone has been down from this side to unlock the doors, there are many ways for people to come and go without you or the rest of the family knowing."

Jade let her eyes wander from side to side and now that she looked more closely she realised that there was lots of work still to be completed.

deVille urged her forward again, and they began to walk down a central isle between a mass of different equipment towards what looked like a stage at the far end. Some of the equipment was standard, some of it was modified gym or playroom equipment, and some of it was custom-made for torturing. All of the larger pieces were custom-made and were fashioned from heavy oak timbers joined with long iron coach bolts which gave them a sinister medieval appearance.

DOMINATING OBSESSION

The cellar was massive, with a high brick ceiling held aloft by huge curved arches. The cellars were more or less the last remaining evidence of an old monastery that had stood on this site hundreds of years before Hubris House was even thought of, and the construction reflected the church architecture of the time with many wicked and mischievous gargoyles peering down at her from every recess.

Jade looked into one of the many tall free-standing oblong mirrors that were dotted around every piece of equipment. Staring back at her from wide frightened eyes she saw a little naked girl being led by the hand by a large, dark, handsome, well dressed man.

Unable to bare the sight, Jade once more looked up at the flowing arches with their intricate brickwork picked out by the spluttering orange torches that were on every wall and every pillar.

All at once she realised it then, and the realisation made her feel even smaller. She was naked and lost and being led into a cathedral - a cathedral dedicated to torture.

23

Jade felt growing trepidation as they approached the stage, but they turned off before they reached it and she gave a heartfelt prayer of thanks.

Now they were approaching one of the many side cellars which she could see through a high curved archway.

They stopped in the doorway to give Jade time to survey it. It was about fifteen feet long by ten wide and had been recently furnished for occupation. Sparsely, though. On the end wall there were two large locked pine cupboards, between which was a marble topped washstand and accompanying buckets, bowls, and jugs.

Along the right hand wall there were two large log effect

gas fires with copper flues. Also on this wall, pushed into the near corner, was a large square box that was probably a chemical toilet. On the opposite wall to this, six large steel hasps had been set into the brickwork about three feet from the ground and at two foot intervals along its length. Attached to the nearest hasp was a complicated heap of chains and manacles.

"This is where you will be living for the next few days," deVille informed her.

"Oh no!" Jade screamed and tried to break free. "No no, Uncle Nick, you can't, you can't leave me down here!" She hammered at his massive chest with her little fists.

deVille caught hold of her wrists in one hand and used the other to swing her up into his arms. "There are no rats - the giant spiders eat them all." He laughed uproariously, so that the sound echoed round the walls of the main chamber.

"You sod! It's no laughing matter, can't you see I'm petrified?" Jade wriggled and jerked at her wrists, desperate to be free.

"Now stop it!"

Jade now knew that voice and stopped struggling at once at his command.

deVille bent and kissed each nipple and then both eyes and finally, her forehead. "You will sleep down here, chained to that wall, and I, and my friends, will teach you to be a perfect little slave, obedient in everything and very proficient with those areas that aren't bared to us due to our need to leave this," he tapped her fanny, "and this," he tapped her anus, "intact."

deVille carried her to the far end and put her down in front of the left hand cupboard. "Now let me show you what's what. Amongst other things, this locked cupboard contains food and water. The food's not very good and it has to be earned so that may not concern you at all."

She gasped. Her voice would not work.

"The wash stand and the unlocked cupboard contain ev-

erything else. There's only cold water, but there is a kettle and a ring to heat it on. That kettle isn't for making tea, it's only for heating water to wash with. You must be scrupulously clean at all times. There's a douche and an enema and every kind of perfume and make up you could want, including your own preferred brand. I think that's about it."

"Please don't do this," she pleaded. "I'll do anything you want. There's no need for this." She was trying to be brave, but she broke down there and ran and threw herself into his arms burying her head in his chest. "If you only knew how scared I am. So terribly scared!"

"Don't tell me you're prepared to fall at the first hurdle. I thought you really wanted Miles?"

Jade stiffened. Then without looking at him she disengaged herself from him, knuckled the tears from her eyes, and walked resignedly back to her designated corner.

"Let's show you how you will be. Kneel on your mattress."

Jade spread one of the double blankets so that half of it would be under her on top of the single palliasse. The other blanket she folded up and put under the pillow, then she knelt down. deVille fixed a bright steel collar round her neck and snapped it shut. She was now fixed to the wall by a ten foot length of heavy steel chain. deVille placed her arms behind her back and clipped her wrists into manacles that were attached to her neck chain. Then he clipped her ankles into similar restraints which were on the ends of thinner chains that were also attached to her neck chain. A shorter chain also ran between each ankle.

"Lie down and cover yourself." Jade did so with difficulty. It was very uncomfortable. The floor was hard, the pillow was virtually none existent, and everything was itchy and scratchy.

"OK, stand up and walk around."

This also was possible, if rather difficult and uncomfortable.

DOMINATING OBSESSION

"You see, you'll soon get used to it," deVille told her. "But that's something for you to look forward to later. First we had better get a note written for your mother. What's it to be, a week in Great Yarmouth with this friend Alison your mother keeps going on about?"

Jade nodded resignedly as he undid her chains. "She will expect me to phone each day."

deVille unlocked the cupboard and took out a mobile phone.

"Will it work down here?" Jade asked without much interest in the answer.

"It does work, perfectly."

"You use it to organise all this stuff with your friends," Jade guessed.

deVille nodded as he produced note paper from his lockable cupboard, and Jade dutifully wrote the note. "There's a suitcase that's already almost packed. I was half thinking of really going to see Alison. If you bring that down, or hide it somewhere Robyn won't be suspicious."

deVille examined the note and slipped it into his pocket. Then he began to undress. "Time to start your training," he informed her. "From now on you will address me as Master at all times." He took hold of her chin and brought her lips to his to kiss. "Soon that's the way you will always think of me."

Once he was completely nude deVille slipped on a pair of slippers he took from the right hand cupboard. Then he unchained Jade, and they went back out into the cathedral cellar.

Jade felt that they were wandering aimlessly like shoppers at a furniture auction, but eventually deVille stopped in front of a padded bench which had a metal frame and several metal arms branching off it, including two adjustable stirrups that rose up from one end.

"Sit in the centre, with your feet at this end, and lie back."

As soon as she had done so deVille grabbed her ankles

DOMINATING OBSESSION

and pulled her towards him. Jade's body slid easily over the polished leather until her bottom was right at the edge of the padded seat, then he lifted her legs and fixed them into the two stirrups. These he adjusted and manoeuvred until she was fully stretched both upwards and outwards. She struggled up onto her elbows so that she could see herself in the facing bronze mirror.

"Oh!" a little cry escaped her as she saw how lewd she looked. Her vulva was fully exposed and totally vulnerable. "I look obscene!"

"Yes, it's nice, isn't it?"

Jade slowly shook her head. To her it looked rude and unflattering, but obviously a man would be looking at her with different eyes.

"That's beyond mere beauty," he said. "That's raw sex and one very available succulent young woman."

He stooped and lightly ran his forefinger from her clitoris through her moist labia and down on to her perineum, before pressing its tip against her exposed anus.

"Ooohhh!" Jade shivered, as her anal ring tried to bite it off.

"I think your little ring is getting as impatient as I am," deVille said happily. He stroked his fully erect penis pensively for long enough to make Jade very uneasy that their bargain wasn't going to hold.

"Better move on," he said to himself at last. "Now - lie back." He secured her wrists to the end of two of the metal bars that protruded from the bench, then removed the unused bars and the section of the bench beneath her head. Her neck muscles strained for a while, but slowly her head sank down.

"That's it - just relax." He knelt and placed a strap around her head, and adjusted it so that she couldn't move at all.

"Your mother's much the same size as you, isn't she?" he suddenly asked.

"Yes, an inch shorter, but we take the same size in most

things." Except shoes, Jade thought, wiggling her toes in the empty space inside her present ones.

deVille found another bench of the same design as the one to which Jade was fixed and manhandled it into place beside her. Watching a well built nude man with a large erect penis flex his well developed muscles was no strain at all and Jade was more than happy to wait while he made adjustments to the other bench. She had to watch him upside down in the mirror behind her head, but it was still great.

"Good," he said at last. "I'm going to teach you to swallow a man's cock. Unfortunately it's a thing that most women never learn to do, but, as any man who's ever experienced it will tell you, it's like putting your most precious part in an organ as powerful as a meat grinder. Any woman who masters the technique can provide mere mortal man with the sort of pleasure that I would have thought should have been reserved for the exclusive use of the gods." deVille laughed at his own over exuberant eloquence.

Jade might have questioned him about it, but her present position made it almost impossible to speak.

"You may be sick and you may panic, but it can be done if you relax and are determined to see it through. First we will have to relax you."

deVille went to her other end and using his tongue he worked first on her vagina and clit and then on her anus until Jade thought she must explode. Rather than relaxed, Jade now felt as taut as a violin string.

deVille returned to her head and Jade could see from his hooded eyes that he was also not far from climax.

Placing his hands on her breasts he slowly crouched down until the tip of his knob was against her open lips. He thrust gently forward with his hips and the full length of his penis slid over her tongue and into her mouth until its helmet was against the gateway to her throat.

"Relax, my love, this will be far easier if you are successful first time." His hands started circling round and round

DOMINATING OBSESSION

on her breasts.

Jade couldn't relax. She was terrified. Despite his assertion that this was possible she knew that it couldn't be. People were sick if the slightest little probe was put past their tonsils, to have a huge lump of living flesh blocking her windpipe was out of the question however much she wanted Miles.

She swallowed and waited. And deVille kept his cock perfectly still while his hands circled her breasts and she knew that he was waiting like a hunter for his quarry to break cover.

And then her nervous throat began to fill with fluid and she began to choke on her own saliva. deVille squeezed both nipples as hard as he could and thrust his cock into her throat. Jade tried to scream and retched as part digested food rushed up her throat and into her mouth and out of her nostrils. deVille squeezed her nostrils closed and Jade knew no more.

When she finally returned to the land of the conscious deVille was shagging her throat.

She tried to panic, but he was so far down inside her that she could do nothing. This was the worst moment of her entire life. Her stomach felt as if it was full of white hot fire, her chest was racked with unbearable pain, and her head was splitting apart. But deVille didn't care. His cock went mechanically up and down inside her throat, travelling for almost its entire length, but never quite re-entering her mouth.

Jade was now so emotionally and physically drained that she couldn't fight him any longer. Her body sagged and she gave up the uneven struggle. As if sensing her submission deVille lengthened his strokes until they were encompassing the full length of her mouth from her lips and deep into her throat for as far as his massive weapon would penetrate.

Jade took no further part in this. She surrendered him her body and waited for it to end. Which way it ended, in death, injury, or success, she no longer cared.

deVille exploded inside her and for what seemed like a minute she screwed up her fists and toes and tried not to

scream as his violence took control of her entire senses. His wildly stabbing weapon was in her throat, his sperm was in her nostrils and all over her face, his groin was attacking her mouth and bruising her lips, his thighs were squeezing her head until she was deaf, and his balls were thrashing at her blind eyes.

She could take no more...

And then it was all over and deVille withdrew and stumbled away to collide with the rear mirror which he dashed to the ground before staggering on like a blind man until he too finally realised that he had nowhere to go and crashed to the floor exhausted.

24

Jade awoke to find that she was dead and gone to Hell.

For a moment that knowledge seemed very real, and when the actual truth of her survival rushed in to replace her false assumption her body instantly bathed itself in sweat. She was alive, but barely. She was still strapped to the bench and now she was in the dark in a dungeon full of torture equipment and constant unexplained noises.

The windows set into the subterranean chamber just below the level of the ceiling showed her that the sun must be low in the sky, so she knew that it was evening. Her whole body ached so much that she also knew that she must have been strapped in the same position for several hours.

Suddenly there was a subdued rumbling sound that filled the entire chamber and the already dark place began to grow even darker. Jade looked up in time to see louvred shutters revolving to blank out all the windows. Then there was the sudden frightening 'woosshh' of the gas torches and she had light, giving hope once more.

"Oh, Master," Jade sobbed, when deVille eventually came

DOMINATING OBSESSION

into sight.

He released her from the bench while she babbled her unquestionable relief at his return. He was immaculately dressed as usual and Jade knew that she was covered in filth of all sorts, but she didn't care as she crushed herself against him as soon as she was free.

"Please, Master, please, can I come and sleep in your bed? I promise no one will know I'm there. I'll be as quiet as a mouse and creep down here first thing in the morning, but I can't bare to be down here in the dark any longer."

deVille said nothing, but he held her very tight and she felt eternally grateful that he had returned to release her from her bonds instead of leaving her until morning.

Eventually he spoke, and Jade heard his voice from deep within his chest as well as more normally from above her head. "Why did you call me master?" he asked. "Was it because I ordered you to?"

Jade didn't have to think about that at all. He was her master. She curled herself up into a little ball and made herself as small as she could on his lap, and with his strong arms around her frail body to protect it, she knew that he was her master and that she needed a powerful master to look after her and keep her safe.

"You are my master now!"

He raised her head and kissed her and Jade began to cry. Somehow she knew that this wonderful man would give her everything she ever desired from life.

"Come, let's get you cleaned up," he said, and rose with her on his lap and carried her effortlessly to the side cellar which he had decided should be her home for the duration of her training. Jade wanted to ask him again if she could creep upstairs and spend the nights in his bed, but she didn't dare.

deVille helped her to get cleaned up. He even helped with warming the water and administering her enema. Then they decided that she would discard her stockings and shoes

144

DOMINATING OBSESSION

and even her watch and earrings and be as naked as the day she was born.

"There's just one more thing," he told her after he had inspected her both back and front, "you must be shaved - here."

Jade's hand immediately darted to her lovely pubes. "No! Oh, no. Why, Master?" she asked in disbelief. "I thought you liked me like this?"

"Oh, I do, but I've decided it must go. You'll still look beautiful with a bare mound. Many men would find you even more beautiful that way, and I'm one of them." He smiled at the doubt in her eyes. "I like the innocence and nakedness of a little bare cunt. It makes me feel more powerful."

He opened the right hand cupboard and took down a well made wooden box with brass catch and hinges. It was similar in size to a shoe box and Jade was curious to know what it contained, but he didn't show her until they were out in the main cellar sitting side by side on a couch like those used by doctors. deVille opened it and Jade peeped in. It contained several packets of wax depilatory strips, some jars, bottles, wiping clothes, and a sponge.

"Oh, no!" Jade said, when she saw them, "the pain is going to kill me."

"Very possibly," deVille agreed. "The agony you women are willing to go through to make yourselves look more attractive to men never fails to amaze me." He was already warming the first strip between his hands.

"You may be my master," Jade said, "but you're still a bastard."

deVille smiled at her, then kissed her on the lips. "I'm glad I haven't crushed your spirit completely. I only want to harness it, and once that's accomplished we can set about the much more interesting task of making you into a very formidable little lady."

He returned to his work and laid the first strip on her pubes near her left thigh. He patted it down for several sec-

onds, and then, wrenching against the direction of growth, ripped it free, and with it a large strip of her luxuriant black bush. Jade screamed and deVille laughed and they continued like that until he was certain that there wasn't a single hair left to mar the perfection of her shiny new little vulva. While Jade still fought with the memory of the pain deVille ran a soft cloth with a soothing cream over her newly created smoothness, then sponged it clean with cool water.

It was done and his eyes told her that he loved it. So did his lips once he laid them on it to cover it with kisses as gentle and as welcome as the caresses of butterfly wings. It could only end one way and Jade lay back and wriggled and thrashed and groaned while deVille used his mouth and tongue to bring her to a long overdue and well deserved orgasm.

"What do you think?" he asked.

Jade sat up and placed her hand where his had been. Her vulva seemed tiny in comparison to the way she wanted to remember it with its springy cushion of soft shiny black beaver fur. She cupped the tiny naked newcomer in her hand and even her own little fist had no problem in hiding it completely. She stroked it. The flesh felt smooth and pliant, but as naked as an oven ready chicken.

"It feels funny - so unfinished," she said.

"That's a good word," he agreed. "That's what it is - unfinished. Come and look."

They stood in front of one of the bronze coloured mirrors and they both looked at the blank space between her thighs.

"It's like a baby's," Jade said.

"Yes, and you are an innocent little virgin too," deVille agreed.

"Not so innocent now, Master. Not since meeting you."

He laughed. "Are you sorry?"

Jade shook her head. "No, not a bit. Even if we don't get Miles it will have been worth it. I'll still be your slave, won't

I, Master?"

"Yes, Jade, you'll always be my slave, until I pass you on. The worst of the training is over, you know that?"

"Yes. I'm still scared, but I know that. And if my throat can take your giant, it can cope with anything, Master."

deVille laughed again, flattered by her words. "You want something, don't you, Jade?"

"I'm so scared of being chained down here in the dark, Master. That's all I ask. I will do anything else, but I'm terrified of that."

"Well, I'm sorry, Jade, I can't let you back upstairs," deVille said. Then he took her chin and lifted her face so that she would look at him. "But I have got some good news. My friends will have to work every night to get things ready for your grand meeting with Miles. That means they will need light and if you like you can stay awake at night and watch them and catch a little sleep during the day."

Jade threw herself into his arms. No one had ever had such a kind and loving master, she was sure of that.

"Come and have a look at this," deVille said and lead her back to the central isle.

Jade hadn't really realised before, but now she could see that the isle that led to her sleeping chamber and the main isle that led towards the stage crossed in the very centre of the cathedral cellar and at this crossroads a large arbour made from rough hewn oak beams had been erected.

Besides the uprights and the cross members there were a dozen beams that were angled towards the ceiling to make the frame for a four sided pitched roof. Suspended in the centre of this was a large glass tank. It had a flat glass floor and circular sides, and its top rose to a point into which a large metal ring had been fitted.

There was a chain fixed to the ring and this ran through a pulley. While Jade watched, deVille crossed to one of the oak uprights and unhooked the other end of the chain and began lowering the glass tank until its base was safely on the

DOMINATING OBSESSION

floor.

deVille secured the chain again and then moved forward and opened a curved door that had been almost invisible when the tank was suspended. He pointed to the tank's roof. "Plenty of breathing holes up there," he said. Then he tapped the sides of the tank. "Yet very much rat proof." He laughed. "And when its suspended way up there, with all the great hulking workmen crashing about below I don't think the black beastie will have much chance of grabbing you, do you?"

Jade suddenly understood the significance of his words. "But they'll all see me - like this!" she exclaimed.

"That's certainly the idea." He was almost laughing again.

Jade trembled. "Will I know them?" she asked.

deVille shook his head. "No, they're not locals and they don't move in your social circles, so you have no worries there. In fact, the whole point is that you shouldn't know them. You will merely be an object to them and they will remain faceless and anonymous to you. Get in now." He stood aside and waved her in.

At the tank's centre there was an elaborately curved seat made of transparent plastic. Jade sat on it. The plastic wasn't cold to her bare skin and the seat was perfectly comfortable. She leant back and deVille threaded her arms through the chair's back and fixed them together so that each wrist was attached to the elbow of her opposite arm. Then he opened her legs as wide as they would go and secured them at knee and ankle. She was now as exposed as a woman could possibly be and Jade was shaking as deVille hoisted her aloft in her glass prison until the tank's transparent bottom was about seven feet from the ground.

deVille spoke in to a microphone that Jade could see was on the post next to where he had secured the chain. His voice echoed hollowly inside the tank.

"The men will be here soon..."

25

By the time the workmen arrived Jade had already worked herself up into a state of high sexual excitement. When they all crowded round she thought she might faint. She understood now what deVille had meant about them being faceless. Each man wore a loose fitting hood like a flower sack with two eye holes and a wide meshed gauze covering the nose and mouth.

Jade couldn't hear much of what they were saying, but she could tell by their body language and the way their bodies shook when they laughed that they liked what they saw. Jade liked what she saw too. The men were of varying ages and all dressed differently, some in overalls and others bare chested and just in shorts, but they were all rough with large muscles and many had tattoos.

After only a few minutes they broke up and once started they seemed to work at an incredible pace. They all looked at her whenever they were near and occasionally one or other would lift his loose fitting hood and flick his tongue at her, but for the most part they were too busy to spend as much time staring at her as she would have liked.

For her part Jade felt mentally as well as physically suspended. She was drifting in a sort of orgasmic dream in which she was the queen of a bustling hive and the one who all the workers longed to mate with.

At last one of the men stopped by the post and spoke into the microphone.

"Hi?" he said.

"Hello," Jade replied after the click.

"How are you doing?"

"I'm doing fine, thank you," Jade replied, and then to prolong the conversation so that he wouldn't rush off she added: "You all work remarkably hard."

"Of course, you know why," he said with a laugh as if he thought that she did.

DOMINATING OBSESSION

"No." Jade shook her head at him.

"You don't? He's not told you?"

"No." Jade shook her head again. She felt like a fool, like a painted doll that had no brain.

"The old bastard!" the man said, and Jade saw him shake his head in disbelief and admiration as he laughed and hurried off to tell his mates.

Now Jade's body hummed with a new emotion. deVille had done it to her again. There was something important that he hadn't told her about. The man was a true bastard, Jade had to give him that. She could see that it didn't matter to him whether the news came as a complete shock when he deigned to give it to her, or whether, as had happened, she was given some inkling of what it might be. In either case it reinforced his lesson. She was his to do with as he liked. She was simply there for his amusement and for that of any of his friends he chose to share her with.

"You bastard, Master! You fucking bastard!" Jade screamed aloud, sure that no one could hear her. "What have you concocted for me this time you pig?" she demanded of thin air.

As if he had heard her after all deVille appeared in the corner of her eye. Jade turned her head and watched him approach. He was still fully dressed and looked as if he hadn't been to bed at all. Jade's heart dropped. He was so very handsome. He seemed to get more desirable every time she saw him. She knew why. She was falling in love with him. Perhaps this was what she had always wanted, a man that treated her like dirt and seemed always to have the ability to defeat and surprise her.

deVille stopped under her glass prison and looked up at her. He was checking on his little prize, staring at her anus through the transparent seat. Jade felt it wink at him and she gave a little cry as her breasts began to burn with embarrassment. The bastard. He was going to get everything he wanted. Already she was his slave and now she knew that when the

DOMINATING OBSESSION

time came his huge monster would take possession of her tiny little passage just as they had agreed.

deVille lowered her to the ground.

"You want to know what's going to happen to you?"

Jade nodded.

"Well, as you suspect, or as someone has told you, these workmen are going to help us with your training."

Jade felt the tension in her body rise to exploding point. She had suspected as much, but it was still traumatic to have the last vestiges of hope shrunk even further by hearing his easy confirmation.

"There are a dozen men working in three gangs with four to a gang. Every two hours one of the gangs will take a rest. How long they get depends on how much work they've already completed. And how much rest they get will depend on you." He laughed. "Within the confines of the conditions we have already agreed concerning your fanny and anus they can pretty much do as they like with you, which includes punishing you if they think you've been holding back. To tell the truth, there are men here tonight who would beat you unmercifully whatever you did, but as long as you're good and do your best to please them, I'm sure some of the others will do their best to restrain them for you. So it's up to you, you see. You need to look out for your own skin. Do you understand?"

Jade nodded, too horrified by the content of his speech and its casual form of delivery to have the strength to make any protest or to offer any other answer.

"Don't worry, you'll do fine. You won't let me down. You know that to do so would mean that I would loose face."

deVille straightened up and waved over a large man who had been standing respectfully just out of earshot.

"All right, Mick, she's all yours."

"Thank you, Mr deVille," the man replied.

He entered the tank and laid down certain objects he had been carrying. Jade's frightened eyes went to them at once.

DOMINATING OBSESSION

There was a small box, like a jewellery box, a pair of swimming goggles with the entire lens area blanked out with black electricians tape. A short piece of cloth that had been folded in to several thicknesses to make a strip about two inches wide and two feet long. And all these were on top of one of the white flower sack hoods.

Mick opened the little box to reveal two plugs that he fitted into her ears. Jade looked at him as he did so. He had soft blue eyes with sandy coloured eyelashes and through the wide mesh gauze she could see a sandy haired beard and moustache and a mouth in which all of the top incisors appeared to have been chipped.

All sound was blanked out and it was like a film with a silent sound track as he fitted the swimming goggles. Now she was blind as well. She felt him fit the blindfold and the hood. Then he released her from the chair and she stood up uncertainly and left the comparative safety of her tank.

Someone secured her wrists together behind her back, and with one man's helping hand on either arm she was taken somewhere.

By the time they arrived at their destination Jade was almost hysterical. With a hand to guide her foot she stepped up on to a padded mattress. The same two men that held her arms used their other hands behind her knees to force her to kneel, then they pulled her legs apart and someone removed her hood, but nothing else. She was to hear and see nothing. Jade began to sway. She was close to fainting.

Many hands began caressing her body. They all wanted to stroke her naked vulva and there was some squabbling and impatience. Someone's head was placed between her legs and she was encouraged to sit on his face. His tongue immediately began exploring her vulva and anus. Her hands were released and fitted round two cocks. The men they belonged to were standing either side of her and they showed her how to grip them as if they were two sauce bottles who's contents she wanted to shake all over her breasts. Then a

DOMINATING OBSESSION

knob was at her lips and she opened her mouth to let a cock inside.

She had only touch, smell, taste - and imagination. The hands moved on her body, on her breasts, on her bottom, on her legs and thighs. The tongue penetrated deep inside her anus; the cock scuttled up and down her throat; her fingers moved frantically on the cocks in her hands; and a powerful orgasm filled her entire being.

It didn't take them long. The cock exploded inside her throat. When it withdrew and its owner stumbled away she showered the contents of the other two cocks on to her face and breasts. As she did so she came herself. The tongue in her anus went berserk. But before she had finished it was snatched away from her and the next moment there was a new cock in her mouth that came almost at once filling her mouth and face with hot squirts of salty semen.

Someone lifted her and laid her face down onto the back of a large hairy man who was kneeling naked on the mattress. Her arms were stretched around his chest and then linked together at elbow and wrist. Her breasts were pressing hard into his back and she could hardly breath. Her ankles were fixed to his legs then he opened his legs wide forcing her legs to stretch wide with them.

Someone began to whip her. They whipped her across her back; on her feet; behind her knees; on her bottom; on both inner thighs; and finally, between her legs. She screamed and screamed and through her deafness the external sound boomed back at her from the surrounding walls, but she had no other contact with the outside world other than through the hot, hairy sweating flesh of her whipping horse and the fine stinging tails of the silk whip.

The man with the whip made her come several times until her tears filled her goggles and stung her eyes. Then many hands were on her body again and they took her down and the cocks, hands, and tongues proceeded to have her in a similar fashion as before.

DOMINATING OBSESSION

When it was over they returned her to her glass display case and secured her to the chair, then Mick removed her hood, blindfold, goggles, and ear plugs. Jade blinked at the unaccustomed light and shuddered at the unaccustomed sound and Mick left her without a word and hoisted her back above the ground.

Her experiences every two hours on this and the following two nights were very similar. Some of the groups preferred to take her to a more public space and to use her in more ingenious ways using more complicated equipment. Some of the men liked to beat her more brutally and with more vicious whips or belts. But at the end of each session she was returned to her tank coated in even more semen and left there without a word being said.

There was never any love or sign of affection, except once, when someone kissed her. She suspected that the man who did it had found himself alone with her for a minute and his kiss was kind and all the more appreciated for being unexpected. The mouth that gave it to her was surrounded by hair and she wondered if it might have been Mick. Who ever it was she thanked him for it and was glad that he had the kindness and courage to do it.

Her experiences by day were in complete contrast to those of the night. deVille visited her quite often. She always washed and prepared herself very carefully before allowing the men to chain her prior to sleep, and she was glad she did so, for on more than one occasion deVille found her still asleep and woke her with a kiss.

Without a watch and groggy through lack of sleep and from an excess of emotional stimulus, Jade had lost all track of time, but at last deVille said, "This is your last day's training for now. You will sleep all day tomorrow and tomorrow night we will put our little plan into effect."

Jade felt the butterflies in her stomach. She had tried on her costume and run through her part in the proceedings a dozen times, but there were still large chunks that she didn't

know about and that lack of knowledge made her feel uneasy.

"Scared?" deVille asked.

Jade nodded.

"No man will be able to resist the sort of woman you have already become. Believe me, Robyn will seem like a little mouse in comparison."

Was that true? Could she defeat Robyn and steal the one thing that Robyn held more precious than all others?

"I see that you're still not convinced. This will need great skill and perfect timing, but more important than that it requires confidence. Confidence on your part, Jade. I'd hoped that I hadn't knocked all of that out of you."

"You haven't, Master, you haven't. I know we can do it."

"Even so, I will show you the rest of the plan and then you will have no doubts."

"Thank you, Master. I love you, Master." Jade hugged his arm.

"I have no worries about that Jade. I'm certain you do. But love isn't enough on its own. Do you fear me, Jade?"

Jade's heart stood still as she recognise his change of tone and mood.

"Do you?"

"Yes, Master."

"You must fear me so much that you will never ever dare turn against me how ever strong the motivation to do so is."

"I do fear you, Master, I do fear you that much!"

26

deVille strode back down the centre isle towards the cellar steps, a large confident man dressed in smart casual shirt and slacks.

Jade ran behind him naked and small, feeling not at all

the confident young lady he needed her to be for her meeting with Miles.

deVille stopped at the foot of the largest piece of equipment in the whole of this cathedral of torture. Jade took her place beside him and also looked up at what at first sight she had thought might be a French guillotine.

It was mounted on a flight of seven wooden steps, a great wooden frame that almost touched the high ceiling. Now that she had the opportunity to study it in more detail she saw that there were actually two oblong frames, one heavy outer one, and a much lighter and smaller one inside it.

deVille took her up the wooden steps on to the platform and told her to look down. The side beams of the main frame went straight down through the planks at the centre of the platform and when directed by her master Jade had to step over a wide gap to perch on the bottom board of the smaller frame.

deVille shackled her wrists to the top corners of the frame, and her ankles to the bottom corners. Then he fitted leather harnesses round her waist, thighs, and shoulders, and attached them to chains attached by shackles to the sides of the frame. He took considerable time and care in the adjustment of the chains so that they held her body almost totally rigid.

By the time he had finished she was almost ready to come. The mix of emotions was indescribable. She was naked, and trussed like a chicken so that she was completely helpless and obscenely open. deVille used one hand to caress her breasts and the other to run round and round over her bottom, inner thighs, and pubes, without ever quite straying to her wide open vagina.

The inner frame began to move and she rose effortlessly to the ceiling. A quick glance confirmed that deVille was using pulley ropes wound around a small capstan to pull her up, but she was far too interested in watching the images of the lascivious young woman that was herself in the mirrors to pay him much attention.

DOMINATING OBSESSION

As the inner frame bumped against the top beam of the outer one she saw a shower of shining bronze diamond break themselves free from her vagina and float gently off in elegant arcs towards the planks of the platform some ten feet below. The frame jerked as deVille lowered it a foot and then she was turning through a three hundred and sixty degree arc. As she went round she saw deVille twisting a large metal wheel like those used to steer sailing yachts.

Then she was on her way down again, this time all the way to the floor. As she disappeared below the platform her nostrils flared at the strong smell of dog and as she once more traversed through three hundred and sixty degrees she saw blankets and a bone that told her that this room beneath the platform sometimes doubled as a kennel.

Her unseen driver turned her cradle to face the floor then lowered her slowly towards it. The unpleasant doggy smell became stronger and she prayed that he would stop her decent before her wide open labia actually came in contact with any of the stinking blankets. The small amount of light that filtered through from above and through the cracks between the planks made it possible for her to see how close she was getting and she was beginning to become anxious when she stopped only a foot from the floor.

Once more deVille righted her, and soon she was popping back up through the oblong hole in the ceiling of the platform and experiencing the curious sensation of seeing her own image apparently rising up from the grave.

"I believe this is the finest whipping frame in the whole of Europe - maybe the world," deVille said proudly.

Jade was pretty certain now that the black hearted bastard intended to use the frame to hold her while he beat her so badly that she would never ever dare risk defying him in any way. But she still had one even more terrifying suspicion.

"Is it used for anything else, Master?"

"What do you mean?"

DOMINATING OBSESSION

"Do you have a dog?" Jade asked, her nose creasing at the memory of the strong unpleasant smell of animal in the hollow base of the platform.

"Yes," deVille replied, "but Cerebus is not in residence yet. We don't want any of the workmen savaged, do we? But that's certainly where he normally lives. He likes it down there. It's dark and he can see out through the gaps in the planks without anyone knowing he's there. It suits his personality."

Jade shuddered as a shocking image suddenly flashed through her mind of a large black hound silently watching her from the shadows while she lay bound naked to a bench like a virgin sacrifice.

"What's the matter with you?" deVille asked. "You look as if you've seen a ghost."

"Worse! Much worse. A black nightmare!"

"A nightmare, eh? Well, see what you think of this for a nightmare. Look through the gap between those two mirrors." He pointed at the two mirrors in front of her.

Jade did so and a moment later at the far end of the cellar she saw a great shower of sparks and red flickering shadows start up, like those of flames from a huge bonfire. In another moment the shadowy flickering flames were joined by other shadows that moved against the brick of the pillars and walls.

Now Jade saw the shadowy outlines of dark giant figures in capes with long pointed beards and short inwardly curving horns. And all this frantic movement was accompanied by the babble of voices, the crackling of burning logs, the tortured screaming of women, and the manic laughter of cavorting demons.

Jade looked at deVille with horror etched on her face. This was her nightmare made a hundred times worse. This was her black beastie, but now he had many terrible friends and many screaming female victims.

deVille lifted a remote control and pointed it and in a second the terrible commotion ceased as suddenly as it had

begun. Jade looked at him and her startled body sagged back in its bonds with relief. She had known it must be a trick, yet her body had reacted to some trigger that had been planted deep within the genes of her ancestors when the world had first begun.

"Good, eh?" deVille asked, as happy as any little boy with another of his gadgets.

Jade nodded feeling the colour slowly returning to her cheeks.

"It was you who gave me the idea for it, of course, and I'm sure it will work a treat. It's just what this miserable old place needs to cheer it up a bit?"

A trick. Another of his bloody tricks. That was what Cerberus would turn out to be as well, thank God. The bastard knew that her own vivid imagination had presented her with a huge black hound that was far more frightening than anything nature could ever conjure up.

"What are you thinking about now?"

"Nothing, Master. I'm sorry, Master," Jade said, hurriedly.

"What's that?" deVille held his hand to his ear.

"I said -"

"Speak up, you'll have to shout."

"I said -" Jade stopped, the sound of her shouting voice was drowned out by a great wailing and screaming.

"What?"

"Where is it -" Jade began, but stopped as her shout was once more drowned out. It was a demonstration of another of his infernal gadgets. Jade returned her voice to a normal conversational level. "I said, where is it coming from, Master?"

deVille pointed at the ceiling above them, the stairs beside them, and then at the pillar that was immediately to the other side of them. Now that he had pointed them out Jade could see the small unobtrusive speakers.

"You can't tell, can you? Wrap around sound, that's what we've got." deVille was obviously pleased with his demon-

stration. "There are sensors all around you that are sensitive to the pitch and the level of your voice. Normal conversation is allowed, anything louder is drowned out."

Jade groaned inwardly. His mood had changed completely again. The little boy had gone and the monster was back.

deVille began unbuttoning his shirt. Then he turned away and descended the steps still undressing.

This was it. All at once she knew that she wanted it to stop. She had been crazy to ever get mixed up with this madman. He was going to beat her into submission, subject her to such horrendous unendurable pain that she would never ever think of defying him. Why was she doing this? Which one of them was crazy? Jade looked at him in the mirror. He was now completely naked and standing at a wall rack selecting a whip.

Jade felt her heart jump and she was instantly wet between the legs as her vagina wet its lips at the sight of him. This man had total power over her. He could do anything he wished. She couldn't stop him now even if she wanted to, and with a knowledge as pure and sharp as a blinding light she knew that the person she needed had to be unstable.

He had to be unpredictable.

He had to be a psychopath.

She had to believe that he was capable of injuring her beyond repair if she provoked him in the wrong way. That was what she needed. That was what she lived for - the challenge. The challenge was part of the reason she wanted Miles, she knew that. But it wasn't the full reason. deVille had been wrong to say that she only wanted him because he was the only man alive that she could never have. He had also been wrong to say that she only wanted him because he belonged to Robyn. She was competitive, that much was true, but that wasn't the whole story. She wanted Miles because she genuinely loved him, not just to prove that she could take him away from Robyn.

deVille had selected a whip which he now held in his left

DOMINATING OBSESSION

hand. As Jade watched in horror he took down a cane and made several practice swipes with it in the air. Christ no! Jade twisted wildly in her bonds. She couldn't bear that much pain, nobody could.

deVille mounted the steps, a large muscular man, completely naked, with a determined look in his eye and brandishing a whip in one hand and a cane in the other.

Standing behind her, he reached past her and held the whip out for her to examine. It had a short leather handle and many, many, tails, each about eighteen inches long. He draped the tails over her left shoulder. Jade turned her head and looked at them from the corner of her eye. They seemed to be made from a variety of materials, some of them leather, some of them thin metal wire, some of them possibly even silk. This whip would bring her pain, but it was also designed to bring her pleasure. This wasn't the one that would be used to break her. This one was the one which would be used to transport her to a high state of ecstasy. Jade shuddered at the prospect and her vagina once more oiled its throat.

deVille pulled the whip slowly down her body towards her bottom. The tails spread out and tickled her flesh with their different textures until they reached the rise of her left cheek, when deVille flicked them away making her shudder. Then he walked to the front of the frame and dragged the whip over her breasts and down into the cleft between her legs. He continued in a similar manner, walking round and round the frame ensuring that the whip left no part of her body unattended.

Soon she was wriggling and writhing with pleasure. Then, with an occasional flick of his wrist, her torturer began to vary the stimulus. The stinging smack of the multiple tails contrasted beautifully with the tenderness of their caress when he dragged them across her skin. Slowly he began to increase the smacks and reduce the caresses. Then he added harder and harder smacks. Jade began to whine. Soon the

strokes became heavier. Then heavier still. He turned the frame through ninety degrees and, stepping between her legs, he beat her on the cheeks of her bottom and the exposed ring of her anus.

Then he stepped free and turned the frame one hundred and eighty degrees and beat her on her breasts until she felt sure her erect nipples must start squirting blood.

He turned her again so that this time her head was pointing straight down towards the floor, and he beat her again between the V of her wide open legs. The multiple tails of his whip cut mercilessly into her swollen labia.

She was screaming now. Screaming, screaming, screaming.

deVille turned her virtually upright again. He threw down the whip, took up the cane, and moved to her left side.

"Now, Jade, I want you to etch this into your mind as surely as I am going to etch my mark into your body. If you ever even think of defying me, remember back to this moment and know what sort of man I am and what I am capable of."

The stroke across her bottom nearly cut her in two. Jade rose up in her shackles and screamed again with every fibre of her body. Then she fell back, slumped in her bonds, completely drained, all energy gone. deVille came near and opened her left eye to check that she was conscious.

"Can you hear me, Jade?"

Jade moved her head slightly so that he would know that she could.

"Now, Jade, this is the one. This is my mark. Once this stroke is made my mark will be on your body and your soul will be mine. I want you to open your mind. I want you to forget the person that you once were and think only of the person you will now become. Remember, Jade. Remember this moment. Remember the moment you were reborn."

He walked slowly to her right side. Her body began to shake. Every fibre of it was terrified. Every minute particle

DOMINATING OBSESSION

of it hammered at her brain and screamed to be let in.

The cane descended like a streak of white hot lightning. The pain was unbelievable and as her eyes shot open Jade saw the disjointed puppet that was herself jerk helplessly in its bonds. But despite the pain she knew that she was whole. She had survived intact.

deVille turned her until she was upside down. Then he came close and whispered in her ear. "I lied, Jade, I have two more strokes for you to endure."

Jade's mental fortress cracked and crumbled into dust. He couldn't! He couldn't! She couldn't stand any more. She began to cry and wail and plead. He had her now and he knew it. Her barriers were down. Her protection was gone.

deVille struck her twice more once from either side. On the fourth stroke her orgasm went out of control as the heat from the cane turned it into a raging fire storm which no amount of thrashing about in her bonds could assuage.

She was a soul possessed now, burning in hell fire, dashing herself about within her bonds with no regard for self injury. She felt herself turned so that she was facing up to the ceiling and a moment later her screaming mouth was full of rampant cock and her steaming fanny was being sucked from her body.

Her thrashing and writhing and twisting and turning reached crisis point. A large part of her fanny was inside deVille's mouth and she had to escape from the unbearable ecstasy of his sucking and chewing. And she had to have his great monster deep inside her, as deep as it would go.

Jade's throat ground on his cock and deVille tore his mouth from her fanny and stood bolt upright with his hands on her breasts. Jade squeezed again at the alien in her throat tossing her head from side to side and drawing it back in an attempt to wrench his member from his body. deVille in his turn squeezed her nipples until her whole throat was wide open and screaming.

deVille's hands moved to the back of Jade's head. He

DOMINATING OBSESSION

could have used her cruelly and callously then as a vessel. He could have fucked her throat like a maniac with fast giant strokes that gave her no quarter and no opportunity to recover and to fight back.

But he didn't. He set the rhythm and she followed. And as they moved closer together Jade learnt the truth of the power this man had given her. She began to fly. She became invincible. She became the most beautiful desirable woman in the world. And the cock in her throat and the god behind it became the only important thing in her life.

27

Miles took one last look at himself in the mirror then closed the silk dressing gown he had purchased on his last trip to Hong Kong and tied the belt with a flourish.

He had a large and wide circle of friends. He took part in many sports, was a member of many clubs, and held executive directorships with many of his late father's companies. He had no problem at all amusing himself by day or night, but something told him that this particular night was going to be something else.

He smiled to himself as he started down the stairs. It was certainly starting well. This was definitely the first time he had ever been invited to a surprise party in his own house and told to come wearing nothing more than a dressing gown.

He opened the kitchen door to the pop of a champagne cork.

"What's all this - celebration?" he asked happily.

"Yes," deVille confirmed. "We heard you coming so we thought we'd start. Here, take one."

Miles took the still foaming glass and raised it above his head so that he could lick some of the sticky liquid from its base. The others looked like they had been started for some

DOMINATING OBSESSION

time, and Robyn had her left arm suspiciously concealed behind her back. She brought out an already finished bubbly bottle and placed it back on the table with a mischievous giggle.

"What's it all about?" Miles asked, anxious to join in their fun. "Aren't I a little overdressed for all this?"

deVille was dressed in white tie and tuxedo. He turned to look at Robyn, and Miles turned to look at her too. It wasn't an unwelcome task. She was dressed in a green satin evening dress with a skirt so short that it appeared to be virtually non existent. With large amounts of smooth, naked, peachy cream skin above, and what appeared to be several yards of lace patterned white stocking below, she was certainly packaged to give a man an instant erection, and Miles had no qualms about being that man.

"We're all dressed up to honour you. This is your night and believe me you're perfectly dressed for the part you have to play. This is a celebration of the future. After tonight there will be no more hanging back."

"Well, I'm all for that," Miles said, chuckling.

"To a new decade and a new age," deVille said, recharging their glasses. "This is a ceremony in recognition of the millennium, even if it is a bit premature, in which everyone will be celebrating a new beginning."

"Steady on, old man," Miles said, "There was supposed to be a similar ceremony here once before in a big old monastery that once stood on this very spot. That too was supposed to herald a wonderful new beginning for everyone. Instead it ended in a ball of hell fire that destroyed the building and pretty nearly destroyed all learning and progress for a hundred years."

"Well we must certainly hope that that doesn't happen this time," deVille agreed.

Miles was very happy. He loved Robyn, he liked and admired deVille. He didn't know what it was that the two of them had got planned for him, but he was certain that what-

DOMINATING OBSESSION

ever it was it was going to include getting his end away and witnessing deVille do the same, several times over. He beamed at Robyn as she curtsied, and as she straightened up she lifted the hem of her skirt to give him a wonderful preview of the delights to come.

deVille was pouring more champaign.

"Hey steady on," Miles said, covering the top of his glass, "I don't want to risk ruining my performance tonight."

"To business, then," deVille said. "Down to the cellars."

"The cellars?" Miles said in amazement. "There's nothing down there."

"Isn't there?" deVille asked, intriguingly.

deVille lead the way with Robyn following and Miles in the rear. Their little procession made an unusual sight. With deVille at the front in tuxedo, walking very fast. Then Robyn next, her white stockinged legs flashing out an erotic message as each flouncing step bounced the hem of the tiny green skirt up to reveal a tantalising glimpse of pert little bum cheeks. And finally Miles, bringing up the rear in a state of excitement and erection.

deVille went through the door into the servants' lobby and stopped outside the cellar door, waiting for Robyn and Miles to catch up. It was still the same old cellar door Miles had always known, but it had recently been given several new coats of paint and now looked resplendent in glistening black with a large letter 'H' in gold coloured metal attached to its centre.

"What's the H for?" Miles asked.

"That's for you to decide - it could be Heaven, it may be Hell," deVille replied, still happy to remain mysterious.

He threw the door back and reached in and pulled down three large brass levers that Miles knew hadn't been there before. Immediately there was a frightening roar, not unlike the sound of an open blast furnace, and somewhere below a fiery orange glow shone out to illuminate the cellar steps and send shadows flickering over Robyn's startled face.

"It sounds like Hell would favourite," Miles said.

"Gas torches," deVille, explained. "I think you'll find they help create a special ambience."

He was right. So did all the torture equipment.

They stood in a group at the bottom of the steps as Miles and Robyn looked around in amazement. Where on earth had it all come from? How on earth had it been moved in without them knowing anything about it?

Miles half expected a conducted tour, but deVille had very different plans.

"As I implied, Miles, we have something very special in store for you. So, I think it's going to be best to restrain you."

Miles looked into deVille's deep brown eyes, watching the flickering torchlight reflected in them and listing to the muted roar of the burning gas, as everyone waited for his decision - including himself. Inside, he felt an excitement he had never experienced before. It tightened his chest and made it difficult for him to breath.

"Fair enough," a stranger within his head answered for him before he was really ready.

"We'll let Robyn do the honours," deVille said, stepping aside.

But Robyn seemed transfixed, staring at deVille with huge glazed eyes and an intense manic stare. Miles realised that she was trembling. She was like a petrified rabbit staring into the hooded eyes of a serpent. Then it was over, and the moment was past.

"What's the matter?" Miles asked her as she came to slip his dressing gown off.

"It's nothing, just a silly premonition."

"And you, my dear, slip that lovely dress off," deVille instructed.

Miles had a strange feeling himself then that the other two had rehearsed this. But why should they? And all fears and suspicions were immediately forgotten as Robyn slipped

out of her dress. Miles heard himself groan with longing and despair. She was lovely. She was his wife of twelve years, but she had never looked so desirable as she looked to him at that moment. No woman had. She was pure and white in her unashamed nakedness. And as his eyes travelled up those long legs in their covering of white silky lace patterned nylon and finally stopped at the sweet pink lips of that most beautiful of all orifices he knew that she was the most desirable woman alive - more desirable than any virgin bride had ever been or could ever be.

At that moment he wanted nothing more than to ram his burning hot prick between those sweet pink lips and fill her to the brim with all the love she had yearned to receive over the years and which he had never quite found the courage to deliver. There would be no holding back. At long last he wanted her to have it all, all of him. Everything that was in his heart. He cried out, needing to tell her that at long last he now understood and was ready to give the full commitment that she had always needed: "Robyn! - Robyn!"

"Chain him," deVille barked.

Robyn looked from one to the other, and for a moment Miles looked at deVille and knew that he wanted his wife back. In that second he was ready to die for her. But in that second deVille grinned that awful secret grin of his and his body grew until he seemed a whole half foot taller than Miles. Something in Miles recognised the uncoiling serpent, and he was still. He couldn't defeat this man, physically or mentally.

deVille took his prize roughly by the arm. She showed no resistance, but stood as still as her body would allow and watched Miles from dull eyes.

"All right, Miles?" deVille asked.

Again they all waited.

"Yes, Master."

deVille nodded, Miles' use of his correct form of address hadn't gone unnoticed.

DOMINATING OBSESSION

deVille took possession of Robyn's body then. He was standing behind her and slightly to her right with his left hand round her left biceps. He used his right hand to caress her body and he and Robyn both watched Miles' reaction as, in a trance, Miles watched deVille's hand twisting and turning each swollen nipple before gliding on down to ruffle the chestnut forest and enter the white valley. Robyn's green eyes said that Miles ought to be happy now that she was giving him what he had always longed for, and deVille's eyes said that he wasn't doing this because Miles wanted him to, he was doing it because Robyn belonged to him now and he could do anything he wanted with her.

Robyn's white thighs parted to let deVille's hand enter and tease open the tight lips, and those lips sprang on it in joyous eager welcome and covered its fingers with their sweet white honey. Then Robyn's knees began to bend and her eyes closed at last as her frame began to shudder. With a cry she was bending and deVille lifted her on to his left hip as she began to curl into a ball. Then his hand returned between her legs, this time from the rear, and continued its sweet torture until she had given him his reward which deVille passed on to Miles, leaning forward and anointing his steaming knob with it.

Robyn uncurled to look fixedly at Miles again, and deVille lifted his hand to her mouth and she obediently licked his palm clean of her liquid gift, then dealt with each finger in a similar manner.

For a moment all was quiet. deVille nuzzled Robyn's neck and kissed along her shoulder, then he released her arm and kissed down her spine to her bottom. Robyn's eyes closed and her mouth opened as he kissed her soft cheeks and then back up again to her neck. deVille's hands had followed his lips on their intimate journey and now with them caressing her breasts and his lips caressing the back of her ear he almost whispered: "Chain him." Robyn arched her spine and leant her head back, but deVille was already gone.

DOMINATING OBSESSION

Robyn watched deVille's departing figure for a moment, then she turned, and pushing Miles back against a set of wall bars, she began anchoring him to them. Before she had finished deVille returned.

He had removed his clothes and was completely naked. He came up quietly and placed his cock between Robyn's legs from the rear and soon his lips and hands were continuing where they had left off. Robyn's thighs took firm possession of deVille's rod and wiggled it up tight into the crack of her arse so that she gave little straining grunts and muffled cries of delight as she struggled to complete her task with scant attention. And now, whenever her flesh touched Miles', whether by accident or malicious intent, the intensity of her arousal scorched his skin and made him recoil at the heat of her passion.

At last Miles was firmly anchored to the wall, his legs and arms spread wide. deVille reached up and tried Miles' wrist restraints then turned away. When his jailor was satisfied that she had finished, she bathed her tongue in her own saliva and brought its glistening tip to supply much needed relief to Miles' baked dry lips and his cock jumped as he found himself gazing into two dark green pools damp with desire for another man.

Glancing once at deVille, she dropped to her knees and took Miles' cock lightly in her left hand.

"Now I want you to be good." She pressed her lips to his knob, then feeling him shudder, took him deep in her mouth for a moment of ecstasy that was gone all too soon. "Have fun!" Her tongue flicked out for the glistening translucent bead that had already formed in his cock's little blind eye. She might have done more, but deVille called out her name, bringing her to heel.

With one last lingering look at her husband, Robyn turned and walked towards the huge whipping frame. As she mounted the steps Miles' balls registered each one she took and he groaned softly to himself as the cheeks of that delec-

table bottom rose and fell alternately on every tread.

28

At that moment something made Miles look up at the stairs. At first he wasn't sure what it was that had caught his eye, then, with a jolt he realised that someone had opened the cellar door and that harsh electric light from the servants lobby was now shining down to strike the wall below the half landing.

The ceiling line cut off his view of the top of the stairs. His available vision stopped just above the half landing where the stairs executed a ninety degree angle before the top five steps that lead to the entrance door. But he was almost positive that someone was standing just out of sight preparing to come in, someone who shouldn't be there in a house that was locked and bolted and with all its legitimate inhabitants already down in the cellar. The hairs stood up on the back of Miles' neck and he wanted to call out to deVille, but he was paralysed with fear and uncertainty and the words wouldn't come.

So he waited, chained to the wall in the nude, while someone entered the cellar and started down the stairs. Although he knew they were there his heart still jumped as a large dark shadow blotted out the electric light completely then slowly shrank to a much smaller blacker shape that he instantly recognised. He was looking at the shadow of a figure that had horns, a cape and a trident. Miles stopped breathing and suddenly his mind was very concentrated and his body very taut. The shadow had something else too, something that made him hesitate to cry out. It had breasts and curves and an unmistakable female form. So Miles watched with unblinking eyes and waited for a female devil to round the corner on to the tiny landing.

DOMINATING OBSESSION

The she devil turned the corner and placed first one foot and then the other on the half landing and brought them together. Miles stared at the bottom of a pair of scarlet patent leather boots which had the tallest stiletto heels he had ever seen. As the boots descended another step, and then another, he watched the legs slowly emerging from below the ceiling line and realised that this was how the whole figure would appear slowly descending towards him from a height of twenty feet, nine inches at a time.

The legs kept coming and coming and the boots went on for ever, way past the knee, then suddenly they stopped half way up the thigh and he had his first glimpse of stocking, red stocking with four inches of lace top. Then at her next step his heart stood still and so did she. Slowly she brought her second foot down to stand next to the other. Her legs were together and he could just see the bottom of what looked like a red lace basque. But his bulging eyes could hardly believe what was between that and the stocking tops. There was only scarlet suspenders and creamy white flesh. It was ridiculous, she was dressed as a scarlet devil, but he could only think of an angel. Where there should have been a triangle of hair, there was only virgin white flesh. And where there should have been a red gash in that flesh there was nothing, no imperfection - no faint crease - nothing at all.

He realised the stupidity of his thoughts. He was a man, he didn't want a woman who offered no means of penetration. But if he had been God The Creator he could never have brought himself to desecrate his own beautiful perfection by providing the means for man's wicked intrusion. Perhaps that was the Devil's ultimate torment to provide a body that was erotic perfection with no means of entry? Or perhaps it was the Devil who had been forced to finish God's work for him and that was why he had fallen from grace?

All at once there was a huge commotion on the far side of the cellar. Someone had laid fire to a huge pile of logs. Miles saw the sparks and the shadows of the flames mingled

with the dark ghostly shadows of many dancing forms. There was a babble of voices and much laughing and screaming. There were a whole host of devils and their female companions or captives having some sort of ritualistic dance.

Who were all these people? Miles looked up at the platform and for a moment his brain wouldn't move. Robyn was strapped inside a frame, her legs and arms spread wide to the four corners. Her back was towards him and her body was incredible. Her white stocking legs led up to a pert thrusting bottom and the deep curve of her waist opened to an angel wing back and wide rounded shoulders. He looked past her to the mirrors and she was looking back at him as shocked as he was. His eyes dropped to her breasts. They were thrust out before her with huge erect nipples and as he watched she began to revolve as the frame she was in began turning through a full circle.

When she stopped Miles found himself looking at deVille, who was playing the part of ring master, and this act over, was holding out his arm to the stairs indicating where the next part of the action would take place.

Right on cue the unknown scarlet devil woman began descending again, and now Miles relaxed, certain at last that her entry into the game was planned and expected by at least one member of their company.

The scarlet basque came in to view. It covered an extremely trim waist and Miles gave a heart felt groan of desire as the next step revealed that her breasts were supported but left uncovered. Unlike the missing genitals there was no trickery or coyness linked to these beautiful expressions of the female form. They were full, firm, and brazen, with large glistening red areolae and nipples. The sort of breasts that perfectly befitted a scarlet she devil.

There followed the shoulders and neck split by the strap of a cape and already he could see that her pointed chin was covered with scarlet leather and he knew that his burning desire to look on the face of this temptress was going to be

DOMINATING OBSESSION

frustrated.

At last she was there fully revealed and she stood with both feet on the same step and her legs pressed firmly together and looked back at him through almond shaped holes in a full leather hood that covered her whole head. The leather of the hood was soft enough to show the contours of the face it was stretched over, and these features had been emphasised by sewing and cutting to provide the line of a pair of arched eyebrows above the almond shaped eye holes, a straight nose, high cheek bones, and a full pair of lips. Whether or not this gave a fair representation of the face beneath the leather was impossible to say, but if it did, she was no one he knew.

On top of the hood there were two short black in-curving horns, and in her right hand she carried a trident with a short wooden handle and stainless steel prongs. In her left hand she held aloft the last foot of her own arrow headed tail

The full effect was devastating, and Miles wasn't at all surprised to feel his cock come up sharply.

The devil woman continued her descent, giving him plenty of time to confirm that she was frightening perfection. If all Hell's tormentors looked half as good as this he would gladly go there at once. Who she was he didn't care. She would turn out to be another of deVille's female slaves, he was sure. But one thing he did know and care about and that was that he had to have her whatever the cost.

She descended with such poise and confidence that he knew that she had behaved in a similar manner to this with other men many times before. But that didn't matter, it was impossible to expect virgin innocence and lustful experience too, and his rampant rod was telling him that he wouldn't give anyone a good thank you for a virgin at that moment.

She reached the bottom step and he was able to appreciate the full glory of those magnificent breasts. They were thrust out before her like a badge of office and even more proud and upturned than Robyn's. And as she got closer he was able to confirm his initial belief that the nipples and

areolae had been painted with bright scarlet lip gloss.

She stopped in front of him and, starting at his ankles, looked critically up his naked body. Miles did the same to hers until he at last found himself looking into a pair of imperious slate grey eyes. It may have been then that he fell in love, all he knew for sure was that his whole body was burning and that he wouldn't be able to think until those eyes gave him permission to relax.

With the little attention left to him he vaguely saw her shrug the scarlet cape from her right shoulder then the next moment the trident was raised and on its way. With a terrible thud the three prongs buried themselves in the boards at the back of the climbing frame six inches below his bollocks. The short shaft swung harmlessly up and down a few times then stopped. The scarlet devil laughed with a sound like tiny musical bells and Miles knew that he had lost one of his allotted lives and wondered how many he had left.

The devil lifted both arms to her throat and began untying her cape. Her eyes were watching his. His eyes were watching her tits lifting and returning. When he next looked at her eyes they were smiling. This time he was sure, he was also sure that he wanted to see her face, especially those full smiling lips. The she devil pressed the handle of the trident down and mounted it like a witch on a broomstick. But like no which he had ever seen. The trident was embedded in the boards at a thirty degree angle so the handle pressed up tight between her legs. Miles watched her slide her way along it sure that the friction must open up at least a little crease in the creamy white flesh.

She came to rest with her nipples pressing against his chest and then she leant forward until he felt as if the two hard little bullets must penetrate deep into his flesh, but it was his tormenters soft flesh that they chose instead and soon he was groaning as he felt the full soft firmness of her breasts rotating on his chest. A moment more and his hysterical cock was sandwiched firmly between their two belies

DOMINATING OBSESSION

and then she began slowly rotating her hips and breast in two synchronised anticlockwise circles.

His cock jerked and deposited a present on her belly. It was only the first tiny indication of more to come, and Miles also instantly jerked, forcing his body high and his mind even higher where it couldn't do any more harm by thinking of covering this beautiful temptresses with his limited ration of seminal fluid.

She gave him a moment to recover, then slowly reversed, letting his cock down gently until it was only at eighty-five degrees, hardly staining at all. And when she returned this time, her belly was well clear of his and her nipples hardly tickled his chest as she tore open the Velcro joint and turned back the flap on the lower part of her mask.

For a moment her sweet pointed chin and full smiling lips were revealed in a striptease more erotically stimulating than any he had ever witnessed before. Those lips were as he had imagined, but to see them uncovered sent his heart racing. They glistened like ripe cherries with the same scarlet lip gloss that had once adorned her nipples but which now formed two round red patches on his chest. And they came to rest against his and he obediently opened his mouth to let in a hot darting tongue that filled his brain with stupefying mists of dizziness.

In a second it was all over, leaving him with only the taste, perfume, and memory, of soft silky paradise.

The she devil reversed away from him and Miles looked up to see deVille descending the steps from the whipping frame. He approached the devil woman from behind and put his left arm round her then lifted a cloth and wiped both breasts free of the remains of the lipstick. She indicated her belly and he wiped that too, and both of them laughed. Then deVille wiped her beautiful bald little mound and when the cloth came away for the first time Miles saw the faintest crease.

deVille pulled the trident free and handed her a small

DOMINATING OBSESSION

key.

Miles shot a glance at Robyn. She was still standing in the whipping frame with her back to them watching them in the large bronze mirrors. Her mouth was imprisoned in a cruel black leather gag, but she was frantically shaking her head, trying to tell him that something was wrong.

The devil woman unlocked the shackle on Miles' right wrist, then handed the key back to deVille. Miles hadn't moved his arm. Taking his hand in both of hers she moved it to her breasts, left one first and then the right. Then she moved it down to her mount of Venus. The skin on her mound was as smooth as that of a baby. Miles had never felt anything as erotic. It was firm and soft and perfectly shaped for his palm, but not at all like a breast and he knew he must come. The devil woman knew too and pressed the long sharp scarlet nails of her left hand in to the flesh of his right wrist almost piercing the skin.

It was enough and his self control returned sufficiently for them to continue. Taking hold of his right index finger between her own fingers and thumb the she devil ran it up and down her seamless mound until it opened for them. Miles felt the wonder of the smooth silicon juices easing his fingers passage and knew he was inside. With many soft murmurs and bright girlish giggles she taught him how to masturbate her, then when she was sure that he had the knowledge and courage to continue alone she removed both her own hands to her hips and closed her eyes, temporarily abandoning her body's happiness to him.

When he saw her begin circling her head and groaning in a regular pattern he tried to finish her, but she stepped away from him and remained with her arms crossed, squeezing her breasts until her approaching climax passed away unfulfilled. Now when the eyes opened they were hooded and misty and green.

He was shaking now, with no possibility of stopping. He wanted her so much that it would have made no difference

DOMINATING OBSESSION

to his desire for her if he were to be told that the price he must pay for her was to be put to death the second after he had satisfied his lust.

The devil woman returned his wrist to the shackle and secured it there then presented her bottom to deVille so that he could remove her tail. Then deVille returned up the steps to the platform of the whipping frame and she turned and walked over to a rack of whips. It was the first time Miles had seen her bottom and he groaned in despair. He would do anything to posses such an arse. Anything. It was no good, he couldn't go on, he had to allow himself to come.

Such an arse shouldn't exist. Such an arse couldn't exist without making a rapist of every man. As the precocious little bum cheeks danced their own sexy polka with each other, Miles felt his cock weeping fluid. Some black hearted bastard had planted four cane strokes on that perfect arse in a perfect cross. 'X' marks the spot, his stupid brain said, as it instantly decided who that bastard was. deVille couldn't resist women's arses. He had freely admitted his weakness to Miles on the first night they had met. And now Miles knew why and fervently agreed. There couldn't possibly be anything in the whole of Heaven and Hell to be compared to screwing that darling little arse.

A frantic movement in the corner of his eye made him look towards Robyn again. She was still telling him No, but he didn't understand. What was it she knew that he didn't? What danger was he in? It didn't matter. Whatever it was, there was nothing on earth that could stop him from shagging this devil woman if he had the chance.

The little minx was taking her time selecting a whip. They both knew that it was only a game for his benefit and he wasn't surprised when she placed her hands on her bum and began gently caressing her cheeks.

She chose a whip at last and retraced her steps, giving him time to fall in love with her breasts all over again. The laughing grey-green eyes were amused by his interest. She

stopped in front of him and flicked the whip against the objects of his present desire. Miles flinched as a crazing of fine red stripes and whirls appeared on the white skin. She held the whip up for him to inspect. It was a cat-o'-nine-tails with knotted leather strands. Miles had no idea how much it would hurt, but judging by the way she had flicked it against her sensitive breasts it probably wasn't much. As if sensing his thoughts she flicked it against his stomach. It was like being hit with a bunch of white hot needles. He jerked in his bonds and cried out, losing all breath.

She flounced away and it was only the knowledge that she was soon going to mount the steps to the whipping frame that allowed him to recover so quickly. As he watched the magnificent bottom making its way up those steps he never once paid any heed to the thought that its owner was carrying that vicious whip on its way to beat poor Robyn. And even when the scarlet she devil reached the platform and handed the whip to deVille his only thought was how good Robyn's bum would look marked with a similar dark cross.

deVille took the whip from his beautiful assistant and looked at it, but rejected it at once, handing it back. But his assistant said something that Miles couldn't hear and after a moment's discussion deVille shrugged his shoulders and stood aside.

Now everyone looked at Robyn. She was no longer looking at Miles, but with her head turned to the side she was looking over her left shoulder at the she devil. She was still franticly shaking her head, but this time it was her own soft unblemished skin she was trying to save. With a lazy flick of the wrist the devil woman dropped the nine leather tails on to Robyn's left shoulder. Miles saw Robyn's body jump in its chains and his did the same in knowledgeable understanding. The devil woman drew the whip across Robyn's body towards the right cheek of her bottom bringing it down the steep arch of Robyn's back and flicking it away at the last moment so that the vicious tails brought red stripes to the

DOMINATING OBSESSION

crest of the soft round cheek.

deVille had moved to the other side of Robyn, and now he lifted his arms and, placing his hands behind her head, removed her gag.

Robyn was sobbing, but when she realised her mouth was free she shook her head to clear it and quickly blurted something out. The distance was too great for Miles to hear what she said, but he heard deVille laugh and shake his head in refusal. Robyn tried again to convince him, this time shouting her plea. But at that precise moment a great wailing scream arose somewhere else in the cellar, drowning out her words before they could reach Miles. And whatever it was that she had said this time had no more effect than her previous entreaty and deVille shook his head and turned away as the cat-o'-nine-tails was flicked on to Robyn's right shoulder by his erotically dressed young assistant.

Once more it was dragged down from her shoulder and across her back and Robyn screamed, then screamed again when it was flicked off at the crest of her left bum cheek leaving that mound gaudily etched with bright red marks to match its twin.

With her next stroke the scarlet torturer brought the whip up between Robyn's legs to flick away leaving the same tell tale red marks on the bottom of her left bum cheek. And then once more between her legs to do the same to the bottom of her right cheek.

Robyn was constantly moving now, her body swinging in her bonds and twisting and turning. She was also constantly screaming and wailing and crying out and her shouts and screams were becoming intermingled with those of the other poor soul who was no doubt being tortured in a similar fashion somewhere deeper into this hellish dungeon.

The scarlet torturer brought the whip down in a backhanded side swipe at Robyn's left buttock, then as her stroke reached the end of its arc, she brought it back again with a forehand on the centre of the other cheek. Except for a small

patch in the middle Robyn's whole bottom was burning red with a web of darker red stripes amongst the bright colouring. The devil woman stood back and with a full swing planted a forehand blow right on this last pale spot.

Robyn screamed and raised up in her bonds then fell back and lay limp with her chin on her chest.

29

The scarlet she devil handed her whip to deVille and turned away from her limp victim and turned her flashing eyes on Miles. Now it was to be his turn, and for the first time Miles realised that she intended to cause him real pain. He had been horrified for Robyn, but he was terrified for himself. He had never witnessed such deliberate premeditated violence in real life before. It shocked him to realise that there were people capable of doing such things. It shocked him even more to realise that he still found her the most erotically attractive creature alive.

She walked down the steps towards him and he watched her in horror at how much his body still wanted her. Her eyes were grey again now and looking at him with that bright steady gaze. There was no remorse for what she had just done, only a mild amusement at the knowledge of what she was about to do next. Miles couldn't hold her gaze, but not to look meant lowering his own eyes to the wonderful glistening globes of her breasts, or to lower them still further to the open lips of her vagina, and to feel his cock immediately jump at the prospect of creeping inside that warm wet paradise.

Suddenly she stopped. Miles looked up and those eyes were laughing at his need again. She ran her hands down her body until her long pointed fingers were spread either side of where her pubic triangle should have been. Miles was

DOMINATING OBSESSION

amazed to see that the lips of her vagina were tight shut again now, but as he watched they opened like a little flower. Then the inner labia also opened until her cunt was like a delicate pink rose head. In a moment her beautiful flower was closing again and then it was gone leaving only a round edged slit that it would have been impossible for a child to slip a penny pocket money inside.

Miles knew that he would never be able to smell another rose without thinking of this moment. He also knew that in his old age it would be pleasant to spend a lot of time sniffing roses and revisiting his memories.

Again he heard that wonderful girlish giggle. It was so bubbly and innocent that it reminded him of all the nice times in his life. But now she was moving again with a determined air, and in a moment she had reached him and Miles closed his eyes and almost cringed in fear. But the touch of her hands on his shoulders was soft and sensuous and the next moment the touch of her nipples on his chest and the sharp tips of her nails in his sides sent a bolt of electricity through his stomach. Now his eyes were closed for a different reason as she began to descend to her knees dragging the soft tips of her breasts and nails down his shaking body as she did so.

Miles couldn't stand it. He had to cry out as grooves of ecstasy were gauged in his tortured body. His cock disappeared into her cleavage and her nails gripped hard to his buttocks. Then her hands sidled round towards each other on his hips until they met her boobs. With one breast in either hand and her index fingers forcing her nipples together on top of his shaft she moved her captive up and down its tight soft prison.

Miles opened his eyes, but he couldn't look. He looked over her head instead and saw Robyn still hanging weakly in the whipping frame and deVille descending the steps towards the rack of whips. His cock was released from its padded purgatory and he heard the sound of tearing Velcro which

made his heart jump.

As his cock disappeared between the lips of that hot warm heaven he knew that he had done his best, held out till the very last second. No man could have done more and release was going to be heaven. But his torturer had other ideas. The index finger and thumb of her left hand was squeezing shut the ejaculatory duct just below his balls. It was her schedule they would be working to!

Miles gave a sigh of relief and after less than a minute he was back in control. Her grip relaxed and her fingers gently massaged the full area between his rectum and balls. Then both hands moved on to his balls and with one testicle folded in either fist she began to pull on them, dragging them down and easing their unbearable ache away. It was ecstasy being in such experienced confident hands - if anyone could prolong his enjoyment and eventually bring him to an earth shattering orgasm it was this magnificent scarlet she devil. He was as happy as a contented milch cow as he turned his attention to the whipping frame to see how his wife was.

Robyn was conscious again, and gagged again, and being whipped again, this time by deVille. He was standing in front of her beating her with a whip that looked similar to the first, but with far more tails. He wasn't beating her hard, more wiping the tails over her body with little forward and backward unlocking movements of his wrists. Robyn's black leather gag was back in place and she was spinning in her bonds and almost mewing under the unceasing caress of deVille's lash. But when she saw Miles watching them she once more began frantically shaking her head and gesturing at him with wild eyes as if there was something she was desperate for him to know.

deVille saw this and hit her hard twice between the legs and then twice more once on each breast and Robyn began to jerk in her bonds and test the effectiveness of her gag. There was nothing Miles could do except watch with horrified eyes while deVille whipped his poor victim in to a frenzy.

DOMINATING OBSESSION

Then Robyn suddenly drew herself up in her bonds and began shaking uncontrollably. deVille stopped whipping her. Robyn's eyes pleaded with him to continue and at last Miles understood the truth, she needed only one more blow to bring her to a shuddering climax.

deVille threw the whip down and without a backward glance walked past her towards the steps. Robyn watched him go with horror. Then her eyes met Miles' and she turned away in shame and closed her eyes until her shaking stopped. The next moment deVille was at the side of his assistant and holding a small wooden bowl and something else which was held hidden in his hand.

With one long last sliding suck of a favourite lolly the she devil removed her mouth from around Miles' cock. She spent a few more moments licking the more obvious globules of saliva from it, then with a final gentle pull on his balls she turned her attention to deVille.

Miles didn't have to wait long to discover what was in the bowl. deVille held it out and the girl dipped both hands in to it. When they emerged they were coated in oil. Then his agony really began, as first one finger, and then another, and another, began to tease their way into his back passage. She returned to the bowl and renewed her coating of oil twice before she was satisfied. Then she turned to deVille and held her hand out. He placed something short pointed and white in it and even before she twisted the base and he heard the soft humming noise Miles knew what it was.

deVille laughed, and in a moment his beautiful young companion found it impossible not to join in. The tip of the small vibrator entered the entrance to Miles' anus and he screamed, then clamped his teeth firmly over his bottom lip. His head came up and he found himself looking at Robyn. Her body was covered in sweat that made it glisten like wet gold in the torchlight. She was hanging completely limp in her bonds, as if all strength to resist was finally gone.

Once more his erotic torturer took a firm grip on his

tube in the area just behind his sac and squeezed hard with finger and thumb to ensure that all chance of ejaculation was nipped in the bud. Then she pushed the small vibrator fully inside his anus.

Miles began to scream again, and this time he couldn't stop. She was driving him insane. He must come or his balls would explode. She opened that beautiful mouth wide. At first he thought that she was mimicking his agonised screaming but then she dipped her head and took the full length of his weapon inside her mouth.

The knob of his cock disappeared into her throat and then she shifted forward again pressing her face deep into his groin. She had taken all of him, plus a bit more that wasn't there to give. There was only one place she could have put him, and Miles waited hardly daring to breath, enjoying the sensation of having his cock tightly held on all sides. She swallowed again. It felt as if his foreskin must be ripped free and shredded back along his shaft. His cock was completely surrounded on all sides by muscles that could crush it into paste. Then the walls of her throat took command of him completely, moving him gently backwards and forwards, all the time squeezing and softly caressing him. Her rippling throat was full of saliva and the ecstatic sensation was too much for any man to live with.

The scream rose in his feet, making him rise to his toes. It ran up his legs which locked tight and grew to use every fraction of their length. Then it coursed up through his stomach and chest, emptying his lungs of every particle of air, and picking up speed all the time, rushed up through his throat and emerged through his mouth to go echoing round and round the brick lined chamber.

In that moment the wicked she devil had mercy and released her grip on his scrotum. The trapped ejaculatory fluid rose immediately in a single great flood that blistered the walls of its narrow tube as it raced towards the single tiny exit and threw itself hurtling into the dark unknown. He felt

her gag and turn back the tide to send it racing back past his thundering cock on its way to her mouth and nose. His cock jerked and bucked and conspired with her throat to cut off her air and for a moment she was as still as death as she began drowning in a few millilitres of glutinous liquid. Then with her nails tearing his buttocks and her head bouncing uncontrollably against his groin she took all his wild fury as he thrust at her with all the power of a demented animal. And when he had no more power, only screams and gushing tears, her throat took his cock and her hands took his balls and she finished the race for him and nursed him back to stillness.

Miles had never known such an orgasm. He wasn't sure if a man was capable of multiple orgasms; this might be a first.

The she devil withdrew the vibrator from his anus and her mouth from his cock, and rose to her feet. Miles looked into a pair of brightly shining eyes that were now almost as darkly green as Robyn's. Those beautiful lips were thick with his come and turned up in a beatific smile. They bumped against his and in a moment his mouth was full of her wriggling tongue and the salty taste of his own thick cloying fluid. Somehow she captured his reluctant tongue and dragged it into her own mouth with such force that he was convinced that she intended to suck it out by the roots.

Then she taught him that it can be as pleasurable to be joined at the mouths as joined at the genitals. For several minutes they remained locked together like that with their tongues chasing each other in and out of their respective mouths and he knew then that however unacceptable the past or future dreadful deeds of this frightening woman, he wanted to always be allowed to remain her devoted slave.

All too soon her mouth released his and still holding his head in her hands she moved her own head back six inches so that her blissfully happy eyes could gaze contentedly into his. Then for the first time she spoke to him.

"Thank you, Daddy," she said.

30

"Jade, Jade, how could you?"

She stepped back then and pulled her scarlet hood off, shaking her hair free and running a hand through it, enticing it back into its rigid uniformity. Beautiful Jade, his gorgeous step-daughter as he had never seen her before. Her face was flushed, her eyes were bright green, and her jet black hair shone with a golden halo of shimmering torchlight.

"I love you Miles, I've always loved you."

She said the words as if they made sense. As if merely saying impossible things made them possible.

"But I'm your father!"

"No! You're my lover and always will be from now on."

She fell to her knees and took up the fiery aching torment which was all that remained of his shrivelled cock. She squeezed it hard with both hands: the pain was excruciating. Then as his scream became a poignant squeal, she left her right hand to squeeze his cock and buried the nails of her left hand in the flesh of his thigh and pulled down towards his knee. He screamed again as three six inch long grooves were torn into his flesh, but Jade had no mercy and clamped her teeth tight to his right thigh and bit down hard until he stopped screaming.

They remained like that, with Jade squeezing the pain from his cock, and adjusting the pains in his legs by moving her nails within his open wounds and modifying the pressure of her biting teeth. When the pain in his legs became greater than the pain in his cock, and Miles felt strong enough to bite his lip and whine through his, nose Jade removed her nails and her teeth from his thighs and stroked and nuzzled and kissed his cock with her face, lips, and throat while her

DOMINATING OBSESSION

hands massaged his balls and the area leading to his anus.

Eventually the pain in his cock became bearable, but he didn't want her to stop. He wanted to spend the rest of his life with this wonderful nurse stroking his genitals and listening to her telling his cock how wonderful and brave it was.

"I'm sorry, Miles, I kept you waiting too long. I was too full of love for you. Next time will be just perfect - like an orgasmic dream, I promise. And I will never hurt you again, my love," she said to his cock, "unless your master wants me to." She squeezed it to her lips and gave it a final kiss then stood up and looked into Miles' eyes again.

"There can be no next time, Jade. You must know that. You can't love me, not that way. It's not allowed."

"It has to be allowed, Miles. I can't live without you. It's no good anyone saying I must. I've tried and it isn't possible."

"It's against the law!"

"Everything worth doing has been against the law at sometime, somewhere, Miles. Don't you know - laws are made for other people by men that think we are all children who shouldn't be allowed to have any grown-up fun. Well I'm not a child, Miles. I don't feel like a child. I didn't enjoy being a child, and I'm not going to be treated like a child any longer. I know what feels right and I make my own laws. You can't destroy your one and only life because some stupid busybody wants to interfere in our happiness."

Jade was right, she wasn't a child. She had grown-up and he hadn't noticed. She was only seventeen but she already knew more and had more common sense than he would ever have. Miles felt very proud of her.

Jade threw herself on his chest and with her arms hugging him tightly round the neck she cried out the frustration and anger of five years of hell.

What could he do? She had sucked his cock. Sucked his cock and drunk his sperm. And done it far better than any-

DOMINATING OBSESSION

one else had ever done. Anyone? He had only really ever known Robyn. With a sudden shock he realised that that state of affairs might have lasted for ever. If it had, he would never have known about this. He loved Robyn, but he had just enjoyed better sex with her daughter than he ever had with her. Jade was only seventeen. Think of all the other women there must be who knew far more than her.

Jade's breasts were against his chest and she was holding his penis again as if she was scared that even now, after all she had said and done, it might still be taken from her. Then they both felt it stir. Miles felt Jade stiffen, but she didn't stop crying or move her head from his chest, she just moved his cock to her fanny and began stroking it up and down between the lips of her vagina.

When it was strong enough she popped it in to her entrance. Then she began to gently squeeze it with her labia. How was that possible? Robyn couldn't do that. Jade was only seventeen and yet her labia were moving on his half erect cock giving it little love bites. And when she had gobbled him, he couldn't be sure, but it had felt as if she had taken him down into her throat.

Jade began to sink to her knees her right cheek sliding down his body and her tears leaving a damp crooked smear on his stomach and belly as she went.

Robyn began to shout and scream, throwing herself about in her bonds and shouting incoherently, the only understandable words the names of her daughter and her husband. She was hysterical. Completely out of control. But what could he do?

Spurred to life, he fought at his own bonds and began begging Jade not to do it. Without a word she popped his cock into her mouth, oiled her fingers in the bowl, and picking up a long string of black beads began threading them slowly up his rectum.

Miles stopped groaning Jade's name and pleading with her to stop. He didn't want her to stop. The harm was done.

DOMINATING OBSESSION

What harm? He was sterile, he couldn't get her pregnant, and if it didn't work out all of them were strong enough and sensible enough to live with the consequences.

Robyn had stopped pleading as well. She no longer hung helplessly and dejectedly in her bonds. It was as if she had come to terms with it: accepted that there was nothing she could do to change things.

Miles was fully erect now, and gently, with a single swallow, Jade eased him into her throat. Christ! This time there could be no doubt. He was all the way in and held by loving muscles that pulsated a gentle flow of saliva up and down his cock. It was heaven. His body turned to jelly. He began to float quietly off towards a wonderful gentle climax.

Jade finished feeding the string of beads in to his anus, and with one last farewell squeeze, stopped massaging his cock in her throat and withdrew from him. His cock felt cold and betrayed. Jade rose, and looked into his eyes.

"I love you, Miles."

She needed his forgiveness for her deception.

"I love you, baby."

Jade smiled, that would have to do - for now, her look said. She turned away and went over to the rack of whips. This time there was no long delay while she made a choice. She seemed to know what she had come for. She selected a thin cane with a curved handle and without looking back at Miles she mounted the steps. Even without the cross on Jade's bum to remind him, Miles knew what was going to happen. So did Robyn.

deVille held out his hand for the cane, but Jade shook her head and when Robyn began screaming again and begging Jade not to do it she looked her mother straight in the eye and said nothing.

deVille gave Robyn several strokes on the back and bottom with his multi tailed whip until her bright red glow returned. Then he moved in front of her and concentrated on striking her between the legs and on the breasts as before. It

didn't take long, and as Robyn's orgasm rose towards a climax again she twisted her head in a vain attempt to see her daughter and started screaming at her again pleading with her not to do it.

The pleading stopped when the first stroke cut its ugly red line across her right buttock. Jade wasn't in the mood to give mercy and with deVille's help to turn their victim at the appropriate times she didn't stop until her mother's bottom was marked with the same sign as her own.

Miles watched Robyn's beautiful body shuddering and twisting and yanking itself about and his head held only a single stupid thought.

X marks the spot.

31

deVille supported Robyn's limp body while Jade released it from the whipping frame. Then deVille eased Robyn on to his right shoulder and carried her with his cheek against her bottom and his arm between her legs holding her almost casually with his hand just below her left knee. His burden appeared totally lifeless with her arms and hair hanging straight down and her breasts and head bouncing carelessly against his back.

Jade followed, but they didn't go far, only as far as the first main pillar. The pillar was round, made of brick and eight feet in diameter. At the top it supported one end of three arches all forty yards across. There were four such pillars in this main cellar with each linked by arches to its two neighbours plus the one diagonally opposite it. As the pillars were each set ten yards in from the walls this provided a subterranean chamber with a ceiling span of sixty square yards.

Jade fitted her mother's wrists and ankles into shackles

so that her body was once more presented in a star shape. This time she was facing Miles and he could see that although her breasts and belly and thighs were red from the beating there would be little to show for it within the space of a few hours.

With her mother firmly secured and hanging limply in her bonds, Jade turned to Miles and took a moment to unbutton her basque. She opened it to reveal her stomach for the first time. A gold ring a little bigger than a curtain ring shone from her navel. Jade pulled it to show him that it was firmly attached through her flesh. She threw the basque on to a nearby settee and sat down, pulled off both thigh length boots, tossing each one over her shoulder as soon as it was free. She stood up laughing, and turned a pirouette like a belly dancer.

"I hate clothes. Will you allow me to walk around the house naked from now on, Miles?"

Miles made no answer, but his cock jumped at the prospect, causing Jade to laugh again. She blew him a kiss and ran off to find deVille.

Miles wondered if they had both gone off to join the other party that he could see was still in progress over on the far side of the cellar, but they returned after only a few moments with deVille carrying a bucket of water and a towel and Jade carrying a little black box. deVille took up position and with a full backward swing threw the contents of the bucket at Robyn. The consequence was dramatic. As Robyn resurfaced shaking and spluttering, Jade laughed and used the towel to dry her mother off and to calm her down.

When Robyn was fully recovered Jade took out the piercing gun. Robyn looked at her in horror, but Jade merely laughed and deVille spoke to Robyn after which she hung her head in resignation. Jade dampened a piece of liniment with disinfectant and wiped her mother's navel with it. She placed the piercing gun in position and Miles heard a faint click. deVille stepped forward with a large gold ring.

Miles was shocked. Shocked at what deVille was prepared to do and shocked that Jade was prepared to do it with him, to her own mother.

Then they did both Robyn's nipples and her clitoris in a similar manner.

While deVille took the gun away Jade wiped her crying mother's body again to remove the smell of disinfectant. Then she sprayed her with perfume.

Robyn was released and placed on the settee where deVille hugged her and kissed her and fed her a long cold drink. Jade came over to Miles and gave him similar refreshment. The glass contained ice cold tonic water with a slice of lemon floating in it and Miles couldn't remember when a drink had tasted so good. As Jade supported his head and tipped the tall glass to his lips he felt all the same familiar excitement as her naked body touched his.

"How could you, Jade?" he asked.

"Everyone should be pierced," she replied un-repentantly. "I'm going to be fully pierced after your special treat," and with that she was gone, leaving Miles feeling that it must be a dream.

The three of them then walked off deeper into the cellar. Miles strained to see, but with all the mirrors and equipment they were soon out of sight.

Only deVille returned to come and release Miles from his chains, and the two men walked over and feasted their eyes on the two helpless women. Now Mother and daughter had been pinioned side by side on two identical padded benches. The back of each bench had been raised so that the women could easily look forward. Their arms were clamped above their heads and slightly to either side in a way which ensured that their breasts were displayed to maximum advantage. Their bottoms were positioned at the very edge of the nearest end of the bench and their wide open legs were held upright at a ninety degree angle with their ankles firmly locked in another set of metal clamps. Both vulva's were

DOMINATING OBSESSION

wide open and the X of the cane pointed to two sweet little bum rings.

"Jade is a virgin. Did you know that, Miles?"

Miles looked at the lewd young woman laid out before him. Then he looked at Robyn. It was unbelievable.

"How about you Robyn, did you know?" deVille leant forward and pulled the gold ring that he and her daughter had so recently fitted through her clitoris.

Robyn jumped and shook her head.

"But you hoped she would be?"

Robyn nodded.

"Always a problem for a mother. Their daughters have got to learn. They've got to experiment. But how to keep them safe while still allowing them to find out about their own bodies and sexuality?" deVille summarised every mother's dilemma.

Robyn looked guiltily at him as if he had trapped her in some deception. She turned away and looked over at Jade. Jade smiled back and winked.

What was going on? Was everybody mad? Could Jade be a virgin? Miles looked at her. It didn't seem possible. She was obscenely displayed with her legs and vulva wide open. She had the marks of a recent severe caning on her bottom and she had already shown him that she had more control of her vagina than he had any idea was possible. Not to mention that he had just seen her whip and body pierce her own mother and the fact that she had given him the best blow job he had ever had.

She was looking at him innocently, as if butter wouldn't melt in that very clever little mouth.

deVille laughed. "It's perfectly true I assure you," he said. "Her hymen is intact, I checked. It isn't even touched, it's going to take some shifting."

He gave Robyn and Miles time to take this in.

"Your daughter is very fortunate. She's not going to lose her cherry in a furtive uncomfortable coupling in the dark

DOMINATING OBSESSION

with insufficient preparation and foreplay. She's going to lose it in front of her family and friends in a glorious demonstration of the true joy of sex. And I'm willing to bet that whatever happens she will orgasm with her very first penetration and have no guilt or regrets and only ever experience pleasant memories of this night. And there aren't many women who could say that about their own first experience of penetration."

deVille looked at Robyn as if seeking confirmation.

He got none. What was happening inside Robyn's head Miles had no idea.

deVille left it. "You find it hard to believe after your earlier experience, Miles?" he asked.

Miles nodded and looked again at Jade.

"She has loved you for five years, Miles. Her love built until it became an obsession. And I don't have to tell you what an obsession can do to people, do I? Those tricks and fireworks" - he lifted a remote control and pointed it towards the commotion in the corner, which immediately faded away - "those are mere illusion, and the rest is the culmination of three days intensive hard work with an inspired pupil." He turned and looked at Jade who beamed happily back at him. "She didn't want to come to you as your little girl. She thought you would be horrified and condemn her to a lifetime of despair. She wanted to come to you as a woman."

She's certainly that, Miles' eyes confirmed. He turned to Robyn then back from mother to daughter. She was even more of a woman than her mother. In every way.

"So there it is Miles, Jade's present to the man she loves. If you care to take it."

Miles looked at him in horror. It was no use trying to pretend that he didn't want Jade's present. His erection was far more secure and upright than the leaning tower of pizza would ever be, and it was nodding like a learned judge at every word deVille said. But how could he? and in front of her mother too! If this was a dream this was the moment

DOMINATING OBSESSION

when he was going to wake up with a sticky stomach.

"It's got to go," deVille said. "If you don't want it, I will be happy to take it."

Miles turned to him sharply.

"It's your choice. Here they both are." deVille moved his arm to encompass mother and daughter. "But you can't have them both - and I will have whichever one you leave."

This wasn't a wet dream, it was a wet nightmare!

Robyn's expression was inscrutable. Surely she would rather almost any man other than her husband should be the one to take her daughter's cherry. It was all his own fault. It was all going disastrously wrong. He hadn't intended any of this to happen. When his tormented brain had screamed its wish for him to be given domination over all women, he hadn't meant Jade to be included.

"Sorry to push you, Miles, but I think it's time."

There was no way Miles could meet Robyn's eyes again. He looked at her wide open vulva with its beautiful muff of chestnut brown hair. The gold ring was holding the hood of her clitoris open, the clitoris itself looked enormous. This would be her first time with her ring in place. The throat of her vagina swallowed self consciously as if already fearing that he would make the wrong choice.

He turned away, straight into Jade's steady gaze. She wanted him and she had schemed to get him, it was all there in those slate grey eyes. And his knob had risen before he had even looked at that beautiful naked body again. Her vulva was creamy white, silky smooth and virgin, and just aching to welcome him in.

"Jade," he croaked, before he had chance to change his mind.

"Good man," deVille slapped Miles on the shoulder and pulled him close for a momentary hug.

Miles turned and walked the three paces that took him to stand in front of Jade. Robyn would understand. He couldn't let Jade lose her precious cherry to deVille. It was too im-

portant to her. As a mother Robyn must see that. Almost in a dream he reached out and ran his hands down Jade's legs to her thighs. Oh, God. He felt like coming. He would never manage to get it in. He would end up creaming her belly and deVille would take her anyway.

Oh Christ, feel how her flesh purred at his touch. He found the courage to look at her. Her eyes were screwed tightly closed and her teeth were biting deep into her bottom lip. It gave him strength to continue caressing up and down her legs waiting for his wayward, dancing, cock to come back under some semblance of control.

"Miles!" Robyn's eyes were pleading.

"She's a virgin, Robyn. She saved herself for me. She wants me. I can't reject her. I can't make her give herself to someone else. You must see that."

"Oh, Miles, it's you that doesn't understand." Robyn began to cry.

"Understand what?"

Robyn continued to cry, biting her lip and shaking her head.

"Understand what?" Miles asked again, but with the same reply. Did she know? Did she know herself what it was that she thought he should be able to understand? He looked at Jade, wondering if she would know. She was crying as well. She looked just like her mother.

deVille ran his right hand down the inside of Robyn's left leg letting the side of his little finger gently touch her labia. She carried on crying. He kissed the sole of her foot in the centre of the instep. She wiggled her toes. He kissed her ankle then down her leg to the back of her knee. She tried to bend her leg, but failed because of the clamp, so she thrust her whole leg and foot as straight as they would go, wiggling her toes and trying to find an impossible extra eighth of an inch.

deVille remained there softly kissing the crease at the back of her knee with his hand gently caressing her inner

thigh as he did so.

Robyn stopped crying.

Miles leant forward, letting his cock slide over Jade's belly and his hands circle her breasts as his lips found hers. They kissed, a sweet dry kiss, then their mouths lunged at each other hungrily. As their tongues danced their crazy dance and chased each other in and out of each other's mouths, and as his fingers and thumbs found those wonderful stiff nipples and teased them round and back, he slowly eased his penis down into her moist little cleft.

He looked at the other couple. deVille was now standing at Robyn's head, kissing her right arm. He had already reached the inside of her elbow. Robyn had her head on its side watching Jade and himself. Her eyes were still hoping that Miles would stop. deVille's lips reached the inside of her arm pit. Robyn screwed up her eyes and tried to pull her manacled arm away. Failing, she had no option but to cry out and shake her head instead. deVille's lips kissed over her shoulder, up her neck, and into her eyes. Robyn's breasts began to swell up large then slowly deflate again as her breaths became bigger. As deVille's lips left, her eyes began to release tears. Each tear appeared slowly from between her lashes, reformed itself in to a glistening liquid beetle, took a quick look around, then scurried off down her cheek to the safety of her mouth.

deVille lowered the rear of the bench and Robyn's head disappeared out of sight. deVille positioned his cock with his right hand, waited for Robyn to give a final hiccuping sniff, then thrust gently forward with his hips, presumably offering that unbelievable monster up to Robyn's welcoming mouth. As deVille leant forward to suck Robyn's nipples he winked largely at Miles.

Jade was shaking, her whole body vibrating in ripples. It was time. Miles placed his arms round her legs and moved his cock deeper into her vagina until its progress was blocked. He left it there for a moment feeling his excitement for his mission grow to fever pitch. Then he gave three strong pushes

DOMINATING OBSESSION

at her door, hoping that it would remain barred against him. Her defences remained intact. His heart flipped over at the thought of what he must do. It was going to hurt her like buggery, but he had to be brave. His thrust needed to be hard and unmerciful, a single penetrating blow.

Miles slowly withdrew and paused for a moment to give his brain time to enjoy the wonderful euphoria of belonging to a superman. Then he brought it to order and made it picture its task.

With a sudden single swift thrust he brought his massive siege engine forward to crash against Jade's interior defences.

With equal suddenness he felt his damaged weapon rebound with numbing intensity from the impenetrable obstacle within.

There was no time for another full build up. His forces were fully committed already and he pressed on with the attack as best he could, thrusting and boring until a small breach became an opening which the point of his knob could just squeeze through. As Jade screamed at his fumbling operation he felt her defences falling away on all sides and at last he was in.

Jade stopped screaming. The bloody deed was done.

Miles' elation was sufficient to rank this moment with the best of his life. He had done it. He was unstoppable, a superman. His lover was red hot and covered in sweat, and for the moment unable to go on. But they were there, complete, lying together as one. It was wonderful, as awe inspiring as birth itself.

Jade began to stir and they were both so excited that he knew that it must all be over in a moment. She was so tight and so wet. There wasn't any blood. He moved quicker and quicker, feeling Jade coming with him. Oh no! Please no! Please, God, give him the strength to hold on. Then he knew that it was going to be all right. He was coming! Coming! Coming! But so was his magnificent partner. Oh Christ! Oh Christ! she was screaming fit to burst. Oh Beautiful. Oh yes!

DOMINATING OBSESSION

It was magnificent. He was a stallion. A roaring screaming bull.

Then deVille pulled the beads from Miles' arse in one quick yank and Miles clenched his buttocks like a mantrap springing shut as a great white light became a firework display and then a huge coloured kaleidoscope with all the colours of the rainbow fading to muted pastel colours.

Miles came then as he had never come before. He was the strongest animal in the universe, a perpetual motion machine that couldn't be beaten. And even if he had wanted to stop, which sometimes he did when he felt that the emotion was just too great to handle, he couldn't have done so because of the animal beneath him that thrust and reeled and writhed and did everything possible to grind him into submission.

But now he had to stop, he couldn't go on, he had no breath left and his strength was ebbing. But the tired weapon rose again, and again they rose with it, and again and again until suddenly he had no strength left.

Miles' last scream burst and stopped before ever reaching the final note, and he clasped down on Jade's body as good as dead. Jade's scream ended too, as if both had depended on the other to survive, and for a few seconds the fading resonance of them both continued to bounce round the vast cellar from mirror to mirror and wall to wall.

Miles lay on his lover, knowing he was too heavy, but unable to move. And now his only concern was to find some breathable air to bring into his dreadfully sore lungs. So he lay there fighting for air and survival and knowing that both were still uncertain. And he knew that he didn't want to die, but he didn't care too much if he did.

He had done it. It was the most important thing he had ever done. His whole life had been leading up to that moment. They could take his life away from him, but they could never take that magnificent moment away.

Miles turned his head to the side. deVille was between

Robyn's legs sending that monster of his in out of her at an incredible speed. It really was an unbelievable length and thickness. And so strong. Miles knew that he would never be able to move inside a woman like that, so fast and so hard. It was if there was no feeling in it, and deVille used it like a weapon to reduce all opposition to quivering, shaking, screaming, jelly.

This was what Miles had always longed to see, this raw naked power reducing his wife to a quivering slave. He should have been jealous of deVille's ability to do this to her. He should have felt intimidated that for ever afterwards she would have this magnificent lover to compare with his own feeble efforts. But he didn't, he felt strong. He felt powerful again to know that he had this man on his side. No woman could defeat deVille. No woman, however accomplished, could stand against him for long without surrendering.

Robyn was screaming and turning her head from side to side every time deVille's groin came in contact with her new gold ring, but her presence there seemed almost immaterial to the proceedings. How would she ever be able to get any satisfaction from another man's shagging after she had experienced this. At some point before starting deVille must have adjusted the top end of her bench back up so that she could watch herself being rogered from every conceivable angle in the many bronze mirrors.

Now despite her restraints Robyn pushed her head and breasts forward as far as she could screaming at deVille.

"Yes! Yes! Yes! Do it you monster! Fuck me, you bastard. Hurt me, beat me. Screw me to death!"

Despite his useless shrivelled dick Miles wanted to accept the challenge. He wanted to urge deVille on. He felt he wanted to jump up and help, but he couldn't bear to miss a second of the action.

deVille stopped. "What did you say, Slave? What did you want?"

"You bastard, you fucking bastard, do it. Do it. DO IT!"

DOMINATING OBSESSION

deVille had drawn his rod right back.

"Where? Where would you like it, my sweat mouthed little rose?"

Miles realised from deVille's jeering words that his knob must now be positioned at the entrance to Robyn's anus, and a quick check in the mirrors confirmed this to be so. Miles knew that Robyn didn't like it up the back passage, but she didn't hesitate, her answer was instantaneous.

"Up my bum you bastard! Screw my arse off! But for fuck's sake - do it! I can't stand any more!" and with this final wailing plea Robyn closed her eyes and waited for him to do his worst.

But deVille wasn't done with her yet.

"Who are you asking, Slave. Who am I?"

Again Robyn's answer was instantaneous and this time it was also unequivocal.

"You are my master! You are The Master! You are the only true Master!"

This time deVille didn't hesitate - his reply was also instantaneous and unequivocal as he rammed his cock deep into her anus and began frantically to bugger her with all the force available to his massive body.

Robyn screamed and fainted, but deVille didn't stop, and in a moment she was back, screaming and wailing and thrashing about like a lioness caught in a net. Her flesh was moving in every direction, but always a split second behind the direction her body was shaking in. And each time the mighty monster rushed up her tight little passage the shock waves travelled ahead of it, like the bow waves from a battle cruiser under full attacking speed, making the flesh shudder in waves as their apex sped towards her brain.

By the time Robyn was finished and reduced to a shaking, wobbling, sobbing, jelly, Miles found that his own cock was already half way to a usable state again.

deVille looked at the mass of tears and vibrating flesh that had once been a woman, and reached up and caressed

down her leg from her ankle to the top of her in...
Then he did the same to her other leg, and he kept
the same until she began to recover. Then he move[d]
head and released her arms and sat on the bench hugging
her, rocking backwards and forwards and shushing her sobs
telling her that it was over, all over.

Jade stirred beneath Miles. He had been supporting his
weight from her, but now that the other couple's drama was
over she wanted to be free and to receive her own loving
reward. As Miles lifted her up he realised that he was covered in blood. It was everywhere, caked to their legs ankles
and bellies and right up to Jade's chest. He looked at her in
horror and then in concern, but the deep green eyes smiled
back with only love.

"Thank you, Miles. You're mine now. You can come and
unlock me. I want to show you how precious you are to me."

32

Jade watched deVille nursing her mother while she waited
for Miles to find the key for her wrists. deVille had his back
to her and Robyn's head was pressed into his chest with his
arms covering her almost completely, so she had to watch
them in the mirrors.

Despite deVille's best efforts Robyn's body was still shaking, and as Jade watched Robyn coughed in her choking distress and more of deVille's sperm emerged from her anus
and joined the rest sliding down the crack of her bottom.

Miles found the key and undid Jade's wrists and then
after a wonderful hug he went off to release her ankles. Robyn
was still again now. At last the hurricane that deVille had
released inside her had blown itself out and Robyn was now
empty of erotic emotion but brim full of love. Jade felt the
twisting screw of jealousy's stiletto blade. It was Miles she

wanted and Miles she'd got, but she also wanted deVille!

deVille leant forward and laid Robyn back on the padded bench. He kissed her on both eyes then on the lips, and finally, before standing, on each resting breast. Robyn knew he was about to leave her and she struggled to open her tear blinded eyes and cried out to him. But he was gone. Gone, surprisingly, to refasten her wrists. Then he readjusted the back of her bench so that she could lie with the top of her body flat, and before leaving her completely he slipped a cushion under her head and planted a gentle little peck in the centre of her sleeping forehead.

Jade was standing with Miles enjoying a cuddle and finding her feet and despite their bloody state deVille came and put his arms around them both and gave Jade a kiss.

"Happy?" he asked.

"Ecstatic, Master," Jade replied, and they both laughed, and Miles joined in.

He took them off then so that they could all get washed down with buckets of ice cold water straight from the tap which they threw over each other with much shrieking and laughing before standing in a circle and drying each other off with huge fluffy white towels.

Then deVille asked Jade if she wanted to be manacled to the pillar for the rest of her piercing, and she decided that she did. It was Miles' privilege really, but he decided that he would prefer to act as nurse and fit the gold rings, so it fell to deVille to excite her nipples and clitoris and to do the actual piercing. Not that she needed any exciting, but deVille took his time about doing it anyway, telling them that it was always as well to do a thorough job.

The actual piercing was brilliant and the sensation in her nipples and clit afterwards was indescribable. It was like having a stranger constantly playing with her nipples and clitoris. A stranger that she could never see, but who she knew was constantly lusting after her naughty bits. Of course there was no stranger, just the memory that deVille had

DOMINATING OBSESSION

pierced her nipples and clit so that he could play with them more effectively, and so that her body would always look incredibly beautiful and erotic for him.

She looked at herself in the mirror and thought that she would swoon. She looked unbelievable. Her tits were fantastic, but her little bald mound was out of this world. So proud, it was thrusting itself forward so much that it wasn't necessary for anyone else to be on the inside of her to know how self important it felt. It was positively beaming with self satisfaction. She could hardly wait to be on her own to try them out, but deVille wasn't one to let her experiment in private and he ordered her to show them how she would masturbate using her lovely new rings.

In all truth she knew that it wasn't really necessary for her to touch them at all, she could easily have brought herself off by just thinking about what he had done to her and how magnificent her body looked in its new jewellery. But she was anxious to put on a good show. She stood at first and putting the index finger and thumb of her left hand through the two nipple rings she pulled her nipples together until they touched.

Then she rubbed them together.

The effect was explosive and totally unexpected. She was hit by a blow from inside her chest that although it was travelling outwards towards the tips of her nipples, knocked her backwards off her feet, and it would have slammed her into the pillar if deVille hadn't caught her in time.

He carried her to the settee, and with much laughter, told her to take it easy, but although she had just come she couldn't bear to leave her nipples alone. This time she was expecting it and not having to worry about not falling over she was able to ride with it, but the effect was still the same, a tremendous surge of tingling energy that made straight for her nipples and down to her clit. And once she had found the courage to pull on the ring in her clit she had to lie flat on the sofa and pant and writhe as she had a most extraordinary

DOMINATING OBSESSION

external orgasm that tingled over her flesh like ten million iron booted centipedes.

She couldn't open her eyes, but she knew it must be deVille who took hold of her navel ring and instantaneously taught her that there was a direct link between it and her anus. He set up such an ache that it made her legs go empty and bowed them out until she felt as if she had spent a lifetime riding a barrel bodied pony. She knew what he was doing, of course, he was preparing her anal cherry. And doing it very well. She needed something up there. Something she could grip with all the muscles in her stomach and arse. Something that could reach the ache and blast its way through making her stretch her legs until she was as straight as a pencil.

And there was only one thing she knew that could do all that. A thing that would be straining to look at her now, and wetting its tiny lips in anticipation of having her. She opened her eyes to check that she was right. Through the narrowest of slits, past lashes flickering with gold rimmed liquid beads, she saw that she was. And the cocky little bugger was so outrageously eager that he had blown her a big bubble that he kept balanced on his bright purple helmet like a football star showing off with a ball.

She was so happy inside that she wanted to laugh, but she was also so frightened she wanted to run and hide in a dark cupboard.

deVille's hand stopped the regular rhythmic twisting of her navel ring and he moved both his hands to cover hers and stop her motion on the other rings. It was time. She would have liked one more orgasm, but she knew that it was better this way.

They walked back to Robyn. She was still almost asleep, but she smiled when she saw them approach and stop in front of her, saving her longest loving look for deVille. Jade immediately felt it again, the stiletto blade of jealousy deep in her vitals being inexorably twisted and plunged all the

DOMINATING OBSESSION

way home until its sharp point was hard against her spine. Placing his hands on Jade's upper arms from behind deVille steered her right up in front of Robyn's wide open legs.

"Bend and give your mother a loving kiss, Jade, while we attach your rings."

Jade felt her body go rigid and she saw a similar reaction in those of Robyn and Miles. This was wrong, he couldn't ask them to do this. But he wasn't joking and he wasn't asking. There was no mistake, and no trick. He was the Master and he was ordering it done. And who was there to deny him?

Jade bent and placed her hands on the bench either side of her mother's breasts. She felt so hot, so swelteringly hot. It was so close. There was no air at all, and she couldn't breath. She couldn't think. She mustn't think.

No one assisted her. She lowered her body down until she made first contact. Her mother's body felt as hot as her own. She could feel the heat rising off it in waves, but when she felt the first gentle tickle of her mother's pubic bush against her own naked hairless mound she went ice cold inside.

Then their fannies were together and boiling each other in hell fire. And then their breasts. She had done her best to ensure that their nipples, and even their nipple rings wouldn't be the first to touch, but somehow she had miscalculated and the unmistakable caress of her mother's firm oversize nipples against her own blew the back of Jade's head off in a blinding flash of sulphurous white light. Both women jumped away at the contact, and Jade knew that it was her fault, she should have kept her eyes open and now it was too late she couldn't stop her arms from shaking, or even stop herself crying.

"Shush, shush, Don't cry, baby, don't cry." Their two hot bodies were firmly together and Robyn the mother was kissing at Jade's tears and comforting her child.

No one stopped them. No one touched them. They lay

like that, both shaking, and both thinking constantly of the other's body pressing hard against their own. Jade knew she was coming only seconds before she did. It wasn't her fault, she didn't want to come, but deVille had ensured that she would.

Robyn's body stiffened. She must be horrified. Jade could understand that, she was too, but Robyn's body was tight against hers and Robyn's gold ring and pelvic bone were pressing into her clitoris and she couldn't keep her body still. So she lay there softly shaking while Robyn lay quite still and waited for the terror to pass.

"Kiss her," deVille reminded Jade.

Robyn panicked then, frantically trying to tip Jade's body from her. deVille was standing above their heads. His right hand came down and smacked Robyn's head in one direction, then his left hand came and smacked it back the other way. It was done with an easy rhythmic action that he could have kept up all day, but to Jade who the blows just missed it seemed the most violent, shocking, terrifying, assault she had ever witnessed. And his blows did what he intended. They broke Robyn's concentration, and her resolve, and she began shaking too.

Everything was forgotten then. Jade knew that she had to kiss Robyn. Not because deVille had ordered it, although that was a big consideration after the swiftness of his violence, but because she now had the opportunity to do so, and she wanted to. She wanted to know what it was like to kiss another woman as she would kiss a man. She wanted to be as close to another woman as she could be to a man.

And once she had kissed her, she wanted Robyn to kiss her back. Jade's tongue would brook no refusal - Robyn had to kiss her back. Robyn, resisted at first, but then Jade's madness spread to consume them both.

Jade's body was on fire and her inflamed brain so busy that she hardly noticed Miles' shaking hands on their breasts and navels. But she knew when he had linked their clitoral

DOMINATING OBSESSION

rings, and she knew what to do with that link. To both give and receive with the same thrust was a concept that was mind-blowingly new to her. It was new to them both, but that didn't stop them from becoming experts at it after only a few earth shattering seconds of experimentation.

Jade felt her legs pulled open and her ankles secured. She knew when her hands were taken away for her wrists to be manacled. And she knew when her bum hole was being prepared by deVille's oily fingers, but she wanted only for Robyn to keep kissing her and bringing her off with her groin so that she didn't have to think about what was to happen next.

Then she felt the bench sinking and saw Miles at the handle of the hydraulic lift lowering and heightening and adjusting it until deVille told him it was just right.

deVille's lips kissed over the left cheek of her backside, starting at the bottom and making a wide half circle to end up in her cleft. Then they did the same to her other cheek, and she prayed that he wouldn't use his tongue on her quivering ring.

He didn't. He stood up and placed his hands on either side of her waist and began easing himself in. The knob stretched her until she thought her tiny ring must snap like a piece of elastic. She couldn't scream. She couldn't breath. She couldn't move. She couldn't think. She could only wait for the inevitable to happen and for her poor screaming anus to be ruptured by deVille's great monster.

Then she did scream. As his huge knob slipped inside and her anus twanged shut, she jerked up her head and gave them both barrels at full choke. The cellar took her stereo sized scream and bounced it back at her again and again from every shocked surface.

Jade's brain returned for a moment and lifting up her head again she looked in the mirror at what she couldn't believe she had seen. Miles was kneeling in a huge parrot cage suspended overhead. His head was pressed against the

DOMINATING OBSESSION

curved wire bars and his right arm was through the gap between one set of wires and curved back to hold his cock which was poking through another.

Jade looked at deVille. He was standing upright and completely still and now his hands were resting on his own hips as he looked back at her reflection in the same mirror. He looked simply magnificent, like a golden Greek gladiator preparing to do battle, standing there with his cock inside her rectum, and she knew that she would always want to see him like that however much it hurt this first time.

It was as if he was telling her something - however close a man and a woman might think they are, they can never truly be as close as when the man has his throbbing manhood firmly planted inside her bottom. She wanted him then, all the way, right up inside, because a woman has no stronger way to show her man how completely she has given herself to him than to let him take her there.

Already Jade felt weaker and less assertive than she ever had in her life before. But she had also never felt stronger, or more loved. He was taking her doggy fashion like a beast of the field. That was only proper, he was her master, and she was his chattel. But he had also provided mirrors so that she could witness her own subjugation and glory in her giving, and so that he could look on her face and know how happy she was to be receiving all of him deep in the heart of her soul.

"Yes, Master - do it! Take me! Bugger me! Make me yours. I am your slave, Master. You are the true Master!" Jade screamed.

deVille looked at her and she knew that he loved her, and that he desired her, and that he would take her - now! This instant. In the arse. In a manner that would ensure that she would never forget it.

deVille began moving: almost imperceptibly at first. Jade had thought she would hate it, sure that her own fear would make her too tight and dry, but it was wonderful. She lay

down and pushed her bum up as high as it would go. Her spine felt like it was broken and the rest of her was turned to water.

She wanted to laugh, but she could only cry she was so happy. Her anus was full of floods of liquid as she kept coming and coming. Her vagina was rippling and her orgasm was everywhere: inside and out. In her clitoris, and in her vagina, but also in her legs making her stand on tip toe and wiggle her bum begging him to come even further inside.

And then he did, and every part of her sucked him in. He was so massive! He wasn't inside her, she was outside him, fitting to him like a thin membrane tube. And now there was no longer any need to worry if her mouth was too big or her hips too wide, or if deVille preferred Robyn to herself. None of those things could ever be possible. She was the most beautiful woman alive. A superwoman with The Master's cock up her bum. And she could clamp it and twist it and bite it and kiss it. She could hold it in and release it out and she could squirt her come at it, and drown it in love.

"Oh no! Oh no! Oh yes, do it!" Yes do it, do it, do it. Oh yes let him come, "Ahhh!" He was coming and coming. Jade thrust at him with her anus twisting and screwing and matching him blow for blow. She wouldn't give in. She would never give in. As she raised up her body Robyn's body came with it. Now she was fighting the two of them grinding and biting and spitting and squealing.

Jade and Robyn screamed in unison. And Jade knew that her mother knew too, what every woman knows deep down: there is, and can be, only one true master - and every man has one.

"Ahhhrrrghh!" deVille cried, and he crashed down on top of them like a fatally wounded bull elephant. A superb ranting male beast brought low by a young girl's token of eternal love - her sweet little ring.

And so they lay in a heap that panted and heaved and frantically steamed. And Jade felt nothing except pain for a

long agonising moment. Then she felt something else that came from above. The hot heavy drops of sperm hit her hair and back and she sensed rather than heard others hitting deVille's body and splashing open on Robyn's exhausted face.

Jade thought for a moment, then she said, simply, "thank you, Miles," and she knew that she spoke for them all.

BONUS PAGES.

Our bonus pages seem to be very popular, judging by comment we have received so far. And why not - you always get the usual full-length novel first, so there is nothing to lose.

Anyway, we are planning to promote the Bonus Pages into a Bonus Mag - watch this space! We mean to make the extra Bonus Mag pages worth the price of the book on its own - double value, same price! Yes, soon our books will be longer and will include a monthly magazine with special features, short stories, reader's letters, whatever you ask for.

We can use letters already, for next month, if you are very quick. We print one now to get you going. We shall forward correspondence where name and address is given in confidence (or print them if direct correspondence is welcome), so that this will be a means of people with similar interests to contact each other - worldwide, for our books are beginning to get around really well. This will be a free service, details next month. In the case of this first letter we have a name only, but maybe the writer will get in touch again? You will be able to write to authors also, and expect replies.

After the letter comes the taste of next months title (ELISKA - a little unusual, but a real treat), followed by the fourth episode of our serialisation of the re-written and expanded ERICA, Property of Rex, by Rex Saviour, currently out of stock. This is the sort of book you can enjoy by starting anywhere, but be warned - it will probably tempt you into seeking out the previous episodes in Plantation Punishment, Naked Plunder, Selling Stephanie and SM Double Value.

At the back we now list titles out of stock as well as those available now. ALL titles (ie including out of print) are now available on computer disc by mail order - £5 (including packing and postage) as ASCII files (which can be read by any word processor). Handy for your journeys with a laptop? PC discs unless Mac requested.

BONUS PAGES.

READER'S LETTERS - NUMBER ONE!
London
31 July 1997

Dear Sir,

I am writing to congratulate Silver Moon for its contribution to erotic domination literature. Particularly, I would like to applaud SM's decision to produce fiction in which the world is presented through the eyes of a dominant heterosexual male.

Nexus books, by contrast, are now almost unreadable in that a masochistic lesbian ethos pervades every scene. Every incident of punishment, restraint, domination and humiliation is prematurely inverted so that it becomes its opposite - a moment of release, of pleasure, of gratification for the victim. I don't know what the object of this manoeuvre is, but it doesn't work. Perhaps the idea is to kill two birds with one stone, to appeal simultaneously to dominants and submissives. Disastrous. It is even possible that books reflect a subversive feminism that has irritatingly become entangled in a fascinating branch of sexuality. Aran Ashe, perhaps the originator of this style, and its best practitioner, has a lot to answer for. Mind you, Aran Ashe is probably a spent force now: both of the Tormunil books are damp squibs. Thankfully, none of the other major writers that I have come across have lost their edge in that way - Richard Manton, Rex Saviour, P.N. Deneaux, and Martin Pyx.

I enjoyed Naked Plunder. The exploitational possibilities of South America, not to mention the exotic sexuality of its female population, make it an exceptional fertile setting for a domination novel. A good balance too between voyeurism and participation is used in the book. The protagonist's soul-searching was perhaps a little excessive, but the magic realism was an apt touch and well handled. The physical attributes of Melissa were nicely sketched too, as was her tragically submissive character.

Plantation Punishment had lots of good things also. The power

BONUS PAGES.

differentials between master and servant are always evoked by Africa and her history, making it a potent location for domination writing. African women too, and their earthy, mysterious sexuality, are often neglected these days. The comic element was perhaps too much to the fore for my taste, but the right buttons were being pushed often enough to keep it interesting.

Other memorable moments over the past couple of years have been Dear Master and The Drivers. Dear Master tackles a taboo subject through a brilliantly conceived contract situation. The Irish 'uncle' character is among the most memorable in domination literature and deserves to be revived. The first half of that book is deeply intoxicating. I hope Terry Smith is writing a sequel.

The Drivers is very original. Nothing could have prepared me for the honesty of this book. The brutal realities of contemporary Northern Britain permeate every situation. First hand experience of the haulage industry is everywhere apparent. Endless journeys across half-empty motorways, where the sexual imagination was unleashed and allowed to run riot, is where this incredible fantasy took shape. I loved it.

I have read, or had a good look, at almost everything published by Silver Moon in the last ten years or so. Allan Oldish's Barbary series was original and began a new genre which has continued to flourish. RD Hall wrote a fine schoolgirl spanking book - a subject that has been somewhat neglected by Silver Moon I feel. The only real turkey has been Rorigs Dawn, where the intention at least was right. Most disappointing have been those few books which really belong on the Nexus booklist. I'm sure you know the ones I mean. As for Rex Saviour's Erica being serialised as bonus pages at the back of recent publications - great idea. It is one of a handful of seminal texts. How I wish he'd write another novel!

Yours
A.Reader

BONUS PAGES.

NEXT MONTH PREVIEW - ELISKA by Graf von Mechtingen - Being an account of his mission to a Bohemian region for the Imperial Court of the Holy Roman Germanic Empire in the year 1528

We give you a small incident from this gripping book:

...during the supper, excellent as usual, an incident took place which is worth recounting if only to stress the strange reactions of these noble hosts of mine.

One of the serving-girls - a very pretty serf, naked to the waist as usual - suddenly tripped, her bare feet catching in the carpets. She spilt the whole contents of a beaker of wine over the young Milan whom she was serving; it ran over the table and down into his lap. Milan sprang to his feet and turned on the petrified culprit with a torrent of abuse in local dialect. The girl, whose name I gathered is Tereza, turned white with fear.

"You foul, slovenly bitch of a whore!" he shouted. "You dirty strumpet." And a few more insults I had difficulty in following.

I was taken aback at the man's fury and the Margravine seemed to share his anger but her voice was controlled as her eyes narrowed. I started to help to mop up the wine as the second servant was called to the scene. The Margravine waved me back.

She addressed the wretched girl. "I have been watching you for some time," she hissed. "You are given the honour of waiting at my high table merely because the bailiffs selected you from among the rabble downstairs, because they think you have attractive breasts, you little scum! But you are lazy, careless and provocative - you have even the effrontery to look me in the eyes."

The wench immediately dropped her terrified gaze to the carpets where the wine continued to trickle. Like the wine, my heart bled for her.

"You will pay dearly for this," Eliska said coldly. "Drop your skirt girl!"

To my consternation - for, after all, the scene was being en-

acted before an emissary of His Imperial Majesty - Tereza undid the cord that held her only garment to her hips (I have noticed that females never wear drawers here) and let it fall. She stood completely naked before us, trying to shield the narrow triangle of fair hair over her sex from our view.

"Stand straight, scullion!" It was Milan who shouted, at which Tereza joined her hands behind her back, jutting out her sharp breasts. She was trembling but looked so lovely.

"Send for Jakub!" Eliska turned to the second serving girl who stood quivering in a corner, as far away as possible from her companion, and now fled at once.

Eliska then addressed the table. "As you see, the bailiffs do their best to provide handsome girls with good firm breasts to serve here, but what do we get in return? I have had my eye on this bitch and her pert habits. This is the way she chooses to repay me for my generosity. I have taken her in as an orphan, fed her, clothed her and sheltered her ungrateful body. Well, her naked body you see before you will now pay for the favours she owes. it will taste the whip as few sluts have tasted it recently."

She spoke with venom as Jakub in his cowl hurried into the hall, obviously fully alerted to the situation. He seized the girl by the arms, bending her backwards viciously.

"Has this slut been pierced?" Eliska enquired brusquely. Her man nodded, squeezing a nipple to show the small insertion hole in the umber flesh.

"Yes, gracious lady, a month ago, along with the other slaves from the six villages," the reply came, precise with intimate knowledge of the bodies that fell to the man's charge. "She can be ringed again for bondage and flogging immediately, if that is your wish, gracious lady." The man took an evident delight in his duties.

"I shall decide later," the gracious lady replied. "Meanwhile take her to the slave stalls below and suspend her by the legs next to the whore."

...my wants are served by a delicious, dark-haired serf girl, naked, as usual, down to the edge of her pubic hair, which is the required dress. This one is the replacement for Tereza and is full

BONUS PAGES.

of smiles. I wonder how long she will last? And thinking back to Tereza, now and then when I am in the courtyard, taking the night air, I can catch the muffled sound of screams from the vault below and the hiss and crack of the scourge on flesh as some miserable wench is flogged for some terrible crime - like slamming a door or talking during Vespers...

The same evening, after a stroll among the fragrant boxwood hedges in the castle garden, I decided to explore more of the underworld. There are some thirty steps down which give an idea of the depth of some of the cellars. At one point I saw a great iron-hinged door, firmly locked, which I deduced was the fateful dungeon where the sex-torture - as they sometimes term it - takes place. To the right stretched a dark corridor which I took, following my instinct of direction (which you yourself admired In me when we got lost in the back streets of Heidelberg one night!). Thus I happened on what they call the slave stalls themselves.

These are a series of rough wooden partitions not unlike a stable except that no animal could be kept down here; each stall has a stone slab across its width. You can imagine my surprise, although I half expected it, to find three of the stalls occupied by females, naked and chained. In the first, the beautiful Tereza was hanging by the ankles, legs apart, her arms bound behind her, so that her head hung at the level of a man's loins, which was to be shown a moment later.

The girl was breathing rapidly on account of the suspension she was enduring. Yet she had not been put to the whip - at least, not yet - for her skin was pristine and free of lash welts. I felt relieved on her account, this little spiller of wine.

In the adjacent stall, her buttocks perched on the extremity of the ledge, the whore Marja was stretched by a chain from the neck to a large ring in the wall behind. Her thighs were wide open, chained to the base of the partitions on each side and purple whip marks over her hips bore testimony to the flagellation she had received in the vault. She sat motionless, her eyes closed, her fair hair cascading down her back.

To my further surprise, I recognized Immediately the third female from her blindfold and body rings. Maryska's legs were

BONUS PAGES.

chained to the metal circles in her sex labia, causing her to sit in cruel tension. I noticed that each partition post had a slender whip hooked to it, ready for instant use on recalcitrant flesh or to satisfy a sudden whim.

As I advanced further with my candle, I heard footsteps approaching and I withdrew into the shadows as Bohumil entered. Without taking note of my presence or feigning to ignore me, he approached Tereza's nudity, entirely at his disposal.

He caressed her body from top to bottom - the belly, buttocks, inner thighs and then the sex - and all at once opened his codplece and brought out a pulsating erection. He thrust the head into the girl's mouth and, as her lips encircled the pole obediently, lunged in deep. Tereza gagged at each penetration but managed to perform a superb fellatio, despite her position. After some minutes I thought one or both must orgasm - particularly when the man rubbed his rough cowl against the open labia and clitoris.

But Bohumil withdrew, leaving Tereza panting, gasping. He moved to Marja. Here he plunged directly into her sex, butting her body against the wall. It was she, experienced prostitute that she is, who accelerated the rhythm, seeking the man's discharge and possibly her own.

But she too was left craving. Restraining himself, the man shifted over to Maryska ...

ERICA - EPISODE 5 (you can start here and enjoy perfectly well, but previous episodes are in Plantation Punishment, Naked Plunder and Selling Stephanie in case you want to locate them):

She stopped complaining about shrinkage when I asked for the belt, but after that I had her kiss it and bring it to me every time she took it off to wash the jersey: little ceremonies like that make for domestic harmony and Erica and I got on fine, no trouble at all. If I snapped my fingers, she would come and stand at attention before me, and then I could do anything with her. I did brought her to me quite often, just to show her that discipline was good.

BONUS PAGES.

So things had been quiet for a few days before that first Saturday night of term. She had made a special effort to look nice for me, and had been especially obedient all evening. Her hair was in the two long pigtails she knew I liked, and after I had bathed and shaved her she pinned a flower to the jersey and put it back on. As the evening wore on she became really strung up until as bedtime approached.

I made it early that night: I couldn't wait!

"Get ready for bed," I said. "And remember - be decent when you come down for your goodnight kiss."

"Oh - well -"

"GO!" I shouted. "DO AS YOU ARE TOLD!"

I made up the fire and waited.

When she came back to the den she stood in front of me, hands clenched at her sides, wearing only the hip length night shift I had bought her, and of course the belt.

"Erica dear," I said. "I am extremely unhappy about this. You know you have to wear your snake knickers, it's the most important part of your desensitization. You want to be cured, don't you?"

She went down on her knees and flung arms went my waist as she buried her head in my crotch.

"Speak!" I said.

She looked up pathetically. "You know I can't wear them, the snake is too horrid, it would come into me."

She was shivering. With fright, not cold, as she clutched at my trousers.

"Don't be stupid. Come into you? Don't you know it's only embroidery?"

"Well, but - it might get fatter, it might get fatter and redder, harder and harder, it might force its way in, all slimy - it might spit in me -"

"You get snakes and penises mixed up in your mind, don't you?"

"I - I - do I?"

The serpent, of course, has a great variety of symbolic meanings, such as the principle of evil inherent in all worldly things, and psychologically it is a symptom of anguish expressive of

BONUS PAGES.

abnormal stirrings in the unconscious. But to represent a penis - that I had not heard before, nor wished to hear again. I suppose she would have a new meaning for the apple also!

"You wicked girl!" I shouted.

"W-what?"

"Suggesting that Eve was tempted by a penis!"

"But - but I never -"

"You wicked wicked girl! Must I take the skin off your backside, you evil blasphemer!"

She was crying now, as well she might. "I don't know -"

"Of course you know!"

"Yes, well, I suppose you have to, then. I still won't wear them, not however hard you beat me!"

"Are you saying I am wasting my time?"

"No, Uncle Rex, not if you enjoy it -"

"MY GOD!" I shouted. Setting a bad example, but there were excuses for it. I grabbed her by her hair and hauled her to her feet. "What am I to do with an ungrateful little bitch like you?"

"I - I don't know -"

"Of course you bloody well know!"

"Yes, Uncle Rex, you're going to beat me!"

"Yes! And then I could paint a snake there. Would that cure you?"

"Oh no!"

"And on your bottom too."

"Oh please not!"

"Perhaps tattooing would be better. You can wash paint off, but tattooing is for always."

She threw herself into my arms. "No, no no!"

"I could get a book on tattooing and buy the needles and dyes. I expect I could decorate you all over with snakes, and a special big one down there, a fat red one about to spit, perhaps."

She was sobbing. "Beat me as hard as you like, every night, two times a night, but don't do that! Oh God, not that!"

"Go fetch the knickers, then!"

She ran off, shaking her head and muttering to herself, but soon she was back with the knickers in one hand, held well away

from her body.

"Kiss them!"

It took a long time, but at last she did. A small victory!

"Now," I said. "Put them on."

I saw the long struggle in her mind as she strove to obey me, but it was no good. "I c-c-can't!" she wailed. She gazed at me, frozen and frightened, utterly unable to obey. "My hands won't do it!"

"PUT THEM ON!"

In the end I had to force them up over her wildly kicking legs. She struggled like a mad person, tearing the shift badly, but in the end I held her by the arms, actually wearing those knickers at last, her chest heaving, the lower half of her squirming as if she was on fire.

I turned her round and pointed her towards the door. "Now go to your room!"

But the moment I released her arms she bent down and pulled the knickers straight off. Then she ran into a corner, sinking to her knees and beating her fists against the wall.

This time I put her arms behind her back and tied her wrists together before I forced her into the knickers. When I released her she scrambled to her feet and ran round and round, her bottom writhing and twisting in their tight embrace.

I took her into my arms to comfort her, but she actually spat at me, and I really thought she was going to bite. So I carried her, a struggling spitting piece of humanity, carried her up to her room, and threw her down roughly on the bed.

Then I went downstairs for a drink and prayer, to calm myself a little.

When I returned, she was tossing about on the bed face down, whimpering. Her small hands clenched and unclenched within their bonds, unable to get near the knickers that were tormenting her so. She was crying, crying and wriggling and writhing and throwing her legs about as if the knickers contained hot coals.

As I took the belt from her waist she peeped up at me, big tearful blue eyes through that tangle of fine red-gold hair. I got a comb and tidied it for her: I was becoming deeply fond of that

girl. It may seem strange, but the more I beat her the more deeply I loved her.

I tied her two pigtails together to make a handle, pushed a pillow under her loins, untied her hands and set them to the pillow, then stood back and cracked the belt down on her defenceless bottom, defenceless because the snake knickers bit deeply into the cleft but were no protection anywhere else, then again and again I struck with increasing pleasure and strength.

She actually stayed in place the first eight times, squirming away from the belt but managing to get back in position each time, until at the ninth blow she tried to cover her bottom with her hands.

Despite her threshing about I tied her arms behind her back again, this time higher up, each hand against the opposite elbow. Her fingers were well clear of her bottom that way, and it held her shoulders back nicely.

On the eleventh blow she heaved about so much she actually fell to the floor.

I picked her up, using the handle I had made in her hair, the other hand between her legs, and threw her back face down on the bed.

She obviously did need to be tied down, something I had never done before, but then she had never fallen off the bed before.

I seized an ankle, pulled it down past the knob at the left-hand bottom corner of the bed, and tied it there. Then I caught hold of the other wildly kicking ankle, and something in my head made me take it outside the other corner to secure it. That stretched her wider and screwed the embroidered snake even more tightly into her crotch.

I stood back to have a good look - she lay there on her stomach, arms bound up behind her, ankles to the bedposts, bottom raised over the pillow, biting the counterpane, well exposed and positioned for punishment even before I pushed another pillow under her hips to raise her backside even further. I got a finger inside the tight knickers with difficulty and twisted them until they vanished into the crease between her cheeks, which were clenching and unclenching all the time.

BONUS PAGES.

What an inviting target it always was, that plump squirming curvy little bottom of hers!

I set to warming it up some more with the belt, but after a few minutes I could not control myself and broke off.

I needed another drink.

As I sat in my comfortable chair in the study, I wrestled with the perverted thought that had insinuated itself into my mind as I had crossed and recrossed at the bottom of the bed, so as to wield the belt impartially on either cheek. The way she was secured she was held very wide open and exposed. The knickers had sunk in so far as to be almost invisible, and her newly shaven sex called to me, its very nakedness drew the eye...

Even so open as she was, so invitingly open ... the belt was wrong, it was too broad ... too broad to get in there...

As I sipped the brandy and listened to the sobs from upstairs my eye was drawn to the riding crop on the wall above the mantelpiece.

I stood up and tried not to walk over there. Tried and failed. I lifted it from its hooks and drew its slim tapering length through my fingers ... there was a little hard loop at the thin end...

I hurled it from me with an oath, smashing a rather nice china dragon, and went back upstairs with the doubled-up belt in my hand and illicit lust in my head.

The resumed thrashing must have done her some good, judging from the screaming which started after a while: nobody lives within miles of us, but I pushed a ball gag into her mouth and slipped the elastic strap over her head, for there was too much noise for my liking.

I was excited by my wrestle with the Devil. I felt elated at resisting the temptation to give her uppercuts with the riding crop, but on a baser level I was bitterly disappointed and still suffering from an almost irresistible urge to go and fetch the crop and that made me really angry with myself.

I wasn't sure if I could resist the temptation next time...

Angry with myself? It was all her fault, the brazen little hussy and the murderess should suffer for it...

I lashed the belt down mercilessly, time after time after time. I had never seen her writhe about so much, with such frantic but useless desperation, but only little gurgles and bubbles escaped from the gag.

When at last I had done with the belt, I undid her ankles but not her arms. Almost as soon as my back was turned she was off the bed and scraping herself against a chair, trying to get the knickers down...

I left her and went down and had another brandy, handling the crop lovingly. Then I went back up to her - the crop made a beautiful swishing sound...

She came crawling to me, her eyes beseeching...

I thrashed her round and round the room and down the corridor and down the stairs as she tried to crawl from the crop, then I picked her up and carried her back and threw her down on the bed again.

As she lay there sobbing I hardened my heart. She must be taught a lesson. I turned her over onto her back. Then I grabbed those flailing legs and tied the ankles to the outsides of the bedpost, one by one...

As I gazed down on her writhing form from the bottom of the bed I saw that the snake knickers were twisted deep into her sex...

Her naked shaven sex! That wicked part of her, cowering before the vengeance of the Lord! Temptation of man! Work of the Devil! Time for chastisement! Time for purification! I raised the crop in the air and saw the terror in her eyes as I stood between her open legs and she arched that splendid body of hers, the vessel of the Devil...

I adjusted the pillows to present the best target, and then I struck... and struck... and struck...

When I untied her, she started to try to scratch the knickers off again, even after all my efforts to discipline her. Just as if nothing had happened!

All my efforts had been in vain!

So I fastened the belt round her thighs to hold them firmly together. She was still gagged, of course, and her arms were

BONUS PAGES.

securely bound behind her back.

Once last look was all I could bear as I hardened my heart against her and left her writhing on the top of the bed in the dim red light of the python's tank.

It was just waking up.

1-11

I left my bedroom door open: she would hear me going to bed. I was still at my nightly study of the scriptures when she came hopping clumsily down the passage.

She knelt on the edge of the bed, made very straight by the way her arms, bound so high behind her back, strained at her shoulders and thrust out her firm little breasts. My bedside lamp glowed on her perfect olive skin, so soft and inviting as she waited for my attention, trembling with fright on the white counterpane gazing at me, big eyed but unable to speak because of the gag.

I returned to my reading, for my study of the Commandments was not lightly to be put aside. Then, when I had finished the passage, I laid the Good Book down and removed her gag: she burst into headlong breathless speech.

"It's too much for me in these knickers, Uncle Rex, if you won't let me take them off please don't leave me alone... can I come in your bed?"

"I've only just cured you of that dependency on me." I shook my head. "It is not good for you."

"Oh please –"

I shook my head again.

"Well then," she implored, "may I lie on the floor by your bed, please? Please?"

I considered this carefully.

"You'd be too cold."

"Couldn't you put a blanket over me? I'd go mad all alone in the dark in my own room, thinking of the snake coming into me."

"Go somewhere else, then."

BONUS PAGES.

"There isn't anywhere else, well no other person, and I'm so frightened alone, so very very frightened, I just can't stand it any more, so I just had to come to you!"

For a while I said nothing - my voice would have revealed my secret delight. It worried me that I would have to go through all this again and again until she gave in - worried and thrilled me. My self-control was definitely weakening in the face of temptation. I must control myself, for I was in constant danger of taking her in the Biblical sense, of becoming as great a sinner as she.

It would be so easy. She was so completely in my power, completely defenceless against rape. No, I must stay with educating her until she was nineteen. That was my target and I would stick to it. I had no wish to taste the eternal fires of Hell, but neither, by failing to correct her adequately, must I allow Erica, an admitted thief, murderess and frequent blasphemer, to do so: thus the Devil laid another temptation before me - she is there to be beaten, you enjoy beating her, so beat her harder and more often.

But she looked so wholesome, kneeling there. "You'd better get in, then," I said gently.

She hesitated a long time before at last wriggling into the bed. She was warm and soft beside me, for I wear no pyjamas and her shift was in tatters, and anyway it slid up as she slid down.

Her pert little breasts brushed my chest and heated my lust, for the rosy tips were hard. I drew her to me, but I felt her shrinking back from that too, unwilling to touch my flesh with hers, and became angry.

"About your beatings," I said. "It is still every Saturday night, and you WILL wear the snake knickers those nights."

"Will you hurt me as much as tonight?"

"More!" I said. "I must be more severe each time or we'll never get anywhere, will we?"

"Oh God, Uncle - no -" She shrank back, turning her breasts from my fingers as I fondled them absently, deep in thought.

"Very well!" I said. "Since you obviously don't enjoy my company, and I don't share my bed with wicked blasphemers,

BONUS PAGES.

go back to your own room and think about it."

"Oh God - oh please - I'll be very very nice to you, ever so nice."

She started to wriggle backwards, deeper in the bed, her bottom still squirming in a vain effort to avoid contact with the snake knickers, and to my shame I helped push her down with my hands on her shoulders.

We had been through all this before...

I felt her lips seeking my sex. It was delicious, the more so as I could sense her flesh still shrinking from mine even as she sucked my penis into her mouth. I almost wished her hands were free. I could sense that strange war in her between wantonness and revulsion which turned me on so, her desperate need to please me battling against memories of the wicked mistreatment she had come to expect from men: the parallel war between God and the Devil continued in me, making me want to unstrap her thighs and ... plunge in whilst I was hard ... or maybe use the razor strop or the riding crop first...

I wished I could rely upon the victory of restraint over lust, but I could not. I feared that my control would snap one day soon, yet the Lord's work still unrolled before me, uncompleted.

So I let her work at me as best she could, with only mouth and breasts...

At last her reluctant efforts gave me a convulsively sweet release. It was a long time before her lips worked their way back up my body to my lips, lingered there so softly, then at last she stopped squirming.

"I do so love you, Uncle Rex!"

"As a Father?"

"No no, as my Master!"

BOOK TWO - PROPERTY

PRELUDE

Along the banks of the busy river Baliknahm, beneath the balcony of my room where I am confined at your Palace, Great Lord, came a huge man on a trotting grey horse, splendidly robed and turbaned despite the hot sunshine, and wearing riding boots and spurs. And running behind, tethered to the saddle of the sweating horse by a cord fastened to a golden ring set in the flesh above her sex, ran a naked young woman, small and curvy, very upright, with no arms that were visible to me from where I watched.

The man dismounted with agility, despite his bulk, and looked up at me, grinning. His face was disfigured by a great evil looking scar that ran from the corner of his mouth, right across the right cheek and up to an eye that was closed. As I watched he unclipped the girl, lifted her by a hand at her crotch and one in her long black hair and flung her down on her back in the dust. Her legs sprawled out, kicking helplessly, but no arms were to be seen as he started to pull her along the ground on her back by her hair up the steps to the entrance to the Palace and out of my sight.

Now I see a cart following behind. On it is some strange machine. The man who rides the cart cracks a whip over the eight naked women harnessed to it as they struggle to catch up with the scarred horseman...

Presently the man with the scar stood in the archway leading to my quarters, the girl wriggling in his arms like a rag doll in distress. He seemed to fill the entrance with his presence. He still had one meaty hand at the girl's crotch, the other wrapped in her hair, which was long, glossy and jet black.

"I am Turk!" he announced, looking down at me challengingly - he towered above me, he was maybe six foot six or seven. He was certainly not a native of Balikpan!

BONUS PAGES.

He held the girl out to me as if she were a gift. "Behold the girl Oi!" he said. When I did not move to take her, he flung her onto my bed, where she curled up into a ball. He inspected me with a frown. "You not like? She very tasty!" He walked over to her and slapped her across the face. "Stand!" he shouted. "Display!"

The girl uncurled gracefully, like a cat, apparently without the use of her arms, her skin smooth and golden, a much deeper colour than Erica's olive hue. She came and stood in front of me, at attention like a soldier except that she was on tiptoes and her arms were behind her back, and I caught my breath, for she was the most amazing thing I have ever seen, even in this barbaric country of Balikpan, where the Marquis is worshipped by men and women suffer so grievously.

She was small but perfectly formed: I think the man's great size made her seem smaller at that moment than she really was. There was a jewel-studded collar at her neck fringed with little spikes to make her hold her head up. Her breasts were firm and high and round, the nipples pierced and ringed, and a ruby shone from her navel. From the larger ring set in the flesh above her sex, which I had already noted, a fine gold chain vanished between her legs, so tight that it looked as if it lifted her from the ground, an impression increased by her standing on tiptoe. Her shoulders were strained back unnaturally, and my yes widened when I saw that she had been circumcised, and how radically it had been done.

"Open!" shouted Turk, and the girl sprang to an open-legged position, still on tiptoe.

"Oi mean sugar cane," he said. "My sugar for canings, eh?" He chuckled as he put a finger to her ravished sex, tracing the links of the gold chain. "You wonder why they cut her so deep?" he grinned. "She very very naked, no? Unusual, yes?"

I nodded. I was speechless.

"She was burned down there," he said. "Spoiled to look at. She have five older step brothers. They enjoy to stub out their cigarettes there. After some years of this and other things she run and catched by State Orphanage." He shook his head. "A mistake, for there she encounter Turk!"

BONUS PAGES.

He grinned at me, fingering his scar.

"Or rather," he said, in that gravelly voice of his, which hinted at unknown depravity. "Turk encounter she!"

The girl was gazing over my shoulder, her deep brown eyes pools of misery and pain, her open legged tiptoe posture displaying her beautiful curvy sleek body to great advantage, and I saw her shudder as Turk's reached out touch her.

"Turn!" he barked.

She turned slowly and erotically, and I saw that the chain between her legs went up between the cheeks of a really splendid bottom and was fastened to some quite elaborate contrivance that held her arms crossed high up behind her back - that was what was straining her shoulders back so far.

It was the most effective form of bondage I have ever seen - and a painful one, I had no doubt. That one little chain held her totally helpless and at the gross man's absolute disposal.

"The Orphanage," continued Turk, "is cheaper than the brothels, if one knows the night watchman. Two thousand baht into his greedy fist and the door to the dormitories is open all night. Turk prefer girls, he go there often, he like this girl Oi best, he think she very beautiful. One night Turk drink a little too much, maybe, he take whisky bottle in, she break over his head then slash slash cut Turk, Turk who was once so handsome and have two good eyes -"

His pent up rage was frightening to see. His whole frame vibrated with it.

"Now she mine. She wishes she had never been born but no way to suicide, Turk too clever. All the time I beat her and torment her, and I sleep with her in ways she hate, she think I am a pig at night if I unlock her from this chain."

He paused.

"Now harken," he said, "Turk was sent for, sent for personally by the great Lord of All the Universes himself, for the Great Lord hear of Turk and his cruelties and of the girl Oi and her sufferings. Turk is to lend Oi to you, white preacher man, to encourage you in your writings about this Erica. And when you have finished the story of this Erica, you are to write for the Great Lord above the history of Turk and Oi. The story of Erica

BONUS PAGES.

will be as nothing compared to the story of Oi, for Turk is a good Sahdist and enraged at what this creature has done to him and she is his to do with as he will, for none care what he do and all fear him."

The girl was shrinking away from him, and I knew that it was true. It must be the worst thing imaginable to be the helpless plaything of a sadist who hates you.

"She is to be with you," he said, "for three days, so you may note down her tale, and later Turk and others will tell you more."

At this point he was distracted by a noise at the doors, as the machine I had seen on the cart was wheeled in by the eight women, driven to great effort by the man with the whip.

"Ah!" said Turk. "Place it there... you are late! One shall be whipped for it!"

The women had already lined up before him, marshalled by the man with the whip. They all stood to attention, and now he stalked menacingly up and down the row. They were pure-blooded Balikanese, small and neat in appearance, with big brown eyes, long black glossy hair and smooth golden skins. I find it very hard to tell the ages of Balik women, but I would guess they were all in their early twenties or late teens. "You!" he shouted, pointing at the smallest of them. "You! It is your fault! You are too small! And you!" - pointing to the largest - "you look strong enough to pull a cart single handed!" He turned to the man with the whip. "Torn, take these two and tie them to the cart, and whip them well."

"How many lashes, Master?"

"Continue until I come down." Turk turned to the other six women. "You may watch from the balcony," he said. "Out with you!" He looked to me to see if I was impressed with his mastery of the situation. I was horrified. Your Majesty must remember that I am not one of your subjects, not of the Sahdist religion, and not familiar with local customs.

"Now," he said, "I leave this creature Oi with you, white preacher man, but not in comfort, no she must suffer still." He pointed proudly to the machine. "This her beating frame, it go by clockwork, it help keep her top of the tables."

He saw I was puzzled. I had not heard of these tables before,

BONUS PAGES.

Your Majesty. I think they are not much spoken of to tourists.

"Every week tables are published," Turk said. It was obviously something he was really enthusiastic about. "They show how often a woman has been beaten, how many lashes you know. There is a table by the week, and one that is - how do you say? - incremental? - cumulative? - yes, cumulative. And Oi, she always in top three, often she win, the most beaten girl, is great honour to her master, much money when he show her."

He paused as a pitiful scream came from outside, followed shortly by another. Then they came at regular intervals, a shrill one followed some fifteen seconds later by one that was a little deeper, then in another fifteen seconds the shriller one came again and so on. Turk walked to the balcony and looked out. "Is good," he said. He came back and patted the machine. "Torn a strong man out there, but this better, beat by clockwork, this dial say how many lashes, so no argumenting the score. Is good, yes? Soon put her in for you, but first we drink to the Marquis, you look not too well I think."

He clapped his hands and the serving girl who waited on me appeared as if by magic with a tray. Like all the female staff in your Palace, Lord King, she was very comely and wore the standard length smock and nothing else. As she was a good deal taller than average and stood very straight it was even less adequate than for most, and she caught Turk's eye at once - I saw a gleam of lust in his piggy eye as he reached out for her.

She turned to run, and he laughed in delight as he headed her off from the doorway. "Many womans run from Turk since he get scar," he said. "But not get far! Womans have no rights in this country! If run away, police fetch back pretty damn quick!" He went over to the corner where she was crouching, lifted her by the smock and threw her face down on the bed, then he was upon her like a hurricane. Or maybe an earthquake. I have never seen a more brutal assault. Ten minutes later he had sated himself and his victim was cowering from him, holding the shreds of her smock together.

He laughed, pointing to the torn garment. "That mean trouble for she," he said. "Big trouble! They very fussy here! Dirty clothes is insult to King, very very bad! Go, go, send other!"

BONUS PAGES.

The girl slunk away and presently another appeared and made a little bow to Turk, palms together, hands raised in respect to her chin, a gesture which is called a wai here. She was much shorter than the other girl, and although I suspected that she would have nothing but a fine figure beneath the smock, whatever she had was decently hidden. She appeared to be more important than the previous girl, some sort of supervisor perhaps. Her smock was very smart, very white, immaculate, starched I think. She had a little black bow tie at her slim neck, and a spray of wild white orchids in her hair. Very fetching I thought, a really nice girl, I wouldn't mind...

"Machine dusty," Turk said, pointing to the strange contraption that stood waiting, brooding over the proceedings like a ticking bomb. He said something in Balikanese, and translated for me as the girl looked round in bewilderment. "I tell her to polish," he said, "she wonder what she use! Ha! Ha ha!" He barked another order at her and she took off her smock very slowly and reluctantly and started to rub the machine with it under his gloating eyes.

She was indeed naked beneath the smock, depilated like all the others I had seen, and her figure was far from a disappointment. I saw that Turk was enjoying her nakedness and discomfort at what she was made to do.

"Ah!" he said. "Oil!" He opened a dirty canvas bag that hung from the machine, took out an oil can, and applied it liberally to the wheels. The girl looked at him in horror, but he merely made a gesture to her and she knelt to wipe the oil carefully away with her smock.

"Good!" He examined the now filthy smock and threw it back at her. "Go!"

As the girl left to face whatever punishment she would receive - and I did not envy her it - Turk paused, wondering perhaps what to do next, and listened. The screams from the river bank had stopped. "What is this?" he shouted from the balcony. "Are you whipping dead flesh?"

"One perhaps," shouted back Torn.

"Throw the live one in the cart. You may complete her punishment later. The other is for the river. I will send down two

more." He clapped his hands. "In line. Quickly."

There was an urgent flurry as the six girls on the balcony returned to the room and lined up before him. "You!" he said. "You were last. Report to Khun Torn. I need one more. Who will volunteer?" There was panic among the girls. Then a hand shot up, then another, followed by the rest. They dare not fail to volunteer I thought, the last will be sent. But no! "You!" he said, pointing to a really beautiful creature who had put a hand up first.

"Go to the cart for your whipping."

He turned to me. "One is crocodile meat already," he said. "Is wasteful, unfortunate."

"You have crocodiles in that beautiful river?" I asked.

"Oh yes. We have races."

"Crocodiles race?"

"No, no, womans race crocodiles. If not win, they eaten. Very funny! Peoples make picnic to watch."

He was pleased with himself as the remaining four girls returned to the balcony. Soon the screaming started again, different screams but to the same pattern.

"Now," he said, "I show you how this creature look in the machine. He turned to Oi. "In!" he commanded.

She stood, straight as a die, and walked over to the sinister looking contraption. She put her feet in two stirrups obviously provided for the purpose, and bent forward, biting her lower lip in pearly little teeth as the chain tightened even further. The contraption that fastened her arms together, and to which the golden chain was fastened, clicked into an overhead arm of the machine, and then she was fixed to it as safely as a pinned butterfly.

Turk slapped her on the rump as he moved the foot stirrups apart. "Is good, eh?"

She certainly did look good like that, her head raised by the neck collar, her arms raised together behind her and fastened to the machine, her legs now wide apart. As to her charming and extremely beatable buttocks, they were offered perfectly to anyone or anything behind her, and as I walked round her I saw that they were twitching in anticipation of some sort of attack.

BONUS PAGES.

There was a strange wheel folded back at one side, and now Turk pulled it out and swung it round, so that it clicked into place behind those twitching buttocks, and I saw that a series of straps, or maybe they should be called paddles, hung limply from it - I think they were made of rubber, and they were shaped at the ends, rather like large fly swats or table tennis bats.

Next he raised her ankles - now some sort of counterweight held them up so that the wheel was in the V they formed.

"Ha!" he said. "What a beautiful machine! How stealthy in her swiftness yet how painful is the result!" His great hands were running lovingly over the mechanism, surprisingly delicate in their movements. "Her English name is 'snapper', as you shall see, for she bites when she is wound up. Oh yes, it is all very -" he paused - "primitive? Is primitive the word?"

It was, I thought. Yes, primitive was the very word. Or mediaeval, perhaps, like a torture machine from the past.

I could see now what would happen if it was turned - the heavy looking paddles would come round and fall on those already twitching buttocks.

It was obvious that Oi knew how that would feel! Presumably from experience. She was very apprehensive of what was happening behind her, although of course she could not see. She jumped whenever Turk touched her buttocks and little tremors of fear were running right through her.

The wheel had a handle to turn it by and Turk grinned at me as he gripped it, and I saw Oi tense as she sensed his grip - perhaps there was small creak that she had learnt to listen for.

But Turk paused and listened. Once more the screams from outside had stopped. Silence again outside and panic as he lined up the remaining four girls. "You," he said, "you choose, Khun Rex." It was a most unpleasant thing to ask. They were all so pretty and they all looked so frightened. I shut my eyes. "Keep changing places," I said. I heard them rustling about. "Now, stop where you are." I kept my eyes shut. "Step forward the middle two," I said. "You are chosen." Then I opened my eyes.

To be continued...........

Our Seven Most Recent Titles

Bush Slave
by Lia Anderssen
ISBN 1897809379

Once again, Lia Anderssen introduces us to a lovely, innocent young heroine to whom pain and humiliation bring ultimate pleasure.
Sold into slavery in Africa, Lisa Carling is kidnapped en route by rebels, and sold to a tribal chief who uses her as a sex slave for his warriors.
Finally Lisa realizes that the arousal her treatment brings is what she desires, and slavery is her destiny.

Desert Discipline
by Mark Stewart
ISBN 1897809387

Follow the beautiful Suzanne, as she is kidnapped by pirates and sold into slavery - where she learns to submit herself totally to the cruelty of the whip.

Training Jenny
by Rosetta Stone
ISBN 1897809395

Jenny. Young and beautiful. The wife every man dreams of. Loyal, obedient, submissive, but not a sex slave - or is she?
Three short weeks change Jenny's view of her life forever. Three weeks of total submission to the will of a cold, calculating teacher. Three weeks that plunge her to the heights of passion she never dreamed possible.
Three weeks of pain and pleasure that leave her lusting for more.....

Voyage of Shame
by Nicole Dere
ISBN 1897809409

Commander Arthur Berman's aristocratic features registered incredulous disgust. Thirty years of iron discipline struggled against choking fury and almost lost. It was as thoughthe navy had planned this as one final insult, the last plunge of the knife into his career to which he had devoted his life since the tender age of sixteen
'A detachment of five WRENS, plus one officer, arriving to join HMS Virago, to form part of seagoing crew.'
The Admiral grinned suddenly, punched commander Berman lightly on the arm. "Virago's your last seagoing command, so make most of it, eh? Give 'em Hell, what?"

Plantation Punishment
by Rick Adams
ISBN 1897809417

Our dissolute hero progresses from control of a Victorian Poorhouse for destitute young females to the purchase of a Caribbean slave plantation where he indulges his vices of cruelty and rum drinking even more freely - but will the coming og the Voodoo God Exu be his undoing?

Naked Plunder
by J.T. Pearce
ISBN 1897809425

Locked behind thick walls in an exotic location in South America a journalist discovers bonded girls and submissive women, and aquires an alluring sex-slave he must rescue at all costs.

Selling Stephanie
by Rosetta Stone
ISBN 1897809433

Abducted on the orders of an obsessively jealous woman, Stephanie finds herself plunged into a nightmare or revenge, punishment and degradation. Her youth and beauty and total submission to the desires of her captors are the assets that will ensure a high price when she is eventually sold at auction. Constant training, total obedience and frequent beatings must be endured for day after day - but deep within herself Stephanie discovers unsuspected lusts and desires that can be satisfied only by total submission to the will of a dominant master.

Out of print Titles

All available on floppy disc
£5/$8 postage inclusive
(PC format unless Mac requested)

ISBN 1-897809-99-9 Balikpan: Ericas arrival *Rex Saviour*
ISBN 1-897809-01-8 Barbary Slavemaster *Allan Aldiss*
ISBN 1-897809-02-6 Erica: Property of Rex *Rex Saviour*
ISBN 1-897809-04-2 Bikers Girl *Lia Anderssen*
ISBN 1-897809-05-1 Bound for Good *Gord, Saviour, Darrener*
ISBN 1-897809-07-7 The Training of Samantha *Lia Anderssen*
ISBN 1-897809-10-7 Circus of Slaves *Janey Jones*

All current titles are also available
on floppy.

This is a mail order only offer !

TITLES IN PRINT

Silver Moon

ISBN 1-897809-03-4	Barbary Slavegirl *Allan Aldiss*
ISBN 1-897809-08-5	Barbary Pasha *Allan Aldiss*
ISBN 1-897809-11-5	The Hunted Aristocrat *Lia Anderssen*
ISBN 1-897809-14-X	Barbary Enslavement *Allan Aldiss*
ISBN 1-897809-16-6	Rorigs Dawn *Ray Arneson*
ISBN 1-897809-17-4	Bikers Girl on the Run *Lia Anderssen*
ISBN 1-897809-20-4	Caravan of Slaves *Janey Jones*
ISBN 1-897809-23-9	Slave to the System *Rosetta Stone*
ISBN 1-897809-25-5	Barbary Revenge *Allan Aldiss*
ISBN 1-897809-27-1	White Slavers *Jack Norman*
ISBN 1-897809-29-8	The Drivers *Henry Morgan*
ISBN 1-897809-31-X	Slave to the State *Rosetta Stone*
ISBN 1-897809-35-2	Jane and Her Master *Stephen Rawlings*
ISBN 1-897809-36-0	Island of Slavegirls *Mark Slade*
ISBN 1-897809-37-9	Bush Slave *Lia Anderssen*
ISBN 1-897809-38-7	Desert Discipline *Mark Stewart*
ISBN 1-897809-40-9	Voyage of Shame *Nicole Dere*
ISBN 1-897809-41-7	Plantation Punishment *Rick Adams*
ISBN 1-897809-42-5	Naked Plunder *J.T. Pearce*
ISBN 1-897809-43-3	Selling Stephanie *Rosetta Stone*
ISBN 1-897809-44-1	SM Double value (Olivia/Lucy) *Graham/Slade**
	*Please add £1/$1.50

Silver Mink

ISBN 1-897809-09-3	When the Master Speaks *Josephine Scott*
ISBN 1-897809-13-1	Amelia *Josephine Oliver*
ISBN 1-897809-15-8	The Darker Side *Larry Stern*
ISBN 1-897809-19-0	The Training of Annie Corran *Terry Smith*
ISBN 1-897809-21-2	Sonia *RD Hall*
ISBN 1-897809-22-0	The Captive *Amber Jameson*
ISBN 1-897809-24-7	Dear Master *Terry Smith*
ISBN 1-897809-26-3	Sisters in Servitude *Nicole Dere*
ISBN 1-897809-28-X	Cradle of Pain *Krys Antarakis*
ISBN 1-897809-30-1	Owning Sarah *Nicole Dere*
ISBN 1-897809-32-8	The Contract *Sarah Fisher*
ISBN 1-897809-33-6	Virgin for Sale *Nicole Dere*
ISBN 1-897809-34-4	The Story of Caroline *As told to Barbie*
ISBN 1-897809-39-5	Training Jenny *Rosetta Stone*

All our titles can be ordered from any bookshop in the UK and an increasing number in the USA and Australia by quoting the title and ISBN, or directly from us for £5.95 each (UK) or $10.50 (USA) postage included. Credit Cards accepted as EBS (Electronic Book Services - £ converted to $ and back!)